John Boyd was born in 1912 in Belfast to a working-class Protestant family. Educated at Queen's University, Belfast, and Trinity College, Dublin, he subsequently became a teacher before joining the BBC as a producer in 1947. A playwright he works for stage include *The Assassin* (1969), *The Flats* (1971), *The Farm* (1972), *Guests* (1974), *The Street* (1977), *Facing North* (1979), *Speranza's Boy* (1982), *Summer Class* (1987) and *Round the Big Clock* (1992). He was literary advisor to the Lyric Players' Theatre, Belfast, and edited its journal *Threshold*, having also co-founded the influential magazine *Lagan* (1942-1946). He wrote two highly-acclaimed volumes of autobiography, *Out of My Class* (1985) and *In the Middle of My Journey* (1990). He died in 2002.

ACROSS THE BITTER SEA

ACROSS THE BITTER SEA

JOHN BOYD

LAGAN PRESS
BELFAST
2006

Published by
Lagan Press
1A Bryson Street
Belfast BT5 4ES
e-mail: lagan-press@e-books.org.uk
web: lagan-press.org.uk

ISBN: 1 904652 27 1

Author: Boyd, John
Title: Across the Bitter Sea
2006

Set in Palatino
Printed by J.H. Haynes & Co. Ltd., Sparkford

Archivist's Note

After the death of John Boyd in 2002, his family graciously bequeathed John's entire library and works to the Theatre and Performing Arts Archive in the Linen Hall Library. The Library is privileged to be the home of this collection. Within the collection is a huge body of correspondence, many works that John was constantly being asked to comment upon, and also the work that John produced throughout his life.

Unlike many authors, John kept almost everything he wrote, ranging from scrappy ideas on theatre programmes to full blown manuscripts. John's method of creation was to write in longhand in lined notebooks, and then have the notebooks typed for more editing and reworking.

Works would often start on a small A4 page and thirty years later surface on the Lyric Theatre stage. Such a work would be *Facing North* performed in 1979 which originally started life as *A House in the North* in 1951. *Across the Bitter Sea* has such a history. We believe that John began this novel in the 1940s when living in Ballymacash near Lisburn. This period coincided with his experimenting with different forms and, a motif that would last throughout his life, searching for his authorial voice. It also saw his entrée into the Belfast literature scene during his co-editorship of Lagan. The novel was reworked, abandoned and reclaimed many times over the next forty years, until there surfaces, typed and bound in green leather, what seems to have been John's final version.

It is that text that is held in your hand. Because of the unfinished nature of the manuscript, the Archive in conjunction with Lagan Press, have made one or two minor changes. These are of the usual editing process, and have not made any substantial changes to plot or narrative.

Across the Bitter Sea owes much to the relationships that John had with his wide circle of artistic friends and acquaintances throughout his life. These relationships influenced his writing in style but also in content. The novel charts the artistic life of an often depressed and forlorn Belfast in which art played second fiddle to the making and investing of money. That it is the first fruit of the John Boyd Collection is of great pride to the Linen Hall, as we feel it will add to the overall understanding of one of our most influential cultural figures of the 20th century, and also to the cultural history of the city, which John had such a passionate relationship with.

Hugh Odling-Smee
Curator
Theatre and Performance Arts Archive
Linen Hall Library

Book One

One

"MARTIN! MARTIN!"

His mother was calling him.

"You must get up!"

Yes, he must. She wouldn't come upstairs and help him put on his clothes: not this morning. He would have to get himself ready. She had told him that last night when she was packing things away. Nearly everything in the house was packed away now.

He hated the thought of leaving Bangor: his bed, the house, the long curving, grey street off the main road. They were going to Belfast: and he didn't want to go there. He was sure to get lost.

"Are you puttin' on your clothes?"

"Yes," he cried, throwing off the blankets.

He got up hastily, took off his nightshirt, and dressed.

"Hurry up, son."

He could hear his mother walking about downstairs: she always moved very quickly, no matter what she was doing. Sometimes she broke things just because she was so quick: a cup, a glass, a bowl.

His father must be away now, getting the house in Chatfield Street ready. He wasn't yet accustomed to his father being home from France. Yet nearly three years had passed since the end of the war. His father sometimes laughed in a funny way when anyone mentioned the war and very often said: "The war to end war! I don't think!"

His father had his medals in the dressing table in the front room. Martin loved looking at them, and was proud his father had been a soldier. But many things his father said were hard to understand.

"I wouldn't do it again! That's one thing sure! They told us anything to get us into khaki!"

He was glad his father was already out: he would now have his mother to himself. Then he heard his mother coming upstairs. She came into the room. She was smiling. He loved to see her happy: this morning he thought she might be sad.

"You were far too late last night. You were indeed ... I shouldn't let you stay up so long ... "

She kissed him. He loved her warm bare arms around him, holding him against her softness.

"Are you sorry, Martin, to be leavin' Bangor—and the sea?"

He shook his head. How could he be sorry?

He wanted to be where she was. And he knew she wanted to be in the home in Belfast. She was tired of living in Bangor. He knew that: she was always saying it.

"You'll like Chatfield Street."

He nodded.

He was dressed and ready. She walked down the stairs and he followed her, wondering how he could possibly like the Belfast street. But his mother was sure he would.

The house they were leaving looked strange this morning: no fire in the kitchen grate, no mats in the hall, no linoleum in the parlour. Everything in the wrong place.

"Is the van coming soon, Mother?"

"Sometime this mornin', the sooner the better, I want to get away."

"Why?"

"To catch an early train."

He had breakfast in the scullery: his mother told him it was handier there, with everything packed ready for the road. The remover's van had two horses, so his father had said. How tired the horses would be, walking all the way to Belfast. He imagined them pulling all the furniture the twelve long miles: past Helen's Bay, Craigavad, Holywood, Sydenham, to Ballymacarrett, on the east side of the city.

That was the part of Belfast where he was born, his mother told him: they had lived in three different houses in Ballymacarrett before going to live in Bangor.

But they had never settled down anywhere, his father said. His father hated flitting: and now they were flitting again.

"Where are you flittin' to, Mrs. Connolly?" Mrs. Anderson who lived next door had asked his mother.

"To Ballymacarrett," his mother had replied.

"You won't be sorry, I'm sure."

"Indeed I won't. But you've been a good neighbour to me, Mrs. Anderson, I couldn't ask for better ... "

Mrs. Anderson was pleased when his mother had said that. You knew she was pleased because she had began to hum. He liked Mrs. Anderson because she was fat and good-humoured and had lovely white teeth.

"They're a dear set," his father had said about Mrs. Anderson's teeth. He had discovered what his father meant one day when Mrs. Anderson suddenly took her teeth out and put them on the kitchen table. She was laughing, her whole body shaking, and she had looked different laughing with her teeth out. And she had looked just as different when she had stopped laughing. Her face was like somebody else's.

"Have you had enough to eat, Martin?"

He nodded.

He heard somebody knocking at their front door.

His mother hurried into the hallway.

"If it's the van men I'm not ready for them yet ... "

But it was Mrs. Anderson.

"Can I help you, Mrs. Connolly?" she said.

"It's very good of you," his mother replied. "I'll be going soon ... I'm waiting on the van."

"Ah dear, flittin' is always an upset, isn't it?"

His mother nodded.

"Won't you come in, Mrs. Anderson?"

"Well, only for a minute or two ... "

Mrs. Anderson came in and sat on the sofa: the springs creaked as she sat down. Martin listened to their talk: looking from one to the other, his mother so small and neat, Mrs. Anderson so large and fat. They talked for a time about Belfast people they knew. At last the van came for the furniture.

"I hope you'll be very happy," Mrs. Anderson said as she was leaving. "You should be a happy woman. Isn't that so? You've a good steady husband. That's all a woman wants."

Martin's mother said nothing: and Mrs. Anderson shook her head.

"Goodbye, Mrs. Connolly. Goodbye, Martin."

She gave him a shilling and left the kitchen, her hands tucked inside her apron.

"Poor woman," Martin's mother said. "It's a pity of her." Martin knew why his mother always looked so sad when talking to Mrs. Anderson: it was because Mr. Anderson was rough and unkind and shouted things.

"She hasn't her sorrows to seek."

"Why, Mother?" Martin inquired; he knew Mr. Anderson drank.

"You're too young to know."

"Why?"

"Oh, never mind, son. Say goodbye to our empty house."

He looked at their home. It was so different, empty. Suddenly he thought of the train journey to Belfast and took his mother's hand.

Two

HE FELT STRANGE IN THE NEW house. He missed the field, which lay at the back of the house in Bangor; he missed the sea which he had been able to reach after a short walk; and he missed the pier, the boats, and the lighthouse. The house in Chatfield Street was surrounded by other houses and streets. All of them looked exactly the same, except at the back, where a few backyards had wooden pigeon lofts. The house next to their own had a loft and when Martin looked out of the backroom window he was able to see the pigeons flying from loft to roof.

He liked to watch them.

"But you miss Bangor, don't you?" his father said.

Martin nodded: and his father said to his mother, "I think he's frettin' a bit."

"He won't fret very long," his mother said.

"The city's not good for a youngster. It upsets him, you can see that." Then, smiling at Martin, he added, "But I've got a surprise for you."

"What is it?"

"Wait and see."

On the Sunday morning, after breakfast, the surprise was delivered: his father had bought a motorcycle.

"It's only a second-hand one. But it'll be good for the runs I want to take. I'll take you for a ride as soon as I can handle it myself."

"Where'll you take me? To Bangor?"

"Yes. And further. To the Mourne Mountains, maybe."

His father loved machinery and spent days tinkering with the engine.

"I've to get it tuned properly. It'll go like a bird when it's ready for the road."

Martin was impatient for his father to keep his promise. At last, early on a Saturday morning, his father called from the backyard: "Come on, I'm ready for you."

"I don't think you should risk it, Bob."

"We'll be all right. I won't go fast, Jean. Honestly."

"Please don't."

"And I won't go very far either. Just a short run over the Castlereagh hills."

His father fixed a pillow on the petrol tank and put Martin astride it.

"Comfortable?"

"Yes."

"Away we go ... "

They soon left the city and were up in the hills. The speed made Martin hold his breath with fear, but when his father shouted, "All right, Martin?" he nodded back.

They halted at the top of the hills. His father propped up the machine at the side of the road.

"We'll walk over a couple of fields," he said.

They left the motorbike beside a gate so that they could see it from the field. Below them the city lay wreathed in smoke.

"We live in that dirt," his father said.

They lay in the field for a long time; but Martin was eager to be on the pillion again; he hated to be still for long.

"Let's go, Father," he pleaded.

"All right, but let me get a good whiff of this."

His father stood up and breathed in the fresh country air. Then they walked down the field to the road.

"Maybe when you grow up you'll own a motorcar."

"Could I have one?"

"Why not? If you've money you can easily buy a motorcar.

An' why shouldn't you have money if you've health an' brains?"

His father was breathless when they reached the gate.

"That's what you need in this world, health and brains. Money's useful too," he added as an afterthought.

Martin held on tightly as the motorbike raced down towards the city. He loved the feeling of speed, and his father never seemed so happy as when on a machine. He preferred machinery to wood, though he was a carpenter by trade, and had worked all his life in the shipyards. He was also interested in something mysterious called trade unionism and went to weekly meetings and afterwards talked about what happened. And Mrs. Connolly had to pretend to listen, but Martin knew that his mother wasn't in the least interested.

"Have you to be fightin' about wages all the time?" she often asked.

"Yes," her husband said, "all the time. If we don't fight for ourselves, who'll fight for us?"

"There should be no call to fight at all."

"No; but there is. An' our class has to do all the fighting. We're fightin' for our future."

Martin's parents settled down to life in Belfast. They had been living in Bangor only because Bob Connolly was under the doctor's orders after his return from France. The doctor had ordered him plenty of air; and the two years by the seaside had improved his health. He had put on weight and now seldom missed a day's work. But he itched to return to his native city where all his mates lived and where all his interests lay. Life in Bangor, though pleasant at the weekends, was dull. He felt isolated, as if already retired. And during these two years he had been forced to take things easy—he even had to drop his trade union activities. By way of compensation he had read more.

"I'd never make a scholar," he said. "I'd never have the patience. Anyway there's too many things to do."

The doctor had agreed that he should return to the city, but he would have to take care of himself.

"You must get fresh air at the weekends," the doctor insisted. So Bob Connolly had bought his second-hand motorbike to celebrate his return to Belfast.

"I never know how to pass Sundays, anyhow," he told his wife.

"You could to go church," Jean said.

He only shook his head and smiled.

"Why should I—when you go for me?"

"We should both attend—both morning and evening."

Martin's mother was a staunch Presbyterian; she enjoyed the services—it was what she lived for, most of all. She had been brought up to respect her religion and she hated half-measures. She sang in the choir; and she loved the minister, Mr. Grayson, to visit her house.

But her husband had no time for clergymen. He often reminded her bitterly that they had supported the war; they all turned jingoist. And fools like himself had been caught up in the war-hysteria. The so-called leaders had misled them. In future he swore he would be wary of them all, the religious and the political leaders. They couldn't be trusted.

Three

MARTIN'S BOYHOOD WAS PASSED IN CHATFIELD Street, and soon his memories of living in Bangor became dim. His world was the noisy life of the street, a street no different from hundreds of others in the district. Each house had a front parlour; two small bedrooms; a living-room, called the 'kitchen'; and a dark scullery, with a few shelves, a gas ring and a brown 'jawbox'. Chatfield Street was considered to be a 'good street', largely because the parlours gave the street a certain tone and most of the families prided themselves on keeping their parlours spick and span. None of the women ever wore shawls; and none of the men wore mufflers. Half-a-dozen families set the standard of behaviour and the others tried to follow. When the Connollys arrived, the neighbours saw the motorcycle and noticed that Mrs. Connolly left her home twice on Sundays to go to church. It was clear that the new family would certainly keep up the tone of the street.

Martin soon thought of it as his street. He loved playing with the other boys—bar-the-door, rounders, football; or walking to the end of the tram-lanes and riding back for a halfpenny on the outside platform of the tram. He was sent to a school which was supposed to be the best in the district and which had the reputation for gaining scholarships. Soon his ambition was to win one of these scholarships. It was also his father's greatest wish. His mother thought that only the best education was good enough for her son.

In each class Martin was near the top. He worked hard at his lessons, mostly because he was afraid to neglect them. When he didn't do his homework properly he was caned. The stinging pain on his hands brought tears to his eyes, but much worse than the pain was the humiliation. He became afraid of the teachers and terrified of the headmaster, but he had to accept the school and counted himself lucky to be there. Still, he began to look forward to the time when school would be left behind. And he often wondered what the future held for him. A day— especially a school day—could be very long; for time in school sometimes mysteriously stopped, and sometimes just as mysteriously disappeared.

At drill-time it always disappeared just because he loved the weekly half-hour 'drill' round the schoolyard, with old 'Baldy' Magee shouting through his silver moustache, "One, two! One, two! Lift your feet, boys! On the toes now! One, two! One, two!"

Martin regarded Mr. Magee, his teacher, with awe. Mr. Magee was in his mid-fifties; but he had, in Martin's eyes, the air and appearance of a prophet in the Old Testament. Added to the air and appearance of a prophet he had the power of a god; he was the centre and circumference of the school ever since he had become headteacher at the age of thirty-eight. His power was absolute: none of the teachers—seven in all, three men and four women—ever questioned his commands. The boys constantly kept watch on his every movement in the classroom or in the playground. They were most aware of him when he stood motionless at his dais, the great black school-roll in front of him, his gaze sweeping across the four classes crammed into the big room.

On a Friday afternoon at the end of school, Mr. Magee called out the names of half-a-dozen boys in the class; Martin's name was called last.

"Wait, you six boys; the others, go."

Slowly and quietly the class filed out of the room, their pace gradually quickening the further they went, until by the time they reached the front door, their slow semi-military march had become a quick disorderly trot. Outside the door, in the open air of the playground, they transformed themselves into boys again, shouting raucously at each other and running madly through the wrought iron gates that guarded the school from the main road.

Motionless, in different parts of the room known as 'the gallery', the six boys waited for Mr. Magee's attention. With a slight motion of his hand he indicated that they were to move together into the front row. They moved. They looked at Mr. Magee: at his rosy bald head, his pince-nez, his white shirt and bow tie, his gold chain, his spats, his gleaming brown shoes. Above all they looked into his light blue eyes. But his expression gave away nothing, except that he was not in a bad temper.

They waited.

Mr. Magee stood in front of them, his hands clasped behind his back. He looked out of the window. Outside a cold blustery wind was blowing, carrying into the classroom the shouts of the released classes. Mr. Magee's thoughts seemed far beyond the noisy games of his scholars in the playground. Indeed he seemed to have forgotten not only the boys outside but the half-dozen in front of him.

Still they waited.

Martin followed Mr. Magee's gaze across the playground over the high wall, to a shapeless brick building from which came the clang of machinery. This was Cosgrave's foundry whose furnace glowed like a great bunsen burner in the afternoons and illuminated the school in the dark short days of winter.

But Mr. Magee's eyes seemed to pierce through the foundry to something mysterious beyond.

At last he spoke.

"Well—"

He paused and stared at the six boys, one by one.

"I expect a great deal from you six boys," he said, measuring out each word.

They knew what he meant. He expected each of them to obtain a scholarship. They were the best six boys in his class; and he was relying on them to do their best for the school's sake, for their own sake. From now till the exam they would get an extra class every afternoon. Today the first extra class would begin.

23

"Take out your jotters."

They obeyed.

"Ready?"

They were ready.

Mr. Magee began to write on the blackboard.

He gave them a sentence to analyse and parse, and while they were hard at work he appeared to sink into a reverie. The six boys soon had their task finished; they waited, silently and patiently, till Mr. Magee gave them his attention again. Then he bent forward and took up the jotter of each boy. Slowly, with a blunt red pencil, he corrected the work.

"Not too bad," he said at last, with deliberation.

The six boys waited. Mr. Magee paused for at least a minute.

"You may go," he said, lifting the tiny bell from the table beside him. It was his symbol of authority. The six boys filed slowly out of the classroom, hurried along the corridor of the main room, ran as soon as they reached the porch, and burst into loud complaints as soon as they were well out of hearing.

They split up into pairs immediately they were outside the school. Martin joined Jimmy Kerr, a boy with a pale oval face, snub nose, and large grey eyes. Martin admired Jimmy, who was the cleverest boy in his class. Nearly every week as a result of an intricate system of marking both homework and schoolwork, Jimmy was first. He was popular, too. He was never known to boast; he was never known to cheat—and cheating was common throughout the school. The marking system encouraged it and the boys thought cheating was worth doing if you could do it without being caught. But Jimmy Kerr had no need to cheat. Whenever he made a mistake in arithmetic or spelling or parsing or analysis, a surprised, pained look came into his face, and for the moment he was nonplussed. He found it difficult to believe in his own fallibility. And so did the rest of the class. They took his superiority for granted.

Yet none of them envied Jimmy. He wasn't robust: he never played games in the playground—relievo or bar-the-door or I-spy. He had to look on. And also he was a very poor runner.

The two boys walked slowly along the Albertbridge Road. They didn't talk much. They watched the trams, open at the front and back, swaying along the lines; the country horses and

24

carts returning from the markets on the other side of the Albert Bridge. Then they stopped for a while at a chemist shop with its two great bottles of coloured liquid, one red and the other green, high up at the back of the window.

"I wonder what's in them," Jimmy remarked.

Martin shook his head.

"Would you like to be a chemist?" Jimmy asked.

"No."

"What'd you want to be?"

"I dunno."

"Neither do I."

A tram clanged past, and Martin suddenly thought he would like to drive a tram, especially on sunny days. He told Jimmy what was in his mind.

"It'd be all right," Jimmy said, adding: "Wait till I show you something—"

He dropped his bag, opened it, searched for something.

"See these?"

He held up two six-inch nails.

"Watch."

He laid them carefully on the tram-rails.

"What are you doin' that for?" Martin asked.

"You'll see."

They waited for the next tram to appear.

"Here it comes."

They could see the red-tram turn the corner at the Ropeworks; it seemed to take a long time to come up the road. At last it ran over the nails.

"Come and see."

Jimmy ran forward.

"Look."

He pointed to the nails. They had changed into two bright shining swords.

"One for you," Jimmy said.

Martin fingered the flattened nail. It was warm.

"Thanks."

And they parted.

Martin ran up the hall, leaving his schoolbag in the parlour, against the side of the piano. He entered the kitchen.

"Where'd you put your bag, son?"

Her voice was sharp.

"In the parlour."

"I told you not to leave it there, didn't I? Bring it in here."

"But where'll I leave it, Mother?" he protested.

"Behind the sofa—that's as good a place as any."

"Oh, all right!"

His mother was so fussy that she continually irritated him. She liked everything and everybody to be neat and tidy. "There's a place for everything," was one of her favourite remarks. It was that kind of remark he found particularly irritating. For it simply wasn't true. Some things—particularly a schoolbag—could be left in various parts of the house without coming to harm or without inconveniencing anybody. He would admit, nevertheless, that it was really best to leave his bag always in the one place; for sometimes, he would forget where he had left it; certainly it was curious how it could disappear within an hour and have to be searched for.

He did as he was bidden.

"That's better," his mother said. "You an' your father between you would clutter up that parlour."

His mother was ironing his father's shirts: it was a job she did slowly and thoroughly. Her husband must always have a beautifully starched white shirt to wear at the weekends.

Martin, having got rid of his bag, lifted his library book from the bookshelf beside his father's armchair.

"I won't be long, Mother."

"What about your homework?"

"I'll do it in the morning."

"You'll do no such thing: you'll do it tonight."

"Mother—"

His protest was cut short.

"You'll do it tonight as soon as you come back from the library so you needn't linger there. Get it done; then you can enjoy the weekend."

"Oh, all right."

She didn't understand him. Hadn't he had enough of school for one day? Old Baldy had kept him, given him extra work, and all because he was one of the first six in the class. It wasn't fair! But his mother wouldn't understand his feelings even if he explained what had happened today.

"Don't stay long in the library," she warned.

"Oh, but I've got to find a good book."

"Well, don't take too long about it. I don't like you wanderin' about that end of the avenue. It's too near the chapel."

"Oh mother, I won't come to any harm!"

"How do you know?"

It was no good arguing with her. So, putting under his arm the book to be returned to the library, he walked into the hall, glad to be alone.

Four

THE PUBLIC LIBRARY WAS LESS THAN a quarter of a mile from Chatfield Street. It was a fine-looking square two-storied brick building, with two massive pillars guarding its portico. At night, when it was lit up, the rows of books could be seen by passers-by in the avenue. It then looked a warm and inviting place. By day its appearance was drabber. Nevertheless, in comparison with the buildings nearby, it stood out boldly.

It was surrounded by nearly a dozen churches of various denominations, from an evangelical hall of corrugated iron known as 'the tin mission' to the more orthodox Protestant churches. There was also the Roman Catholic chapel, tall and austere: the most imposing building in Ballymacarrett. Martin, when he had to pass it, would glance at it apprehensively: especially if crowds of worshippers were leaving. He had often heard his mother say: "One thing's sure: they think more of their religion than we do of ours."

The library was also near the Presbyterian church where Martin's mother worshipped. Westbourne church, though forbidding as the chapel, was a building that Martin loved. He only wished that its appearance could miraculously outshine that of its adversary; clearly, however, this miracle was beyond its power.

The chapel dominated the whole district: it was taller, more spacious, more frequented than its competitors. Altogether an object to inspire envy and awe and fear among one section of the community: and love and reverence among the other.

But neither the chapel nor the church which held Martin's loyalty stood on the avenue itself. Both were on the Newtownards Road, of which the avenue was a mere offshoot. In Martin's eyes the avenue was the more important thoroughfare: it had the public library; it had the public baths where he had learnt to swim twenty lengths of the second-class pool; and it had the waste ground where he played football.

He walked along the avenue, slowly and thoughtfully carrying a greasy Rider Haggard in his left hand. His thoughts were no longer tied to school or to his own future. He was wondering what sort of a story he would take to read during the weekend. He often found the problem of selection a painful one. Allowed only one book on loan, he was unable to make up his mind: an adventure story or a school story or an annual ...

He looked up. Something unusual was happening in the avenue. A crowd had gathered just below the public baths, and people were shouting and singing.

He ran towards the crowd. "What's up?" a woman with a basket asked him.

He answered that he didn't know. A man joined them, and the three stood watching the crowd on the other side of the avenue.

"Where are you going?" the man asked Martin.

"To the library."

"Better go home," the man advised. "That's a Catholic shop being raided. There'll be trouble before the night's over."

While Martin stood watching, a piano was dragged on to the pavement; he then noticed that chairs, tables, and other furniture were already piled up on the road.

"Take my advice, and get out of this," the man said. "This is no place for a nipper. The police'll soon be here."

Martin, now scared, retreated up the avenue.

It was the first raid he had seen. It excited and exhilarated him; for as soon as he was out of sight of the raided shop his courage was miraculously restored.

He told his mother what he had seen, but she only shook her head, "Thank God you'd the wit to come straight home."

Then she finished off her ironing and went to the front door. "They're at it again," she called to Mrs. McClure, who lived on the opposite side of Chatfield Street, two doors nearer the avenue.

"I've just heard," Mrs. McClure replied, "in the avenue—O'Rourke's spirit-grocery."

Mrs. Connolly went across to Mrs. McClure's door; then Mrs. Richardson from up the street joined them. The three women stood gossiping, and Martin went out and sat on the parlour window sill. He tried to overhear what they said, but their voices didn't carry far enough. He took out of his pocket a set of cigarette cards called 'Cries of London', and examined them carefully to make sure the set was still complete; he then put them away and examined the sword made by the tram an hour or so earlier. He turned it over and over again, admiringly. He had seen a dull rusty nail transformed into this—a silver gleaming sword! Then an even greater surprise—he had seen the piano being dragged into the avenue!

His mother went on gossiping with her two neighbours. It was a source of amazement to Martin how women could talk for so long about so little. They would go on and on, repeating themselves! And men were little better than women.

Still, he loved to hear his mother and father talking about the riots in the city. They said they were living through a terrible time; all the home-rule trouble; the war in France; and now the country divided into north and south, with Protestants and Catholics fighting each other. And every night now there was the curfew at half-past ten, when everybody had to be indoors; and armoured cars were patrolling the streets.

His mother left her neighbours.

"I wish your father was home safe," she said. "He's to pass through a lot of Catholic streets on the way. I don't trust the Catholics."

"What would they do?"

"Shoot him."

"But why would they?"

"They don't care who they shoot! And our ones are no better! They're all a pack of hooligans!"

She began to set the table for the evening meal; Martin went into the parlour and did his homework until the evening paper arrived.

The newspaper reported a quiet day. Nobody had been shot; no bombs had been thrown; and the looting of the small shop wasn't even worth a paragraph.

Nevertheless the unreported event stuck in Martin's mind. He had seen the crowd in the avenue, the piano on the pavement, the furniture on the roadway, the crowd shouting and singing. That was all. He had missed the bonfire; he had missed the looting and the drunken revelry that followed.

His father arrived home from the shipyard, a little later than usual.

"What kept you, Bob?" his mother asked, immediately her husband got inside the door. "I've been waitin' for you. I didn't know what had happened to you."

Her voice was so sharp that Martin knew at once his father resented it. His father sometimes was very quick-tempered, and Martin often wondered why his mother had never learned how to deal with this.

"What kept you?" she repeated.

"Nothin'," her husband snapped back.

"You're late."

"What about it?"

"Oh nothing, but I've been worrying—that's all."

Martin's father sat down to his meal of broth, boiled potatoes, a chop, all washed down by a mug of tea. The mother told her news.

"They looted O'Rourke's shop in the avenue."

"So I heard," he said, busy with his broth.

"A shame, isn't it?"

"Senseless."

His father was disgusted with the course of events in the city, and Martin had often heard his angry comments on the shootings; his father mostly blamed the workers for their backwardness and bigotry.

"They don't know any better," he would often say. "But their so-called betters do—and they encourage them."

Martin knew that his father was more intelligent than anybody else in Chatfield Street; for the neighbours often asked his advice on all sorts of problems—insurance or unemployment or even domestic disputes. He was respected because he hadn't any of the failings of his fellow-workers—he didn't drink, or make scenes at home or in the street. He lived quietly, was interested in reading, in trade union affairs, and liked an occasional game of whist. And he often went to the Opera House to see a good play—by which he meant Shakespeare or Bernard Shaw. He seldom went to the cinema; and he seldom attended church.

But he preferred not to talk about religion; for his views annoyed his wife.

In other things too, his parents differed. His mother had become more socially ambitious, she wanted to live in a semi-detached house with a bathroom and a garden.

"We could afford a bigger house than this," she told her husband.

He disagreed.

"You don't understand," he said, shaking his head.

"What do I not understand?"

His obstinacy made her attack him, but he always retaliated.

"I'm only an ordinary worker; I could be paid off any day. Anyway I won't pay any landlord a big rent."

She hated him to say this. He seemed to have no regard for her feelings as a mother: she resented that Martin was growing up in a narrow side street.

More and more she came to dislike the district, though she admitted that some of her neighbours were decent enough. But now that the shooting and rioting had come close to their home she was determined to have her own way.

"I belong here," her husband cried; "and I'm staying where I belong."

But Mrs. Connolly knew that despite such protest he might move house if he thought their son would be in danger. So she made Martin tell his father what he had seen of the raid on O'Rourke's shop.

As Martin told his story, his father listened attentively until the end, making no comment at all. Then he rose from the table and went upstairs to change from overalls into his clean clothes. Mrs. Connolly tidied up after the meal; and Martin settled down to his homework.

He enjoyed doing his homework in the quiet kitchen. It was warm and cosy; and no sounds penetrated the small room. He especially enjoyed working at problems in geometry and algebra, and writing his weekly essay. Schoolwork came easily to him, and he loved the concentration it required.

His mother, looking at him bent over the table, thought of his future. Several times Mr. Magee had told her that she could expect great things of Martin, and the headmaster's words were balm to her. All her hopes were centred on her son. Secretly, devoutly, she wanted him to become a minister, but she kept her aspirations to herself. She knew her husband better than to expect him to share them. Despite her husband, Mrs. Connolly held fast to her aspirations; and sitting in church, she often allowed her aspirations to run riot. Instead of the clergyman in the pulpit she imagined her own son, wonderfully handsome in his gown and clerical collar, his voice ringing out beautifully clear to a crowded congregation. She would 'sit under' him, not in the third seat of the gallery towards the back of the church which was her usual place, but somewhere downstairs, in the middle pews, in not too prominent a place, of course, because she would have to take care to avoid any suspicion of being over-proud. Yet she would, inwardly, be exceedingly proud. If only Bob could be persuaded to share her pride. After all, Martin was his son as well as hers; and to have a minister as a son would be a great and splendid thing!

But when she thought about her husband, her expression became strained. Their marriage hadn't turned out as she had hoped. And yet her friends often reminded her of her luck in getting Bob Connolly. She supposed she was lucky, compared with some. Yet things had turned out different somehow, and difficult to explain, even to herself.

Martin had his homework finished just before eight o'clock. He put away his books and went out to the front door. He stood there, in the semi-darkness, looking up and down the street. He felt lonely. Half-an-hour ago his mother had gone out. She was probably in a neighbour's house, gossiping. And his father had gone to his 'branch'.

Martin always felt uneasy in the empty house at nighttime. He preferred to stand at the front door than to sit by himself in the kitchen. In the street there was always something happening; people passing up and down; customers going in and out of Geary's grocery at the corner; neighbours lighting up the gas in their parlours. And usually another boy would join him.

But no other boys were out. He wondered where they were; probably at the pictures, or maybe at the other end of the street, playing bar-the-door or relievo. But he couldn't see as far as the avenue end of Chatfield Street, where they usually congregated.

Suddenly he heard the 'ding' of a door and caught sight of his mother: she was coming out of Geary's shop. She was carrying a few groceries in her hand. She saw him and called, "I'm going into Mrs. McIlroy's."

Mrs. McIlroy lived next door to Geary's: she was a plump rosy faced woman who often stood at her doorstep, arms akimbo. She was Mrs. Connolly's greatest friend: Martin knew that once his mother went into the McIlroy house she wouldn't come out of it for at least an hour.

He made no answer to his mother's call: and before she disappeared up Mrs. McIlroy's hall she called out again, "I'm not far away, if you want me."

"I don't want you," he called back, meaning the opposite.

She didn't care what happened to him, he thought, else she wouldn't leave him alone. She had deserted both the house and himself. After all the house wasn't his responsibility; and if she left it anything could happen ... He felt forlorn and cold. He wrapped his hands in his navy-blue jersey for comfort.

He heard again the 'ding' of Geary's door, and a boy appeared; Sam Geary, whose granny owned the shop and whose father and mother served behind the counter. Sam was twelve, a year older than Martin, and much taller.

"Hello."

He crossed the street and approached Martin.

"Your mother forgot this."

He handed Martin a bar of soap, turned, and disappeared into the shop. Martin gazed at the oblong bar of pale-yellow soap, smelt it and then looked towards Geary's shop twenty-five yards away. He knew the shop was twenty-five yards from his own doorstep because he had often paced out the distance, carefully adjusting his steps so that each one was approximately one yard.

Geary's was a friendly shop, and he liked being sent there for messages. He had been in the shop hundreds of times and must have spent hours looking at the display of goods on the shelves above the two counters. He was familiar with everything to be seen from in front of the counter: and the boxes and tins of goods appeared to him to be of infinite variety.

The shop smelt differently according to where you stood as you waited to be served. And yet it was very small, not much bigger than the parlour of his own house. But it contained everything that his mother required for her everyday needs: indeed it was so handy that she would run in and out of it for a box of matches, a packet of starch, a half-pound of bacon, making three separate journeys for the three items.

After her home and church, it was the centre of her world. Mrs. Connolly loved talking to old Mrs. Geary, who owned the shop, and had the reputation of being the wisest and richest person living off the avenue. Mrs. Geary couldn't of course be compared with the wife of Dr. Williams, but then the doctor owned by far the biggest house in the avenue and his wife certainly had the reputation of giving herself the most airs: Martin had heard his mother make this remark many times.

He smelt the soap again, and was about to leave it in the scullery when he heard Mrs. McIlroy's high-pitched laughter and then his mother appeared at the McIlroy door.

The two women crossed the street.

"What are you doin'?" his mother asked.

"Nothing."

"You shouldn't be standin' out here. It's too cold a night."

"Let me feel your hand," said Mrs. McIlroy, holding his right hand in both her hands, before adding, "It's freezin', Jean."

"What's this in your other hand?" his mother asked.

"Soap from Geary's."

His mother laughed as she took the soap from him.

"I don't know what kind of a head I have! I forgot all about this. Who brought it over?"

"Sam Geary."

"A nice boy, Sam," remarked Mrs. McIlroy. "I wish there was more like him in the street."

Mrs. McIlroy spoke better than the other women in Chatfield Street: and they said she had married beneath her. Her husband, a small dark man of less than five feet, was a boilermaker.

Mrs. Connolly invited Mrs. McIlroy into the kitchen; and Martin followed the two women.

"What a poor fire!" his mother said. "Why didn't you put on a shovelful of coal?"

He made no reply: he had forgotten about the fire; anyway if it was nearly out the fault was his mother's, not his.

"Dear, dear," she muttered.

And away his mother went, into the backyard, where the coal was piled up.

He sat down on the sofa, away from the table, which he knew would soon be set for a cup of tea.

He liked Mrs. McIlroy, and he knew she liked him. He had often noticed her staring at him and sighing; and occasionally he had listened to the two women talk about Mrs. McIlroy's dead son: she had had a stillborn child a year before Martin's birth.

"It wasn't to be, I suppose," she said sadly. "If only we'd been able to have another."

She asked Martin questions about school while Mrs. Connolly got the tea ready.

"You'll turn out a credit to your mother," she said in her precise squeaky voice. "A real credit."

"I hope so," Mrs. Connolly said, pouring out the two cups, and looking at her son: Martin had picked up from the sofa a motorcycling magazine and was trying to pretend that the subject of their conversation had certainly nothing to do with him.

Then the kitchen door opened and his father entered.

"Hello, Mrs. McIlroy! Turned cold, hasn't it?"

"Very cold now, Mr. Connolly."

"Not a very good fire for a coul' night like this, is it?"

He picked up the poker from the hearth and carefully cleaned the grate; then he turned to his wife and said slowly, his manner very serious:

"Have you heard about your cousin—Joe Reynolds?"

Mrs. Connolly lowered her cup so suddenly that it almost smashed the saucer.

"Anything happened to him?"

Martin's father turned towards the fire again and gave it a vigorous poke.

"He was shot—about an hour ago."

"Oh, my God—"

Martin saw his mother's face become very pale; her hands trembled slightly; she couldn't speak for a moment.

"Tell me what happened, Bob."

"I don't know the details—"

"Is Joe dead?"

Martin's father nodded. Mrs. McIlroy sat staring at Mrs. Connolly, who suddenly broke into sobs.

"Poor Joe! A man that never hurt a soul in his whole life!"

The funeral of Joe Reynolds was on the following Monday at half-past two. Mrs. Connolly had been very fond of her cousin, a bachelor of thirty-five, and a cooper by trade; a thin, good-humoured man, with black curly hair.

Martin learnt that it was called an act of reprisal for a Catholic workman who had been killed a fortnight earlier. Joe Reynolds had worked for a firm near the docks, in the district where the previous murder had taken place.

Joe Reynolds was known as a quiet man, well liked by his mates. He was shot in the back during his lunchtime, his unfinished cheese sandwich in his hand, and no one confessed to seeing his murderers.

The circumstances of the death embittered Mrs. Connolly so much that the expression on her face sometimes frightened Martin. When he was at his homework, he noticed her staring into the fire, clenching and unclenching her hands. She told her husband, "I'll never trust one of that sort again, as long as I live!"

Her husband only shrugged his shoulders and replied, "Is the wrong all on their side?"

Five

THE MORNING OF THE EXAMINATION ARRIVED—a bright sunny May morning; and Martin woke early, after a restless night. He looked out of his bedroom window into the backyard, glad that the day had come at last. Soon it would all be over.

He looked into the backyard of their next-door neighbour, Mr. Montgomery, who kept pigeons. Already the birds were cooing in their loft, freshly painted dark blue. Martin loved to watch the pigeons from the vantage point of the back bedroom window; he had spent hours sitting on the edge of his bed from where he could see the birds enter and leave the loft. Sometimes they flew over the roofs and out of sight, and sometimes they merely perched on top of the loft, apparently undecided what to do.

"Are you awake, son?"

"Yes."

"Your breakfast's ready."

"All right."

He hopped out of bed, put on his trousers, and rushed downstairs. He looked at the clock.

"You've plenty of time," his father said.

It was half-past seven.

"See and take a good breakfast," his father added, as Martin sat down, after having quickly washed himself under the cold scullery tap.

"How are you feelin' this morning, son?"

His father was already dressed and about to leave for work: he had put on a pair of clean overalls. Martin replied that he was feeling all right, though inwardly he felt excited. He was sure that he would remember nothing as soon as the examination began.

"Well, I must be goin'," his father said, stuffing his 'piece', wrapped in brown paper, in his pocket.

"Here," he gave Martin a half-crown.

"Don't worry, mind, whatever happens. You can only do your best."

He patted his son on the shoulder and left the kitchen.

Mrs. Connolly made Martin eat two boiled eggs for his breakfast—and then made him put on his Sunday suit. She wouldn't let him go to the college of Technology in his everyday pants and jersey. The occasion was far too momentous. And she oiled his hair—for after his bath on the previous evening his fair hair was sticking out like tufts of feathers.

She was proud of Martin as he walked up the street at a quarter-past eight. And she watched him till he turned into the avenue and was lost to her view. But before he disappeared he had turned to give her a wave. She had waved back, before going in to wash her dishes.

All day her thoughts were with him.

The six boys in Mr. Magee's scholarship class had agreed to meet at a quarter to nine outside the Technical College. Martin judged that he would be the first to arrive; for the clock on Robinson & Cleaver's was at twenty-five to nine when he passed the City Hall. So he slackened his pace up Wellington Place.

In front of him lay the grounds of the Academical Institution, backed by the long, low façade of the school itself. To the right rose the massive 'Tech', overbearing in its massiveness: a much more recent building. The site of the long, low school, built at the beginning of the nineteenth century was completely spoilt by the newer building.

He crossed the street at the Black Man statue and

approached the steps at the front of the 'Tech'. A crowd of boys, some wearing their school caps, others bareheaded, were already gathered round the door. They were chatting in groups; but here and there on the fringe of the crowd stood lonely figures, eagerly seeking companions who hadn't so far turned up.

Martin spotted Jimmy Kerr and rushed over to greet him.

"Hello, Jimmy."

"Hello."

"Anybody else here?"

"Not yet."

They fell silent, both thinking of the ordeal ahead, and looked round the crowd.

By a quarter to nine the other four members of Mr. Magee's extra class had arrived; and almost immediately the crowd of boys swept into the hallway of the 'Tech'.

"Let's go in together," Jimmy said.

"I only wish we were coming out," Martin replied.

They were ushered up a stairway, along a corridor with glass cases displaying machinery, and into a large hall.

A voice from a dais addressed them, "Go to the desk which has the same number as your card."

In the excitement Martin had forgotten all about his card. He groped in his pocket. It was there, safe. And then he had to search for desk one hundred and nine.

It was in the middle of the hall. He sat down, surrounded by strange boys who stared at him and didn't appear to be in the least scared.

He felt his face with both his hands: he was burning; and his knees were trembling. He was glad he hadn't to speak; for the roof of his mouth was dry. He wished it were all over.

A severe-looking man, wearing a stiff white collar, shouted out instructions about the examination; another younger man was handing out the first paper—the essay. Martin wrote his name, address, and school on the front page of his script, as the severe-looking man had instructed him. How could he be expected to write an essay now? Impossible to think of anything! Even his hands were trembling. He wished he could go home.

The essay paper was now in front of him. He glanced at it,

eagerly. There were six essays to choose from! And they looked fairly easy too!

He quickly made his choice: 'My Favourite Hero'. He would write about Horatio Nelson.

No longer nervous, he began writing slowly and carefully; and in what seemed a surprisingly short time he heard the voice again.

"Five minutes to go ... Finish off your work now ... "

He scribbled a few sentences to round off his essay and sat back, waiting for his work to be collected.

He felt happy as he waited for the next paper.

The papers were easier then Mr. Magee had led him to expect—even the arithmetic paper which Martin had dreaded most of all.

Walking home with Jimmy Kerr, Martin discovered that they had given the same answers to most of the problems. And Jimmy Kerr would have them all right! Of that Martin was absolutely sure.

"I may be wrong in them," Jimmy kept on saying.

Martin shook his head.

They walked quickly from the centre of the town and caught a tram at the Fruit Markets; they were anxious to have their headmaster's opinion of the papers.

Mr. Magee was still standing at his desk in the main room though it was now five past six and school long over. He looked tired.

"Well, boys ... "

Mr. Magee's right hand eagerly reached out for the papers, and for a few minutes he studied them.

"Hm ... "

"What d'you think of them, sir?" a boy called Todd had the effrontery to ask.

"What did *you* think of them, Todd?"

"Not too bad, sir."

"You mean—they were easy?"

"Yes, sir."

"So you are pleased with yourself?"

"Yes, sir."

"I certainly hope you've good cause to be. Now, you, Kerr, read out the answers you got in the arithmetic paper."

Jimmy Kerr took a rumpled page of paper from his pocket and read his answers; and the others chimed their agreement or disagreement.

"How many think they've them all right?"

No one dared to raise a right hand.

"Well, we'll see in the morning. Now, hurry on home, boys ... for I want to see you all at nine o'clock as usual."

And as soon as they were dismissed their excitement ebbed away. The scholarship examination was over at last. And suddenly Martin felt hungry.

Once through the school gates he ran home.

Excitedly he told his mother, in great detail, all that had happened since he had left home in the morning. And she listened to him eagerly, her pride shining forth. She listened without ever daring to interrupt him, and his experience was very vivid in her imagination.

He was flushed. Unconsciously she stretched forward and felt his forehead with the palm of her hand. Yes, his forehead was certainly hot; but she didn't think he was feverish.

"You've told me enough now, Martin," she said, rising from the sofa where she had sat still for half-an-hour, her hands in her lap.

"But mother—"

"No more now. You can tell me the rest tomorrow. Your tea's ready."

She had prepared a special meal for him. She had spent the whole afternoon baking soda and wheaten bread, a large apple-tart and a plateful of cream buns. He was very hungry; and he was aware that his mother had made for him everything he liked; yet he never appeared to notice what he was eating.

"Take your time. You're in no hurry now. Don't bolt your food."

"I'm finished now, Mother."

He rose from the table.

"I think I'll go out somewhere," he added.

"You're not too tired?"

He shook his head.

"Better change out of your good clothes."

He went upstairs, changed from his grey Sunday suit into his everyday jersey and pants, and came downstairs again.

"Don't go too far, you're lookin' a bit tired."

"I don't feel tired."

He felt extraordinarily elated.

"Mind what I say," she warned as he put on his everyday shoes.

"I'll only go a walk along the avenue."

As he spoke there was a knock at the open front door, and his mother went into the hall; Martin peeped through the kitchen door after her, and saw Sam Geary standing outside.

"My grandmother says would you please let Martin go to the pictures with me?"

"Come in, Sam," Mrs. Connolly ordered, allowing the boy into the kitchen.

The two boys faced each other sheepishly.

"It's very kind of your granny," Mrs. Connolly said. "Of course Martin would like to go. Wouldn't you?"

She was eager for her son to become more friendly with Sam Geary, but somehow the two boys had never seemed to be over-anxious for each other's company. Martin was over a year younger, and Sam was not usually encouraged by his parents to play with the boys in Chatfield Street. After all, the Geary household was socially above the working-class families in the streets surrounding the shop. The shop and dwelling house occupied the corner site; and Mr. Geary owned a pony and trap; and the house had a bathroom and a front sitting-room. Old Mrs. Geary, Sam's grandmother, talked like a real lady and acted like one, too, though she never gave herself airs.

Mrs. Connolly was proud that the Gearys considered Martin a suitable companion for their Sam.

"Wouldn't you like to go with Sam?"

Martin hesitated. He didn't really want to go to the pictures with Sam Geary.

"Yes," he said at last.

The two boys walked along Chatfield Street, then reached Temple Avenue. They hadn't spoken yet.

"Did you want to come with me?" Sam asked, as they were crossing the avenue. Martin nodded.

"You didn't seem to," Sam added; then as an afterthought: "You can leave me if you like. I can go by myself."

"I want to go," Martin replied.

"It's a good cowboy picture," Sam went on.

"That's what I like," Martin said.

"So do I. We've got a pony, you know."

"I've seen it."

"But my father won't let me ride it."

"Why?"

"Because it's dangerous."

They reached the cinema.

"I've to pay for both of us," Sam said, as they approached the box office.

"Two balcony seats," he told the girl.

They climbed the soft-carpeted stairs flanked with portraits of film stars. Martin had never before sat in the balcony with its comfortable seats which allowed you to see the film without putting your coat beneath in order to have a better view.

Two hours later they came out, hardly able to adjust themselves to the reality of their own neighbourhood. They were by now quite talkative.

"See you again sometime," Sam said in parting.

"Yes," Martin answered.

And before he was able to say thanks, Sam ran off homewards.

"How did you enjoy the pictures?" his mother asked as soon as he entered the kitchen; and he told her he had seen Tom Mix in the big picture.

"Then you're glad you went?"

He nodded.

His father lay stretched out on the sofa, reading the evening newspaper. "Well?" he asked, dropping the paper on the floor. "How did everything go?"

"I don't know."

"Was it as hard as you expected?"

"I don't think so."

"I don't suppose you can tell. How could you? Anyway, you did your best, an' that's all any of us can do. If you win through, well, I'll be glad to see it; an' if you don't, no one's any the worse ... "

"It's time you were in bed," his mother said. "What d'you want for supper?"

44

He took a glass of milk and a biscuit; then took off his shoes and went upstairs.

"Goodnight, Martin," his father called, lifting up the newspaper again.

His mother looked at him proudly as he closed the door and felt his way up the familiar stairs into his own room.

He undressed, put on his nightshirt, and tumbled into bed. He lay awake for a few minutes and remembered hearing the throaty sigh of a ship's siren echoing over the city.

Six

A MONTH LATER A LETTER ARRIVED, inviting Martin to go again to the College of Technology; he was to be interviewed by the Education Committee. When he heard the news Mr. Magee shook his head and smiled approvingly, and said, "You're safely over the first hurdle."

Three other boys received similar letters, and Mr. Magee elaborated on the purpose of an Education Committee called to make a final selection of scholarship boys.

"They just want to have a look at you; to see whether you're the right type. I needn't tell you, of course, how to behave; you all know. And you know the kind of behaviour I expect of you."

Then, as an afterthought, having scrutinised them from top to toe: "And remember, Sunday suits once again. You must all look spick-an'-span."

"Will they ask us any questions, sir?"

"Yes of course they will."

"What sort of questions, sir?"

"Easy ones, I hope."

"But what like, sir?"

"What d'you want to be—that's the kind of question they're likely to ask."

"But I don't know, sir, what I want to be."

Mr. Magee looked steadily at his four boys: then added grimly, "Then find out before you're interviewed. They want boys that have minds to make up, and have them already made up. No shilly-shallying."

So they made up their minds.

A few days later Mr. Magee brought the four together again after school hours.

"Well, Kerr, what have you decided to be?"

"A post office official, sir."

"Good. And you, Bailey?"

" A clergyman, sir."

"Excellent. Is that what your parents want you to be, or are your own inclinations in that direction?"

"I'd like to be a clergyman, sir."

Benevolently Mr. Magee stared at his pupil: a curiously aged-looking boy of eleven, the son of a small draper.

"I can see you in the pulpit, Bailey," he said, changing his own voice to a clerical tone. "You somehow have the look."

The other three boys took this remark, as they took everything Mr. Magee said, with exceptional seriousness: to them Mr. Magee could never be guilty of levity, either in speech or deed; for within the precincts of the school he assumed an air of infallibility, of profound seriousness of purpose. He seldom smiled, and when he did so his face appeared unnatural, as if he were sickening for some disease.

He was a man of fifty-four, of no great intelligence and with little culture.

"Ah!" Mr. Magee said to himself, meditating on the fact that his own career had been a disappointment. He regarded his own reflection in the classroom window: and what he saw satisfied him. Surely he had been cut out for better things than to teach classes of grubby children, the sons of labourers, artisans, and small shopkeepers ...

"Ah!" he repeated, "Where were we? Kerr—a post-official; Bailey—a clergyman. And you, Connolly?"

"A civil servant, sir."

"Good."

Martin had no idea what a civil servant was, except that it was somehow connected with the government. It sounded important; and his mother told him that it was important. It was a safe job (and his parents agreed that he should seek such a job). Martin, for his part, wanted a life with plenty of risks. His ambition was to be a sailor before the mast, or if that was impossible and he had to remain on dry land, he wanted to be a steeplejack. However, he thought that the words 'civil servant' sounded pleasant enough.

Mr. Magee then raised his eyebrows, his mute invitation to the fourth boy, Willie Jamison, whose parents owned a fish and chip shop.

"A commercial traveller, sir."

"Really. Why?"

"Because it's a good job, sir."

"Who says so?"

"My father, sir."

"And he should know."

But his irony was unnoticed.

Mr. Magee knew Willie Jamison's father by sight—and by smell; for the Jamisons, father and son, had the stale odour of the shop clinging to their clothes. Mr. Magee was a fastidious man by temperament: his own clothes were kept scrupulously fresh and neat. He detested any suggestion of uncleanliness. The Jamison boy certainly smelt.

"Ah," he said, looking at his four aspirants and sighing.

"We'll see how you all turn out."

As Martin entered the room he was afraid that he would be unable to speak; and his mind was a blank. As through a haze he saw five men sitting in front of a table, all of them with white papers in their hands. A voice called his name.

"Yes, sir," he answered, not sure which man had spoken. It was the man in the middle, who had a grey moustache and grey hair and who suddenly smiled.

Martin tried to smile back but somehow couldn't. He felt his knees trembling.

"You look a bright boy," the man said, still smiling.

Martin said nothing, waiting for what was to come.

"What do you want to be?"

Before the question was finished Martin had shot forth his answer.

"A civil servant, sir!"

The man broke into a laugh.

"Well, well, it didn't take you long to answer that one, did it? You've your mind made up, then?"

Martin nodded slightly in reply.

"And nobody's made it up for you?"

Martin shook his head.

"Then would you tell me why you want to be a civil servant?"

Martin paused. His mind wouldn't work. He couldn't think why he wanted to be a civil servant.

Oh, he remembered the answer—

"I would be serving my country, sir."

It was now the turn of the smiling man with the moustache to nod his head slightly, before adding; "And any other reason?"

"It's a safe job, sir."

The man nodded again, then closed his eyes for an instant.

"Thank you. That's all we require."

The man opened his eyes as he spoke, smiled again, and Martin left the room.

Seven

IT WAS OVER. MARTIN COULD HARDLY believe that the ordeal was now, finally, at an end. He would be asked to do no more.

The interview had been less terrifying than he had imagined. Still it had been terrifying enough. And he had trembled all during it: he had been quite unable to prevent himself from trembling. He wondered if they had noticed him.

He hoped not. And he hoped he hadn't disgraced Mr. Magee. He hoped there was still the chance of a scholarship for him. It was what he most longed for now. Everybody said it was the most important thing that could happen to him. It would make all the difference to his life.

He vaguely sensed what the difference would be. He would be given the chance of an education until he was eighteen years old. He would be given the chance to study while other boys would be at work. Yet he wasn't sure whether he wanted to study. He felt that work would probably be better than staying on at school.

Of course his father thought that he wasn't ready yet for work, that if he failed to get a scholarship he should go to the Technical College. Then after the 'Tech' he should serve his time to a trade. Become a carpenter or a draughtsman. He was fond of drawing. Only last Christmas he had won a guinea prize in the *Belfast Telegraph* competition.

Three weeks passed, but Mr. Magee made no reference to either the examination or the interview. He appeared to have completely forgotten both. The only change in the school routine was that Mr. Magee now paid no special attention to the scholarship candidates. They once again merged into the anonymity of the class of forty-seven boys.

Mr. Magee worked as hard as ever. Once he caught Martin daydreaming, looking through the classroom window into Cosgrave's foundry to see the red-hot furnace.

It was a sight which fascinated him: this rich-red column of naked flame, like an immense bunsen burner, less than a hundred yards away from the school. He was unable to keep his eyes from it.

"Connolly!"

"Yes, sir."

"Give me your attention, not the foundry. Unless that's where you want to find yourself. Would you like a job in there?"

"No, sir."

"I hope not."

He would like a job in the foundry, though he dared not confess it. The foundry was full of noise—the clanking of machinery, the shouts of men, the roar of the furnace. It was in complete contrast to the quietness of school where the three classes, huddled together in the main room, worked silently; the silence broken occasionally by a teacher's sharp command. Martin envied the workmen, their faces and hands grimy with dirt and oil, as they moved freely about the foundry yard, shouting and laughing at one another. Their world seemed infinitely preferable to his; just as his father's world in the shipyard was infinitely preferable.

Martin pretended to give Mr. Magee his whole attention; but instead of concentrating on a silent re-reading of Act I of *Julius Caesar* he began thinking of what he would do when school was over. This was the last half-hour of the day; and the last half-hour seemed the longest. Sometimes it seemed to go on forever: it seemed that he would have to spend the rest of his life ...

Then the small bell gave its tink-tink sound, half-muted because it was held in Mr. Magee's right hand, and the class almost jumped with delight though they only dared to raise their heads slightly and look imploringly at Mr. Magee. Mr. Magee then gave in return the most economical of his movements—a slight inclination of his head—and the class put away their Shakespeare, very quietly, and fastened their bags. They waited, not yet free.

"Now."

They rose. They marched out slowly, and with orderliness, into the hall and towards freedom.

At last the official letter arrived, addressed to Robert Connolly Esq., and with the words EDUCATION AUTHORITY boldly printed on the envelope. Martin's father had already gone to work: it was twenty past eight.

As Mrs. Connolly took the letter from the postman, her hands trembled. She stood looking at it, afraid to open it. Martin was in the kitchen, at breakfast; his mother stood quite still in the doorway, her face pale, the letter in her hand.

She opened it. It informed her husband that Martin had been successful in the scholarship examination.

"Martin!"

She ran up the hall.

"Son—"

"What's the matter, Mother?"

His mother threw her arms round him: she was weeping.

"You've won!"

"Mother, you're nearly choking me—"

She showed him the letter. She was almost delirious with delight.

"Aren't you excited? Oh, you should be! I'm proud—oh, so proud of you!"

She embraced him again.

"Oh, your father'll be that pleased! I can't wait to tell him! Oh, Martin!"

She sat on the sofa, her cheeks burning.

"I don't know what to say. Aren't you pleased?"

He was. His pleasure was so intense that outwardly he displayed only calmness. She watched him with wonder as he coolly finished his breakfast.

"I suppose I'll have to tell Mr. Magee," he said.

"Of course you'll have to tell him! He'll be as pleased as punch!"

Martin had never seen his mother look so happy: she looked so different, radiant, almost like a girl. She took off her apron, hurriedly fixed her hair, and cleared the dishes off the table with remarkable speed.

She kissed him as he left for school.

"I'm the happiest woman alive now! Hurry home, won't you?"

"Why?"

"To tell me what Mr. Magee says! He'll be the proud man! Away you go!"

She released him: and immediately she ran across the street to tell Mrs. McIlroy and all the neighbours.

Mr. Magee was at his desk when Martin entered the big classroom.

"Well?" Mr. Magee said quietly. He was smiling. He seemed to know about the letter already, for the boys sitting at their desks were smiling too. Everybody seemed very happy.

"Did you get one too?" Mr. Magee went on, before Martin could give his answer.

"Yes, sir."

"Oh, good! Good! That's three this year! Kerr, Jamison, and Connolly."

He advanced towards Martin and held out his hand.

"I knew you wouldn't let me down," he said, taking Martin's hand firmly.

Somehow the day passed. The school atmosphere was quite different from normal: the teachers talked to each other between classes; and Mr. Magee once laughed when a boy made a silly spelling mistake. Martin found that his classmates and even the teachers were already treating him with deference. He had gained a new status; he seemed to be walking about the school as if on air. It was a very pleasant feeling: a feeling of happiness. And it persisted, wonderfully, throughout the entire day.

His father, on hearing the news, was unable to speak for a moment or two; he contented himself with patting Martin's shoulder, then stooped and took off his working boots.

Mrs. Connolly handed him his slippers.

"Isn't it great, Bob?"

"Great news," his father said, shaking his head vigorously.

That was all he said. And it was enough. Martin had never seen his parents so pleased: pleased with him and with each other. His mother had laid a beautifully white tablecloth for tea; and had bought herself a bright new apron. She had the whole house shining, within and without. The brass door knocker was gleaming; the red tiles on the kitchen floor were spotless; everything was dusted, swept, polished.

Mrs. McIlroy called after tea and was brought into the kitchen. She shook hands with Martin.

"We'll all be proud of you yet," she said.

Afterwards he went out. There were few people about the street, and he walked to the top and turned into the avenue, glad to be alone. He was wondering what the new school would be like. It was more than a mile from his home. Mr. Magee had already told him about it: it had fine playing fields of its own, and a large staff of teachers, all with degrees, some with degrees from Oxford and Cambridge.

Martin knew the building by sight, but its weathered appearance had by no means impressed him. It looked neglected and forlorn. Still, Mr. Magee was of the opinion that it was the best secondary school in the city; the sons of doctors, lawyers, businessmen, and teachers were proud to belong to it; and among its old pupils were well-known people, distinguished in public life. To be given an opportunity to attend it was certainly a privilege ...

Martin turned towards home as a few drops of rain fell on the pavement. He had gone as far as the Albert Bridge: and he stood for a while looking at the Lagan. The river was at high tide, the mudbanks hidden, the sluggish water like a dark mirror. He often walked as far as this. It was a kind of boundary for him.

Beyond the river lay the centre of the city: almost unknown territory; he felt a stranger over there.

But soon it would be familiar to him; and he turned and looked towards the bridge once more.

Eight

IT TOOK MARTIN NEARLY A YEAR to become accustomed to his new school. But from the first day he was happy: the atmosphere was completely different from anything he had ever experienced. Most of the masters were on friendly terms with their classes; and the boys looked upon the staff with humorous respect.

It was only with difficulty that he adjusted himself to this new atmosphere. He didn't dare to joke with any of his masters yet, though it was clear that a joke was sometimes actually encouraged. There was no caning, except very occasionally by the headmaster, a Welshman whose passion was for music and who was often seen in the quadrangle talking loudly and laughing with the staff.

Martin liked his English teacher best—a man with fair wavy hair, a stoop, and a gentle voice, who taught in the most casual fashion, sometimes wasting a whole period idly chatting about school affairs, at other times teaching with enthusiasm— especially poetry. It was Mr. Gray who made Martin aware that poetry could give pleasure and should be read only for pleasure. The class was supposed to read Scott's 'Lady of the Lake'.

"I dislike this poem intensely," Billy Gray confided to his class. "Shall I go on with it?"

"No!" shouted the class.

"I'd hoped you'd say no," he replied. "If you don't like Scott, and I don't like Scott, what's the use?"

While the whole class gave a shout of approval, Martin hardly dared to smile.

This kind of behaviour seemed so wrong inside school that he could hardly believe it possible.

"What shall we do instead?" Mr. Gray continued.

"Read *Kidnapped*, sir."

"Does that meet with the approval of the whole class?"

"Yes, sir," the class yelled in chorus.

"All right then, Stevenson today, poetry tomorrow ... I'll read you some good poetry tomorrow ... "

"Please, sir, some short ones."

"Of course, very short ones. I agree with you: short poems are really the best. They don't bore you; they don't bore me; anyway people like us can't live for long on the heights ... "

Martin loved these informal English classes, and at the weekend enjoyed writing his essay for Mr. Gray.

When he received praise he blushed so violently that one afternoon Mr. Gray asked him to stay after the class.

"Well?"

He sat down on a desk beside Martin.

"What have you to say for yourself?"

After a long pause, Martin said, "Nothing, sir."

"Did you think I was angry with you when I asked you to remain behind?"

Martin made no reply.

"Look at me."

Martin looked at Mr. Gray.

"Do I look angry?"

"No, sir."

"Good. I'm not. I've no occasion to be. I like you. I like your work. Don't be afraid of me. See? If you are, than I will be angry—very angry. Now go! Hop it!"

Martin grabbed his bag and after carefully closing the door ran downstairs into the quadrangle. He glanced up towards the classroom; Billy Gray was standing at the window, smiling.

It was a friendly, easy-going school. Most of the boys were the sons of Belfast professional men but some had to come by train from villages and towns round about. There was, throughout the school, a sprinkling of scholarship boys.

During his first year Martin made few friends: he usually played with Jimmy Kerr and Willie Jamison. While walking home the three boys often compared their old school with the new.

"It was like prison," Jamison often said, "only we didn't know it." The others agreed.

"Anyway we're out of it," Jimmy Kerr said.

"I wouldn't like to go back, would you?"

"No fear." Martin's reply was firm. No, he wouldn't like to go back; he would hate their old school—the canings, the silences, the discipline—yet his hatred was mixed with affection. Baldy Magee was a tyrant; everyone stood in terror of him; but all the same Martin felt he owed the headmaster a great deal. Old Baldy wanted his boys to get on in the world. He wanted them to be proud of him: and he wanted them to remember him.

At home Martin was constantly questioned about his new school. His father was always anxious to hear about it.

"You're gettin' your chance, son, and not many of our class are as lucky as you, so—take your chance. I only wish I was in your shoes."

Still, some things puzzled Bob Connolly. He found it hard to understand that there could be no snobbery in such a school; but Martin reassured him.

"No, Father, you're wrong, there's none of that." His father seemed to find it hard to believe.

"None?"

Martin shook his head.

"Of course there's not, Bob," Mrs. Connolly said, "educated people don't bother about such things."

"Aye, but I know they do, Jean. That's where you're wrong."

His father was usually right: but now he was certainly wrong.

In his second year Martin became friendly with a boy called Tom Taylor, the son of a linen merchant. Tom was physically the opposite of Martin: Tom was tall, inclined to be plump, and rather awkward in his movement; while Martin was small for his thirteen years, thin, and agile. Both boys were rather shy, and at lunchtime would roam about the front of the school, seldom speaking. Tom, who wore spectacles for his astigmatism, seemed to enjoy Martin's company.

One day Tom invited Martin to his home.

"Come on Saturday—at about three o'clock," he said in his rather gruff voice.

"Where to?"

Martin had no idea where Tom lived; all he knew was that Tom took a Malone Road tram when school was over.

"I'll write the address down—it's not hard to find."

He gave directions on how to find the house; drawing a little map to help.

"Try and come, won't you?"

"Yes, I'll try."

Martin told his parents about the invitation; they received the news with a flurry of excitement, then agreed that he could accept.

"Let's see where they live," his father asked, consulting the pencilled map. After he had read the address out aloud he gave a whistle.

"Well, well!"

"D' you know the avenue, Bob?"

"No, but I've a fair notion where it is—at the top of the Malone Road, where there's nothin' but large houses standin' in their own grounds."

"What'd you call your friend?" Mrs. Connolly asked.

"Tom—Tom Taylor."

"Goodness gracious!" His mother suddenly flushed.

"You know who that is, Bob—the son of Mr. Taylor—"

"That's not surprising," Bob Connolly dryly commented.

"Mr. Taylor," his wife emphasised. "Thomas Taylor and Company where I used to work ... Oh dear! ... "

Martin's mother was quite breathless. Imagine her son invited to the house of her former employer! She, once a hemstitcher in Mr. Taylor's firm, now had a son who mixed on equal terms with such a family as the Taylors. It was almost incredible. She remembered that when Mr. Taylor entered the hemstitching room the girls at once ceased their chattering and gave their work all their attention. Yet they knew him as a kindly man, who had their welfare at heart. He was softly

58

spoken, with the reputation of being of a religious turn of mind. Of course he never referred to his beliefs—at least Martin's mother never recalled his ever mentioning such a subject.

"But he wouldn't remember me—I'm sure of that—I hardly spoke to him twice all the years I was there. He was a very nice man—everybody thought that—an' I'm sure his son's bound to be a very nice boy too."

On Saturday afternoon Martin took the tram up the Malone Road. He was unfamiliar with this part of the city: it was very different from his own. There were no shops, no factories, and all the houses had large well-kept gardens. The tram, having passed the University district of Botanic Gardens, reached the end of the road. It was here that the Taylors lived, in a leafy avenue on the left-hand side. With the aid of Tom's map, Martin had no difficulty in finding the Taylors' house.

Tom was in the garden, beneath a tall chestnut tree. He lay reading a book.

"Hello!"

"Hello!"

The silence was broken by the appearance at the front door of a large grey-haired woman, who called out, "Tom, aren't you going to introduce me to your friend?"

Mrs. Taylor advanced down the lawn and shook hands with Martin.

"So this is Martin Connolly. I hope you'd no difficulty in finding your way out here. It's very good of you to come and play with Tom."

It was a fine May afternoon, with the sun throwing dark shadows beneath the trees.

"What are your plans, Tom? You'll have to entertain your guest, you know. It's up to you to make suggestions. Well, what have you in mind?"

Tom finally decided on a walk.

"Where?"

"To the river, Mother; along the towpath as far as Shaw's Bridge; then back by the road."

"Good. That'll take you at least an hour; then we'll have tea out here in the garden, and afterwards you can show Martin your playroom."

Two girls appeared round the side of the house; they were Claire and Ruth, Tom's sisters.

"Where's your father?" Mrs. Taylor inquired.

"At the back," Claire, the elder, replied, shyly.

"What's he doing? Weeding?"

"Yes."

"Tell him to come here."

Mr. Taylor was brought to the front garden; and Martin was introduced to a small brown-faced man in shirtsleeves.

"Now, Martin, you've met the family," Mrs. Taylor said, "so off you go, the pair of you."

They walked along the towpath of the sluggish river as far as Shaw's Bridge, and watched the horse-driven barges, laden with coal, glide slowly towards Lisburn. Then they turned to the right, past a great mansion belonging to a famous owner of racehorses, and reached Tom's home.

They had tea in the garden; and afterwards Martin was brought indoors. He was no longer nervous; the chatter of Mrs. Taylor and the two girls was incessant—they appeared to have forgotten his presence—and the whole family seemed to have known him for years.

Shortly after seven he said goodbye.

"You'll come another day, won't you?" Mrs. Taylor inquired.

He promised he would.

The three Taylor children left him at the tram-stop, and when he boarded the tram they stood watching it disappear, waving until it passed out of their sight.

He arrived home. His mother was eager to hear everything; she only wished she had been there, invisible, to see her son among the Taylors. She was very proud of him; and very sure he would take his proper place in the world.

Bob Connolly was more sceptical. His view of the world was far different from his wife's. For her, their son had now his feet firmly on the first rung of the social ladder; she wanted him to climb as far as possible. But Bob Connolly merely saw Martin in danger of leaving the class into which he was born; of being educated by and for the middle class. He didn't want his son to desert his own class. And yet he wanted Martin to be educated, to have a trained mind.

He listened to Martin's account of how the Taylors lived. He sat quiet, nosing the evening paper. Despite himself his own curiosity was aroused.

"Did you hear that, Bob?" Mrs. Connolly interposed.

"No," he lied.

"The Taylors have another house somewhere by the sea."

"I'm not surprised. Only one?" he answered.

"They spend the whole summer there—June, July, August, and September."

"Fancy that!"

"They asked would Martin be allowed to go to the seaside house."

"And would he?"

"Why not? I've no objection. Have you?"

"Why should I have?"

No, he'd no objection to his son having a summer holiday with the Taylors. The boy needed a good holiday; and it was kind of the Taylors to invite him as a companion for their own son; but all the same he didn't want his son to be unduly influenced by this middle-class family and all it stood for.

Nine

TOWARDS THE END OF JUNE, JUST after school had broken up for the holidays, Martin went to stay with the Taylors.

Their summerhouse was on the outskirts of Bangor, on a hill overlooking the golf links. Mr. and Mrs. Taylor were keen golfers and encouraged the two boys to take up the game; but Tom had no interest, and Martin, who was secretly eager to try, refused to play by himself. Tom's passion was for swimming and exploring among the rocks.

"I see no sense in games," he said, "especially golf."

Martin rarely talked about his own home, and the Taylors never questioned him. He mentioned that he had once lived in Bangor.

"Really!" Mrs. Taylor said, her curiosity aroused. "Where?"

He had to confess that he had forgotten the name of the street, but remembered that it was off the main Belfast road; his parents had come to live in Belfast because it was too inconvenient for them to live by the seaside. But the Taylors didn't pursue the subject.

It was a very different world he was entering: and it made him ashamed of his own background. He was becoming aware of how his parents spoke, and of how their neighbours and friends spoke: and the working-class accents he heard at home now appeared to him as ugly and offensive.

He wished he'd been born into a home similar to Tom's: and yet Tom didn't seem to be very happy—or at least he didn't often laugh out loud. Perhaps it didn't matter so much where you were born—whether in a rich home or not—what really mattered was what you felt like inside yourself.

As the week came towards its end, Mrs. Taylor asked Martin if he was enjoying himself. He told her he was.

"Would you like to stay longer with us—perhaps for the months of July and August?"

Martin answered that he would like to stay.

"We'd like to have you. So if you'd ask your parents when you go home on Sunday, and if they agree you could return next week, and stay as long as you like ... "

The upshot was that Martin spent the whole summer with the Taylors. It was the first time he'd ever been away from home for such a long time.

The Taylors lived well. The whole family seemed to do exactly what they wanted. Mr. Taylor played a lot of golf; so did Mrs. Taylor; they often took Claire, Ruth, Tom and Martin on motor-boat trips; and they had friends in for dinner two or three times a week, and often went out themselves to dine, leaving the children with Mrs. Piggot, their middle-aged maid from Dublin. The children rather disliked Mrs. Piggot because her temper was short, especially when she was left in charge.

So July and August passed quickly for Martin, so quickly that when the last few days of August came he was astonished.

"School again next week," Tom said, mournfully.

"Martin doesn't mind, I'm sure," Mrs. Taylor said.

"You'll have to settle down, the both of you, and do some real hard work next year," Mr. Taylor said, because when the summer reports had appeared Tom's was not as good as his previous ones; and Martin announced that his had not been very good either.

"The trouble with you lads is that you get things far too easily."

Though he knew Martin was on a scholarship he never gave

any indication of the fact: instead he told both boys that he considered them good-for-nothings.

It was an easy-going household: even the two girls, Claire and Ruth, were good fun. Martin liked Claire especially, but the two girls had their own friends and only mixed with the boys in the evenings, mostly to play card games.

Martin learnt that Mr. and Mrs. Taylor had plans for their children: Tom was to go to Oxford to study classics and perhaps read law; the two girls would be sent to English schools in a year or two.

"Do you want to go to Oxford?" Martin asked Tom.

"I think so," came the unsure reply.

As Mr. Taylor hadn't had a university education he was anxious for his son to have one. He didn't want Tom to enter the linen business; its future was too uncertain: and all the competition abroad and at home was becoming keener. During the war business had been very good, but the period of temporary prosperity was long over and a slump was now likely. Still, no one could tell what might happen; and Mr. Taylor wasn't unduly worried. As for his wife, she didn't concern herself with the business matters which she heard her husband and his friends discuss.

Mrs. Taylor was completely absorbed in her children and in her social activities. She had plenty of confidence in herself, her children, and in her husband. She appeared to enjoy herself, to be secure in her social position; and while she had parties to organise, friends to entertain, children to bring up, the world beyond her home was of little significance. Anyway, she had little to do with it. She was content to leave that side of life to her husband.

On his return home, Martin had grown a couple of inches and he looked sturdier; also he spoke better. He saw a good deal of Tom during that autumn and winter; especially on Saturdays when, if the weather was fine, he would visit the Taylors' house. Only once did he bring Tom to his own home for tea. He felt ashamed of the narrow street, the small kitchen where his mother prepared tea, and the cramped parlour where they sat afterwards and talked about school.

"Tom's very quiet," Mrs. Connolly said, after their visitor had left. "Is he always that quiet?"

"Usually," Martin said.

"But he's very good-mannered. Did you see how he got up every time I came in and out? He's very well brought up. Anyone can see that."

She was very impressed; more impressed than her husband was.

"I doubt if he's brains," Bob Connolly remarked.

"Why d'you say that?"

"He hasn't enough spunk in him."

"How d'you know?"

Mrs. Connolly was constantly irritated by her husband's cocksureness.

"He's a very nice boy, I thought," she said.

"Oh, I agree ... I didn't say he wasn't."

"And I'm glad he's made friends with our Martin."

"He won't spark Martin off—an' that's what he needs," Bob Connolly said.

"I don't know what you mean."

"No?" He raised his eyebrows.

"No, I don't."

"He'll not teach Martin much, but Martin'll teach him a lot."

Mrs. Connolly thought over this remark. She was prepared to accept it. She believed in the ability of her son; and she believed that he had more ability than any other woman's son—even Mrs. Taylor's. But she must not be too proud.

"He'll teach Martin good manners," she said at last.

"I didn't think your son needed that."

"He doesn't—but he forgets himself sometimes."

She only wished that Martin was as punctilious in his manners as Tom. It pleased her greatly to see the son of the Taylors rise from his chair as soon as she entered the room. It gave her a rare feeling of satisfaction; she had accomplished something important, or more truly, her son had done it for her.

As Martin reached the senior forms his confidence grew. The school was imperceptibly doing a great deal for him. Instead of being so shy that he hardly dared to speak to boys whom he didn't know he became friendly and assured in manner and bearing. And he was growing fast. He had entered the school physically undersized and mentally precocious, with little to offer except a quick eager brain. He was completely pliable and malleable; he wanted to succeed in the world in which he found himself: and it seemed as if he were going to succeed.

Luckily, he was good at games and success at rugby football and cricket made him popular. He was better than Tom at both games; Tom, being short-sighted and slow, tried very hard but had little success. Their friendship, however, remained unimpaired: but more and more Martin became leader. Tom, it seemed, was quite content with following, and from time to time he had his successes too. For example he won more school prizes than Martin did. He worked far harder, and took his lessons far more seriously. Martin worked only spasmodically. He had a strong streak of indolence in his nature, and sometimes for a whole term he hardly did a stroke of work. He was given to sudden enthusiasms: first of all for woodwork, then for watercolours, and finally for music.

He discovered music by chance. On wet Wednesday afternoons when a rugger match was rained off he sometimes called in at the new Museum and Art Gallery on the Stranmillis Road. It was on his way home and he liked to spend an hour or so wandering about the different rooms.

One Wednesday afternoon when he reached the top floor he heard the sound of music. An orchestra was playing Schubert's *Rosemunde* overture. He sat and listened.

The *Unfinished Symphony* followed. He could hardly contain his excitement when the music ended. Why had no one told him about these delights offered so easily and so freely? All you had to do was to sit and listen; it was very mysterious! And he was unable to identify at least half the instruments being played!

That evening he went immediately after tea to the public library and took out a book on music which he read till nearly two o'clock in the morning.

He tried to make Tom share his enthusiasm.

"I only wish I could play something!" he exclaimed with excitement.

"You could learn the piano, couldn't you?" Tom replied, coolly.

"No, no, I couldn't!"

"Why not?" Tom went on; "I learnt for a couple of years. Then I gave it up."

"Why?"

"Because I hated it. Anyway, I've no ear for music. Claire has. She's the musical member of our family."

"What does she play?"

"Oh, I don't know—you'd better ask her."

"I mean—what instrument?"

"Oh, the piano, of course. I thought you meant what music. I don't know what pieces she plays. All I know is she practises a devil of a lot. Far too much, I'd say. There's never peace in the house, you know."

Strange, but he had never heard Tom's sister play the piano. Or if he had, he hadn't noticed her. Come to that, he had hardly been aware of Claire—or of Ruth either. Yet he liked them both. They were quiet, rather like their brother indeed, but not quite so serious-looking. In fact they sometimes took a fit of giggling that came on both of them— or seemed to—simultaneously, and made them appear absolutely ridiculous.

"Claire's away now, you know," Tom added.

"Is she?" Martin asked.

"At school, you know. In England."

"Oh."

"I told you; I must have. And Ruth's going next term. The house'll be a lot quieter then, with neither of them at home."

"Yes."

Martin had forgotten that Claire had been sent to boarding school somewhere in the south of England. He recalled that Tom had told him, casually, and that at the time they had discussed what it would be like to be at an English boarding school. Tom was not in the least anxious to be sent away; he preferred to remain at home; and he had explained why his father hadn't sent him across the water to be educated. The explanation was simple. Mr. Taylor wanted his son to be educated at a local school so that Tom should be at home in his native city; and have his friends at school as his friends in adult life. For it might happen that Tom would have to enter the commercial life of the city; and, if this happened, it would be useful to have plenty of 'connections'.

So Tom, unlike the girls, was not sent away to England.

"When will Claire be home?" Martin asked.

"Next week. Probably next Saturday," Tom answered. "That's the end of term for her."

He discovered that Claire was travelling by the Heysham boat on the Friday night and arriving home on Saturday morning; and as he often went to the Taylors' house on Saturday afternoons he suggested to Tom that he might call, and that in the evening they might go to the cinema.

"What d'you say?"

Tom nodded in agreement.

"See and have your homework done, won't you?"

"Yes, all right."

During the week Martin found himself thinking of Claire. It was curious, thinking of a girl: and it was curious that he should be thinking of Tom's sister. Claire had never struck him as an interesting girl: she was not at all good-looking, he thought. For one thing her nose was snub; and her teeth were irregular; and her hair was never really tidy; and her walk was rather ungainly. He wondered if she were any other girl than Tom's sister, would he be attracted to her? For he realised that he was attracted to her. Else why should he be constantly thinking of her? There was no reason why he should.

It was very curious that he was allowing a girl like Claire to occupy so much of his thoughts. Of course he had often thought about girls before; and he had talked about them too, talked about them in a way that would have shocked Claire, would even have shocked Tom. For he had never talked to Tom about girls: Tom was very reticent about such matters and would blush if they were mentioned. He hated to hear coarse language and avoided boys who used it. Most boys used it at some time or another, especially after a rugger match when they were changing in the pavilion, running in and out of the shower baths naked, yelling at one another, and whipping one another with damp towels. It was all raucous and rowdy, with the senior boys parading their bodies in front of the staring juniors.

Some boys in the first fifteen boasted of their conquests, giving full particulars of their techniques. What they said they did with the girls amazed Martin; he could scarcely believe that girls would allow such intimacies. A boy called Stephen Carter was the most outspoken and claimed the most experience. He was a lithe, thin-faced boy with a pasty complexion and hunched shoulders: he looked delicate yet he was remarkably good at football. He kept a notebook in which he alleged he kept a list of his girls. Grinning, he often said: "They all like it, believe me."

But he refused to allow any of his companions to examine this notebook.

"Why should I?"

"Oh come on, Steve!"

"Share my women with you lads? Not bloody likely!"

"D' you think we believe your yarns?"

"I don't care whether you do or whether you don't."

"You've never had it."

"Haven't I? No, I've never had it! What d'you think I carry these for?"

He displayed a small cardboard box, holding it aloft in his right hand.

"What d'you think I do with these?"

He put the box quickly in the inside pocket of his jacket as one of his companions tried to snatch it from his grasp.

"No, you don't," he cried.

"Where'd you get them?"

Steve pretended to stare incredulously at the speaker.

"Where'd I get them? Where everybody gets them! Where your oul' fella gets them!"

"Where?"

"In any chemist's."

"Did you get them yourself?"

"Why not?"

"You did?"

"Of course I did. D'ya think I sent my sister?"

"Never knew you had a sister."

"I haven't."

"Just as well."

There was a loud laugh at this.

"But you have, Harry, haven't you?"

Steve addressed the last speaker, a tall boy called Harry Campbell, who was wearing nothing but his glasses.

"You have, Harry, haven't you? I know her, as a matter of fact, I know her well."

"You're a liar, Steve," Harry burst out, "you don't know my sister at all."

"I don't? You think I don't. But I do, I know her very well. She's here—her name and address."

Steve tapped his breast pocket.

"She's in the book."

Harry gave a loud grunt of disbelief.

"You've never seen my sister in your life."

"I've seen far more of her than you have," Steve said, leering.

"If I believed you—"

"Don't or you won't sleep tonight," Steve interjected.

"You're a liar," Harry Campbell shouted, "if I believe you." Harry Campbell had suddenly become angry, his fists flying. But Steve Carter took refuge in the lavatory, taking care to bring his jacket with him.

"Wait till you come out, Steve Carter!"

"Pax," Steve called.

"No blinkin' fear. No pax."

"I don't know your bleeding sister," Steve called, "I wouldn't touch her if she asked me to."

"You wouldn't get a chance."

At last Steve Carter confessed that he was leg-pulling: he had never met Campbell's sister.

But Martin often wondered how much experience of girls Steve Carter really had.

Ten

THERE SHE WAS! SHE ENTERED THE gate after her
mother; he watched her close it carefully behind her.

It was the moment he had been waiting for all Saturday
afternoon. When he had arrived at the Taylors, shortly before
three o'clock, Tom had greeted him as usual and the two boys
had gone upstairs to what Tom called his 'den'—the attic in
which he did his homework, entertained his friends, kept his
belongings, and which he forbade his sisters to enter without
his permission.

As it was a showery April day they had decided to stay
indoors. But they had been rather bored; they had played chess
for a while, read for an hour or so, and finally went out into the
wet garden.

As they were walking they discussed a new French master
who already had a reputation for jokes. Then Martin looked up.

It was really Claire! She was wearing a fawn raincoat and no
hat. How different she looked! He was unable to keep his eyes
off her as she walked slowly up the path, smiling.

"Hello, Martin. Showery, isn't it?"

But it was Mrs. Taylor casually greeting him: and he had
hardly noticed her, so engrossed was he with the
transformation in Claire. He immediately became conscious of

his rudeness and limply and shamefacedly returned Mrs. Taylor's greeting.

"Hello, Martin."

It was Claire's voice. Even her voice had changed! Her accent was definitely English now: and it completed the transformation that had taken place.

Mrs. Taylor stood for a short time chatting to the three young people, then went indoors.

"Well, Martin, how are you?"

Claire stood facing him, opening her fawn overcoat, and smiling. He was conscious only of her clear light-blue eyes at first: then of her figure. She had left home a scrawny girl, all awkwardness; and she had returned six months later, completely transformed. It seemed a miracle to him; and he could hardly breathe for a moment or two. Then he became aware that she was waiting for an answer to her question.

"Very well," he answered.

"Good," she replied, her eyes shining.

Her response was decisive: she seemed pleased to see him. At any rate his pleasure at seeing her was extraordinary. He felt hot and was wondering if his discomfort were apparent to the others. He wondered, too, if he were blushing.

"And what's your news?" she added.

"Nothing's been happening here," Tom said, "nothing ever happens here."

"Nonsense," Claire retorted, "the same things happen here as happen elsewhere."

She turned to Martin as if appealing for aid.

"Isn't that so, Martin?"

He nodded his agreement.

"You see, Martin's on my side," she said.

How could he be otherwise? She appeared to him perfect— her coat open in the breeze, displaying a blue dress with a white collar and her hair caught by her left hand as she swirled round on the path facing first of all her brother, then turning towards Martin.

"Won't you come in and tell me all your news?"

The rain had cleared away; the sky had great patches of blue; now, suddenly, a perfect April day.

"Afterwards," Tom said.

"I didn't ask you," Claire retorted, "what does Martin want to do?"

How could he tell her that he longed for her company, that he wanted above all to look at her and to listen to her voice? That was all he wanted. But how could he tell her with Tom there, digging his heels into the damp soil at the edge of the path, and anxious not to go indoors now that the sun was shining.

"I don't mind."

And how he minded!

"Well then, see you afterwards—"

"All right," and she ran up the path.

The opportunity had gone. He had so wanted to hear her news: what her new English school was like, how she had spent her time, what she was studying, oh, it didn't matter what she told him as long as he was in her presence!

Tom was talking about their coming Easter holiday: they were going for a week to Donegal, staying in an hotel at Portnablagh. The whole family was going. Martin heard the news with dismay. When were they going? On Monday morning.

She would be leaving him again.

At last Martin insisted that they go back, though their walk had only been as far as Shaw's bridge.

"Have you to be home early?" Tom inquired.

"No; not particularly."

They reached the avenue where Tom lived.

"Coming in for a while?"

"Well, I don't know—"

"It's only a quarter to five."

"For half-an-hour then?"

They went in. The family was in the drawing room, entertaining visitors, who had called to see Mrs. Taylor. The visitors were two middle-aged ladies, and Tom whispered that he wasn't sure whether they were cousins of his mother's or not, but that they were related to her in some way. The two boys were presented and then were allowed to make their escape.

"I think I'll go."

Martin's tone was mournful. He had seen Claire again; but only for a moment. And she had appeared not to notice him: her attention was on her mother's visitors. It was maddening!

Tom left him up the avenue as usual.

"Anything wrong?"

"No," Martin replied. "Why?"

"I just thought there was."

Tom's answer was matter of fact. Indeed, to Martin, Tom's character was remarkably unemotional: nothing upset him; he took everything calmly; he never became moody or acted unpredictably. He was as reserved as his father and thought it bad form to show his emotions. His mother, however, was the opposite: her emotions continually bubbled over, like a boiling kettle; but her emotions were, in Martin's view, trivial in the extreme.

The Malone tram came into sight.

"See you soon," Tom said.

"When?"

"As soon as we come back from Donegal."

"You'll be away a whole week?"

"Yes."

The tram approached the stop.

"I'll call next Monday. Would that be all right?"

"Yes."

He mounted the platform, climbed upstairs, and waved to Tom. A whole week more! He took his seat on the upper deck of the almost empty tram and as it swayed drunkenly down the winding road he reflected on his misfortune. When he had no interest in Claire he had plenty of opportunities of seeing her. But now—now that he wanted her presence, life was conspiring against him to keep their paths apart.

A postcard arrived from Donegal. It was from Tom. It contained only three sentences: 'Enjoying myself here. Bathing every day. See you next week?' He examined it. A glossy photogravure of a mountain with the unromantic name of Muckish; in the foreground a winding road with a donkey and cart. It told him nothing, yet he was glad it had come. It was something, after all, to remind him of her.

The week passed slowly. He longed for the Easter holidays to end. He longed for school to begin. Above all, he longed for his next visit to the Taylors' house.

Eleven

THEY RETURNED AT LAST. IT SEEMED to Martin as if an age had passed since he had last seen Claire. It was incredible to him how incomplete, how unsatisfactory, how meaningless his life had become without her! He was her slave. It was as if she had captured him. And yet she had done absolutely nothing. She had hardly spoken to him; all she had said were a few commonplace remarks; and yet she had him in bondage.

He called on a Monday afternoon. He was trembling as he turned in through the gate, walked up the path to the front door, and rang the bell.

Claire opened the door.

"Hello, Martin!"

For a moment he was unable to answer her greeting.

"Is Tom in?" he asked, his voice uncertain.

She shook her head.

"No. Won't you come in and wait for him? He won't be long. He's expecting you, of course."

He went into the hall; and Claire closed the door after him.

"I'm all alone," she said.

She was alone in the house! He felt his heart pound with excitement!

She led him into the drawing room. She sat down; he sat down almost opposite her. Immediately he felt shy, extraordinarily shy. He could hardly speak to her! He was afraid of making a fool of himself; and yet he had so much to ask her and so much to tell her. Mercifully she seemed unaware of his lack of confidence in her presence. At once she began to describe her holiday in Donegal. All he had to do was to listen; and he was quite content to listen. Fervently he wished that he had such confidence: she appeared perfectly at ease in his company. And yet he—

"Well now—"

There was a mischievous glint in her eyes; and she paused.

"Why are you letting me do all the talking? I'll go on and on if you let me, you know."

"I like to hear you talking," he murmured.

"Oh, come!"

"I do," he said, with more assurance.

"I don't believe you," she retorted, "and I'm not going to bore you."

"But you don't bore me," he replied.

"You're only being polite."

He shook his head once more. Oh, he was making a perfect fool of himself! Imagine not being able to talk to Claire Taylor, Tom's sister! It was ridiculous. He was afraid of her. That was it! He was absolutely terrified of this girl. Why? There was no reason at all except that he was in love with her and it was impossible to tell her so. She ought to guess. She ought to know.

"Tom told me you'd taken up music. Is that right?"

So they actually discussed him, she and Tom; and she actually remembered this particular fact.

"Yes," he replied, he had indeed become interested in music; and he told her about the concerts in the Museum and Art Gallery.

"I must go to one, some time," she murmured.

It was surely his chance!

"Would you?" he asked, his voice a little tremulous.

"Of course I would; I'd love to."

He wondered if she had misunderstood him.

"I mean—with me?"

"Yes."

Her affirmative was definite; it was spoken quite naturally too, as if young men were in the habit of inviting her to symphony concerts and she was in the habit of accepting their invitations. He looked at her; the expression on his face suddenly made her laugh.

"Well," she said, "please don't look as if you'd done something pretty awful—you haven't!"

He didn't know what to reply.

"Maybe you've changed your mind," she added, "or maybe you didn't expect me to accept."

"No."

"Whatever do you mean, Martin? I don't know what to do now."

"Oh, please come!"

"You really meant that?"

"Yes."

"When?"

"On Wednesday. At three o'clock."

"Where'll we meet?"

He thought hastily of two or three possible places to meet.

"The Botanic Gardens," he said, "at the front gates. At a quarter to three."

"All right," Claire replied; then, as an afterthought, "what about Tom?"

Martin was nonplussed; the idea that Tom should accompany them had simply not occurred to him; or if it had occurred he had dismissed it at once. He looked at her. What did she mean? Did she really want her brother to tag along with them, as a kind of chaperone? Had she really been only teasing him and now was withdrawing her offer? He didn't know; but he took his courage in his hands.

"No!"

He had been examining, with eyes downcast, the plush red carpet with its lines and circles, but as soon as he uttered the 'no' he looked straight into her face. He had spoken louder than he had intended and he gazed at this tantalising girl, waiting for her reply. Now, as least, she knew what he wanted: he had made perfectly clear that he wanted her company, alone.

"Just the two of us?"

She was still playing for time; or perhaps she was still

teasing him; but he had made his desire clear and he had by now conquered his timidity.

"Yes."

He noticed that her eyes were remarkably blue and clear; and her face with its high cheekbones was beautifully moulded. And now it was her turn to be serious. She gazed out of the window for a moment or two.

"Here's Tom coming," she said.

"Well?" Martin's voice was eager now. "Will you come?"

Without looking in his direction she answered, "Yes, I'll be there."

Then she waved at her brother.

"Is this a secret meeting?" she said quickly.

"Yes," Martin answered, his voice low, "yes, I think so."

She nodded as her brother entered the room.

He arrived at the Botanic Gardens and looked up at the clock on the squat redbrick tower; it was at half-past two. So he was early; a quarter of an hour until she was due.

He wandered into the gardens, past the statue of Lord Kelvin and towards the conservatory with its great bulb-like glass dome. On his left was the Queen's University; on his right the white building of the new Museum and Art Gallery.

It was a fine spring afternoon, and Martin took a seat on one of the benches near the conservatory. People were strolling along the paths or lounging about on the grass; young working class mothers with prams or go-cars; old age pensioners with dark crumpled suits and the patient resigned look of the old; small children sitting or tumbling about the lawns; and middle-aged women with forlorn withdrawn faces.

This part of the city, centred on the University and the Botanic Gardens, was more attractive to him than any other part: it had an air of leisure which was lacking elsewhere.

Exactly at a quarter to three he saw Claire approaching him; she was walking down the Malone Road. He watched her: she walked with a slight swing, her head very slightly tilted. She had no hat and was carrying a light green mackintosh. He crossed the road to meet her.

"Well, I've come," she greeted him. "Have you been here long?"

"No, not long."

"I wasn't late, was I?"

"No, just in time."

They crossed the Malone Road and made for the Museum and Art Gallery.

"I've never been here before," Claire said.

"Haven't you?"

"I didn't even know about these concerts."

"Well, they haven't been started very long. I've only been to one, in fact."

"Was it very good?"

"I thought it was," Martin said, "very good."

They climbed the stairs to the Art Gallery and Martin boldly took one of the front seats. They waited for the concert to begin, hardly speaking at all and pretending to be fully engrossed in their programmes.

It was over. They filed downstairs with the audience, mostly middle-aged people, and found themselves in the sunshine of the late afternoon. Already they had expressed their enjoyment to each other: it was as if the music had given them powers of speech. They had heard Beethoven's *Seventh*.

"I love it better than any other symphony," Claire cried. "It makes me want to get up and dance."

Martin nodded.

"I've never heard Beethoven before," he admitted, "never before."

"Haven't you?"

"No."

She waited for him to say something more about Beethoven; instead he invited her to tea in a café near the university.

It was not a particularly attractive café; the tables were marble-topped, the floor was grimy, the waitress slatternly. But to Martin, normally inclined to be fastidious, these deficiencies were of little importance. For the first time he had taken a young woman out by herself, and so far everything had been successful.

They talked. At first they talked about the concert; then they talked about Tom; and then they talked about Claire's school in

England. She told him she hadn't liked it at first because the other girls had made fun of her Irish accent, and this had made her miserable.

"Silly, isn't it," he said.

She looked puzzled; so he added, "Silly, I think, sending you and Ruth to school in England. There are plenty of good schools here."

"I suppose so."

"Why were you sent there?"

"I don't know, really; it was mother's idea; she wanted us to be educated—at least for a year or two—in England. It's quite a common thing to do—"

"It is?" Martin said, "Well, I think it's just a bit of snobbery."

Claire made no answer; she looked rather serious, indeed a little displeased.

"Yes, I suppose it is. But I don't think we're snobs."

"You aren't!" Martin replied hastily; "I didn't say you were either."

"I thought you meant—"

He interrupted her.

"I only meant I wish you weren't at school in England. That's all."

They left the café and walked slowly along University Road under the foliage of the horse-chestnut trees. They reached the front gates of the Botanic Gardens where they had met. Martin looked at the clock. It was just after five.

"I must go soon," Claire said.

"How soon?"

"Well—"

"Couldn't you stay another half-hour or so?" he pleaded, "We could go into the Gardens for a while."

She hesitated; then she appeared to make up her mind.

"All right. For half-an-hour only."

They walked to the far end of the Gardens and sat down on the grass. There was a long silence before either spoke.

"You don't talk much about yourself," Claire said at last.

Martin pondered this statement. It was true, he thought, he didn't talk much about himself and what he was doing and thinking. He nodded his agreement. Eagerly she took up the significance of the gesture.

"You see? You won't even admit it. That's why you nodded, isn't it?"

"Yes," he answered.

"You're almost a stranger to me," Claire added. "I hardly know you at all. And when I once asked Tom about you he only shrugged his shoulders." She paused; "I don't think Tom knows you either."

"I don't mean to be secretive," Martin protested. "What do you want to know about me?"

He faced her.

"Oh—lots of things," she answered, amused.

"But you do know lots of things. You know I like games; you know I like books and music; you know your brother's my best friend at school. What else can I tell you?"

"I don't know."

"You see!"

His voice was triumphant. He looked at her. What lovely, long brown legs she had! She had half-turned away her face and was gently stroking the grass.

"You're a mystery to me, too," he said.

"Oh."

She looked surprised, and glanced at him.

"Why?"

He paused: he wanted very much to ask her one question.

"Do you like me?" he asked.

"Of course I do."

Suddenly he bent forward and captured her hand; she allowed him to hold it.

"You do?" he continued, eagerness in his voice.

"Why shouldn't I?"

Before he knew what had happened he found himself close to her, his arms round her, and his mouth to hers, in a long passionate kiss.

In another week Claire had to leave home again, to return to England for the summer term. Twice Martin saw her alone: once they walked to the Giant's Ring, a mile or so beyond Shaw's Bridge; and the second occasion they went to a cinema. They kept their assignations secret. After the cinema, Martin took her to the Malone tram.

"You'll write to me, Martin."

"I promise."

"I promise too."

He had her address, and she had his, and they promised to write every week to each other. The term would soon pass; Claire would soon return home and they would be together again. He gave her hand a squeeze as the tram approached, and he waved till she disappeared from sight. Disconsolately he turned down Chichester Street, crossed the Albert Bridge, and slowly walked home.

Twelve

HE FELT FORLORN THAT SUMMER. AFTER all, he had little to show for his early promise. He had no job; he didn't even know yet what he wanted to be. Other boys of his own age in Chatfield Street were serving their time at trades, or were working in shops. And yet he was seventeen years of age! In the autumn he would be eighteen!

Mrs. Connolly was disappointed at the upshot of it all. She had buoyed herself up with hope during the last five years; she imagined her son must be of a different mould from the sons of other women. She was intensely proud of him! It had given her a glow to see him leave the house in the morning wearing his school cap and blazer and carrying a strap of books under his arm. She used to watch him with pride as he walked up the street. She was aware, of course, of what her neighbours thought, though they very seldom dared to speak their minds to her; they knew she had her answers ready for them. They certainly didn't believe in all these new-fangled ideas about the sons and daughters of working-class people getting educated! Working-class people were working class, and that was that! No good in trying to get above yourself! Oh, they knew Martin Connolly had won a scholarship, but what of that? He shouldn't have taken it! No, he certainly shouldn't! He shouldn't have been allowed to either! Well, see what happened, after all! Here he was, at seventeen, and never yet had he earned a penny piece, and what was he going to be, anyway?

The neighbours were going to be proved right; so Mrs. Connolly began to fear. Her Martin had not turned out as well as she had expected. She had once hoped he might become a clergyman. And now he didn't go either to church or Sunday School! He was just as bad as his father so far as religion was concerned; indeed when she had dared to discuss religion with Martin he had told her that he was an agnostic. She was not quite sure what the word meant, though she had heard her husband use it. It was something the same as an atheist but maybe not quite so bad. Often she had wished that she had a daughter as well as a son; for girls were not as difficult as boys, and they had more common sense. Men got all sorts of queer ideas into their heads and once in there was no driving them out. And if she had had a daughter she wouldn't feel so lonely either ...

Bob Connolly was also worried about his son's future, but he wasn't a man to display his feelings readily, and his wife was scarcely aware of her husband's anxieties. In his different way he was as proud of his son as his wife was; though Martin had not the least suspicion of what he meant to his father.

Just before Martin left school, he had a talk one Sunday evening with his father; the two of them had gone for a walk to Holywood and back. Walking home they could see the gantries of the shipyards silhouetted in the sky like huge gibbets, against the darkening Antrim hills. The evening sun, now set, was a furnace hidden somewhere in the heavens.

It was seldom that father and son had spent so long in each other's company; and yet Martin admitted to himself that he enjoyed his father's conversation. They were returning by the Old Holywood Road, along the hills, when they stopped for a rest and looked down at the city.

"What do you think of it?"

It was the kind of question that Martin found irritating; but it was one of his father's conversational mannerisms, and Martin had long since become accustomed to it.

"What do you mean?" he replied, knowing that his father would soon make his meaning quite clear.

"Is that where you want to spend your life?"

"I really don't know."

His father took a deep breath.

"There are many worse places, mind; many worse places."

Martin nodded; he knew perfectly well that any comment from him was superfluous; for he knew perfectly well his father's views about the inhabitants of the city, he had heard them often enough. His father regarded some of his fellow-workers in the shipyard as the salt of the earth, as human beings; but as political beings they made him despair. Of course they were all organised as trade unionists, and were loyal to their trade union principles; but the organisation of workers into trade unions was surely only the beginning; he considered that the workers had still a world to win.

"What do you actually want to do, Martin?"

Martin looked across the lough.

"I don't know."

No, he just had no idea of how he could earn his living in an agreeable way. How could he know? How could anybody of seventeen know such a thing? Really, adults were preposterous; they expected you to make the most difficult of all choices, the choice of how you were going to spend your life, and they expected you to make your choice without any real guidance and without any real experience! No wonder the world was in such a state ...

"It's difficult," his father muttered, "I know it's very difficult." Martin nodded.

"I never really wanted to be a carpenter," his father went on, "I was just given this trade because my father thought it'd suit me; but it never did—I never had any feeling for wood; I never had any feeling for it." Now this was a confession Martin had never heard before! He suddenly felt a warm rush of sympathy for his father. How he must have suffered! And suffered in silence too! Martin felt he must not be sentimental: he had no wish to exaggerate, to see his father as a kind of martyr. And yet, he thought, it was really a kind of martyrdom to live in a way that was against your desires, your instincts.

The sky had gradually lost its molten red and had turned to leaden grey.

"What did you want to do, Father?"

There was a pause.

"I don't know, son, that's the truth," he chuckled; "and you're the first one that's ever asked me."

Once a friend of his father's called Malachi Hegarty, a painter by trade, called at the house. Mrs. Connolly liked Malachi, a fat good-natured Catholic who constantly referred to himself as a 'papist'.

She liked the man, although she detested Roman Catholics in general. Since the death of her cousin, Joe Reynolds, she had sworn never to allow a Catholic to cross her doorstep. But Malachi Hegarty was the exception. He had won her over easily merely by agreeing with her about the iniquities of priests.

"They keep the people in ignorance," he said. "You needn't tell me that, Mrs. Connolly, don't I know it?"

She secretly relished Malachi's anti-clericalism, though she couldn't abide her husband's attack on her own clergy.

"Well, Martin, when are you going to join me?" Malachi greeted Martin.

"What do you mean?" Martin asked.

"Oh, not what your mother thinks. I'm not trying to convert you to the true church. Not at all. I don't care what religion you profess—any or none—so long as you'll fight for your rights!"

Mrs. Connolly, who was in the scullery cutting bread, called in: "None o' that talk in this house, Malachi."

"Why not, Missus?"

"Because I tell you I won't listen to it."

"Ah, go on wi' you. You don't mean it. Does she, Bob?"

"Oh, she does," Bob Connolly said.

"I don't believe it," Malachi cried. "Isn't this a good Protestant house? Well then if it is shouldn't you be protesting all the time? Christ knows there's plenty to protest about these days!"

He lit a cigarette and scrutinised Martin.

"Have they bourgeoisified you, lad?"

"I hope not."

"But you're not sure?" Malachi persisted.

"Should I hate them?" Martin asked.

Malachi looked at him without answering. Then said

passionately, "Yes you should—you should hate them! I do! Oh God, how I hate them!"

"That's the trouble with people like you," Mrs. Connolly shouted, "you're full of hate for people you don't know."

"No, no, no," Malachi cried, "We workers know them all right. We slave for them—when we're allowed to. Oh, I've cause to hate them!"

"But you don't hate individuals?" Martin said.

"Individuals?" Malachi screwed up his small greenish-grey eyes. "I'm not concerned with individuals; there's good an' bad among us. That's only common sense. It's the bourgeois as a class I hate."

"Why, Malachi?" Mrs. Connolly called. "Hate never does any good."

"Listen to that woman o' yours," Malachi retorted. "Does she want to drive me to drink? Hate never does any good!"

He repeated the remark, giving it all the scorn of which his deep voice was capable.

"Of course hate does good! Of course it does! You hate dirt, don't you?"

Mrs. Connolly was about to make a reply when Malachi interrupted her.

"Let me finish, woman! I haven't done with you. You hate dirt, and a doctor hates disease, doesn't he? And a socialist like me hates the system we're under! So—there y'are—in a nutshell! Take it or leave it—ye can't ignore it."

He gave one of his great hearty laughs.

"Come in wi' the tea, woman, an' talk some sense."

Mrs. Connolly loved the robust manner with which Malachi always addressed her.

"An' as for you, lad, I want to see you in the movement! I want to see you in the vanguard of the working-class. That's where you belong! Understand? There's only one fight worth fighting these days—the fight for a decent society. It's the only hope we have, isn't it, Bob?"

He turned to his friend, rubbing his great hairy hands together; and Bob Connolly, though he agreed with every word, considered that enough had been said and so contented himself with a nod by way of reply.

Thirteen

IT WAS AS IF HE HAD two selves. One self he kept for his home: the other belonged to his life with the Taylors. And now that he had left school and as a consequence saw less of Tom, his home life was as it had been before he won his scholarship.

He found living at home more and more irksome; it gave him a feeling, almost physical in its intensity, of being hemmed in. The street was too narrow; people had no room to breathe properly: they were crammed in on top of one another.

He continued to visit Tom's home once or twice a week, generally at the weekend; but he had a feeling that their friendship would wither. He was beginning to find Tom's company a little dull; indeed the Taylor family he now thought very staid and unenterprising. Tom had begun to read biographies of famous advocates such as Marshall-Hall, and liked to relate, in boring detail, the stories of famous crimes and trials.

The Taylors, having lent their seaside house to an English business acquaintance of Mr. Taylor, were planning a holiday in the south of France. They were to leave home early in August and would be away for about a fortnight. Martin learnt with dismay that the whole family was going abroad. It was from Claire that he first heard this news; also the news that she would be home for only ten days.

She arrived home at last, and they had arranged by letter to meet in an Italian café near Castle Junction on the afternoon following her day of arrival. She explained that to see him alone before this was almost impossible: she just couldn't disappear from home without an explanation, and she didn't want to tell lies. She would, therefore, do her shopping quickly, then go to their rendezvous.

Unable to control his eagerness, Martin arrived early at the café and took a corner seat. He ordered tea and biscuits for two and waited.

Half-past three arrived. She failed to appear. He became anxious; she was always punctual. To keep anyone waiting she thought extremely bad manners. Five minutes went slowly by; then ten. A quarter of an hour and no sign of her.

He was in despair: she would certainly not turn up as late as this. Something serious must have prevented her coming at the last moment; otherwise she would have written to him. His mood of expectancy had vanished: he felt utterly dispirited.

From time to time the waitress serving him passed his table; she was a small brunette, with a bright inviting expression.

"Would you like tea now, sir?" she inquired.

"No, thank you," he replied. "I'm waiting for someone."

"A young lady, sir?"

"Yes."

What business was it of hers? He felt himself blushing; he was half inclined to tell her to mind her own business: to tell her to get on with her own work and leave him alone.

"There's a young lady over there, sir."

The waitress pointed to another part of the café, past the long metal-topped counters, where people were perched on high stools.

"Where?"

"I'll show you, sir."

He followed her. The café was L-shaped, and beyond the counter was a kind of annexe, recently built. He had never noticed it. And, in any case, he had entered by the back entrance facing St. Mary's Hall.

"There, sir."

It was Claire. She was reading a magazine. She looked up. "I was just going to leave," she said.

He thanked the waitress, who now had a look of pleasure on her face, and sat down beside Claire. The waitress left them.

"I've been waiting round there," he murmured, indicating the back of the café. "I'm very sorry."

What a fool he was! Here Claire was, patiently waiting for him and all the time he was waiting for her!

"It doesn't matter, does it?"

"No, but—"

He looked at her, eagerly, hungrily, with intense joy, hardly capable of further speech. He was only half-conscious of the little waitress bringing the tea things.

"Shall I pay?" Claire said.

"Why?"

Claire indicated the waitress who was standing at Martin's side. He wasn't aware of her presence!

"Oh, I see!"

Hastily he groped in his pocket, found a half-crown, and gave it to the girl.

"Thank you, that will be all right."

"Thank you, sir." And she left.

They spent an hour together. For Martin it was ecstasy to be in her company. She was looking superb and he was unable to keep his eyes off her. She had changed her hairstyle: it was brushed straight back from her forehead, revealing the whole shape of her head. He had scarcely noticed her tiny well-shaped ears before; or the slim line of her neck. And he was conscious of her shapely breasts underneath her white dress.

It amazed him that she resembled her brother so little either in temperament or in physique; for while Tom was reticent and awkward, Claire was frank and graceful. She also differed from Ruth, her younger sister, who was more like their brother.

"You're looking sad," Claire suddenly remarked.

"Am I?"

"Yes, you are."

"I shouldn't be, should I?"

"I hope not; I hope I don't make you as depressed as you look."

Although she spoke the words seriously she didn't look

serious, but serene. Curious how sensitive she was to his moods! She seemed capable of reading his thoughts.

"I was thinking," he began, paused and looked up at her. Suddenly he took her hand and caressed it between his own two hands. Her hand, pale and slender compared with his own squat, square hands, looked fragile. He loved the velvety feel of it and caressed it tenderly. His emotions always seemed to be just below the surface, he thought, as he held Claire's hand; he couldn't help himself. He couldn't understand why a girl could have such power. He was quite sure he wasn't soft or sentimental by nature; he considered himself tough; but yet, with Claire, he was absolutely helpless. He looked at her as she spoke.

"Yes, go on; what were you thinking?" she said.

"Of us."

He spoke the two words emphatically.

"Well, what of us?"

He took a deep breath.

"What do you think will happen to us?" he asked, his voice sombre.

"I don't know. Do you?"

He shook his head.

"What are you afraid of?" she asked.

"Of being separated from you, Claire. Separated for good."

How seldom he mentioned her name! Hardly ever! And yet her name was constantly in his mind. When he was alone he often murmured it to himself, like an incantation.

By now she had surrendered to his mood.

"I wouldn't like that to happen," she replied. "I'd hate it."

"So should I."

"But it needn't happen, need it?"

"No, I hope not."

"Why do you think it should?"

He needn't know why the differences between their social background should come between them; but all the same he experienced a sense of foreboding. He shook his head, puzzled.

"I must go now," she said, glancing at her wristwatch. "Don't think of such things till they happen."

"All right, I won't."

"Promise?"

"Yes, I promise."

She rose; they left the café.

"When shall I see you next?" she said as they entered the street.

They met three times in those ten days, secretly. And no one knew; no one suspected. It was wonderful, the secrecy. They felt they had known each other, intimately, for years. They wondered how many people had ever had the same feelings of ecstasy as they had. And, in addition to meeting alone, they were able to see each other when Martin called at Claire's house, ostensibly to see her brother.

Tom had recently taken up golf—his father's favourite game—and tried to persuade Martin to play. But Martin refused: he protested that golf was for the middle-aged and the old; and though he didn't mind caddying occasionally—in fact he liked to watch Tom's awkward efforts at the game—he had no desire to try the clubs himself. As Martin's pocket money was only half-a-crown weekly he couldn't afford to take up the game; and he wouldn't ask his father to buy him a set of clubs.

However, Martin wasn't at all sorry when Tom set off for the links; because as a result he had more of Claire's company. Ruth, of course, was usually in the house, but occasionally she drifted off and the two were left alone.

On these occasions Claire liked to play the gramophone— she had bought some recordings of Beethoven, Mozart and Haydn—and they would listen together, enraptured. And once or twice Martin persuaded her to play the piano. She was always reluctant to play for him.

"I'll never be any good," she told him; "because I don't practise enough."

But her playing pleased him; he didn't mind in the least her faults in technique; in any event he wasn't aware of them. He loved to watch her at the piano, loved the movement of her fingers and her arms; the whole movement of her body. And she had a curious habit of breathing deeply as she played.

"You mean to say I snore?" She pretended to be piqued.

"Yes, almost."

"Then I won't play any more for you!"

He kissed her.

"But I want you to play!"

"Then don't make rude remarks!"

So he promised not to comment on her playing again, and embraced her.

Their brief idyllic interlude was soon broken by the Taylors' holiday to France. The whole family was going to Bandol, which Claire showed to Martin on the map of France.

"I only wish you were coming with us."

"So do I."

He had never crossed the Irish Sea, and was impatient to do so. And here was Claire at school in England and now bound for France!

He felt a stab of envy at the thought of the Taylors' expensive holiday: it contrasted with the holiday his own parents had—sometimes a week in a boarding house at Bangor, Donaghadee, or Newcastle; or sometimes they had no real holiday at all, but had what was called, "a day here and a day there."

These days usually took the form of charabanc excursions, organised by a few neighbours; a couple of charabancs would be ordered, and on a Saturday afternoon would arrive at Chatfield Street, to be enthusiastically boarded at once. Then the whole street would depart with singing and shouting to places as far as the Mourne Mountains or the Glens of Antrim, forty or fifty miles away. Martin had never gone on one of these trips, but both his father and mother had helped the street committee and arranged for the collection of fares, which were contributed in sixpences each week before the outing.

The evening that the Taylors left for France, Martin felt himself completely at a loose end. He left home after tea, a library book under his arm; and having returned his book—*The Return of the Native*—he walked along the Newtownards Road towards the Queen's Bridge and the quays where the cross-channel boats departed.

He walked slowly. Occasionally he halted at a newsagent's shop and looked at the magazines on display. He felt himself above such highly-coloured trash—stories of horseracing and lurid crime and incredible romances. He had indeed a good opinion of himself and he certainly believed in his own ability;

but his self-belief and self-confidence had developed only very gradually, almost imperceptibly; and were revealed, if at all, only in his rather jaunty style of walking and the way he threw his shoulders back. He was now just above average height, and slim, and rather pale; but he gave an impression of character; of latent strength; of being able to walk along a street more alive than anyone else.

He passed the little shops, dozens of them, that lined each side of the main thoroughfare through Ballymacarrett: little family grocers, drapery shops, hardware shops, fish and chip saloons, newsagents; a post office; at the corner of the road a cinema where he had once seen a hypnotist perform; then on past the Sirocco works which manufactured machinery; past the many pubs, each easily recognisable by the red paint invariably chosen to give it prominence. And outside each pub was its group of 'corner boys' as his father called them— miserable lost-looking groups of men, standing aimlessly outside the bars, as if waiting for something or somebody to turn up.

All the same, Martin liked the sights and sounds and smells of the Newtownards Road: the shawled old women accompanying their daughters and talking in the harsh accent; the shipyard workers walking slowly along after their day's work: the loud drunken talk that could be heard from the pubs; the acrid tang of porter; the smell of vinegar from the fish and chip shops. And from the side streets the shouts of children playing games, and the cries of neighbours addressing each other in shirtsleeves. It was a place full of bustle, of vigorous movement and speech; and it was the place to which he felt he belonged. And he both loved and hated it. It was a mean district with hardly a building worth giving a second glance to; except the Roman Catholic chapel and St. Patrick's Church and Westbourne Presbyterian Church.

At the Bridge end the Newtownards Road changed its character. He had often stood on the Queen's Bridge to watch the ships leaving for Ayr, Ardrossan, Glasgow, Heysham, and Liverpool. There were nearly always a few people standing at the bridge. And no wonder! To the left could be seen the steamers, the long line of docks, the sheds, the custom house, the Albert Clock, the buildings of the port and in the distance the Antrim Hills; and to the right the coal-boats, the County Down railway station and the shipyard beyond. Here, on the bridge, was the smell of the Lough; and the sky, almost hidden along the Newtownards Road, suddenly became visible. Here Ballymacarrett ended.

Martin approached the bridge, saw the Liverpool boat hadn't yet left the dockside and quickly walked towards the sheds. A policeman prevented him from getting near the gangway, so he idly strolled about, waiting for the steamer to depart.

At last the gangway went up, the steamer left, and he made his way forward. People on the quays were waving their handkerchiefs and shouting farewells; the passengers on the deck were shouting and waving back.

He couldn't distinguish Claire in the surge of people crammed on deck. She must be below, in her cabin. Yet she had said she would stay on deck in case he should come to see the steamer depart. He had half-promised to do so, but didn't want her family to spot him among the crowd.

He saw her! She was standing on the top deck, beside a lifeboat! She was waving her scarf!

His heart leapt with excitement. There she was, on the slowly departing steamer, waving at him frantically! He waved back. She was smiling and waving. Then she threw him a kiss!

Then the ship slowly gathered speed, churning up the muddy water of the Lagan, and he stood watching it till her face became only a blur and he could see only her white scarf still waving. Then the scarf too became a blur, and she was gone.

Fourteen

A WEEK OF BOREDOM PASSED. HE felt in despair. He decided to take any job that came his way; anything would do for a start, he didn't care what it was.

One evening his mother handed him over the *Belfast Telegraph*: she had just seen two advertisements in the Situations Vacant column, one for a clerk in an insurance company, the other for an assistant in a bookshop. Insurance didn't interest him in the least, but books certainly did. So he sent in a letter of application, stating his age and education.

A couple of days later he received a reply: he was to be interviewed. He showed his father the letter; the notepaper was headed THE NEW BOOKSHOP: the signature was Frank McCracken; the address a street near Shaftesbury Square, between the university and the centre of the city.

"I don't know any bookshop there," his father said.

"It must be a new one."

"If it's a new firm—not a well-established one—then it'll be chancy; it's bound to be."

"I know."

"Don't take it, Martin, if you don't like the look of it."

"I won't," he assured his father.

But he was determined to accept the job if it were offered to him.

He entered the new shop and looked around him. No one to be seen. He gave a cough; no one appeared.

Behind an opaque glass door Martin heard footsteps; so he walked across and knocked on the glass. A man's head appeared almost at once. "Yes?" the man asked, folding a large piece of brown paper across his knee.

"My name's Connolly—Martin Connolly."

"Means nothing to me, son," the man replied, with a chuckle. "But, go on, tell me more. You see I'm not busy."

"I've an interview here for a job."

"Have you indeed! Well, I hope you get it. I like the look of you."

The man paused and deposited the brown paper on the counter where already a pile of new books lay strewn.

"I've to see Mr. McCracken at eleven o'clock."

"You're seeing him, son. How d'you do? Hell of a mess, isn't it? I don't know how I got myself into it, and I don't know how I'm going to get myself out of it."

Mr. McCracken spoke with a slight Scots accent. He was a slightly-built man with grey hair and eyes and remarkable bushy black eyebrows. The butt of a cigarette dangled unlit from his lower lip.

"Well, Mr. Connolly, you're the third this morning. The other two were no bloody good."

He paused.

"Well now, tell me this first of all: do you really want this job?"

Martin was taken aback by the question.

"I don't know," he replied, "it depends—"

"Depends on what?"

"On a lot of things."

"Such as?"

Martin frowned.

"First of all, whether I'm suitable—"

Mr. McCracken gave a chuckle, went to the front door, threw away his butt, and took out a new packet of cigarettes.

"Have one?"

"No, thank you."

Mr. McCracken lit his cigarette.

"Well now, Mr. Connolly, as to your being suitable, you look to me perfectly suitable, that is to say, you look to me perfectly sober and sensible. And that's all I want. So that question resolves itself. But it doesn't resolve another question, which is this—"

He took a long draw of his cigarette, threw back his head, and exhaled smoke.

"The question of whether I suit you. An' that's just as important a one as the other one. Maybe more so, indeed."

He stared at Martin and grinned.

"Don't you agree, Mr. Connolly?"

Martin hesitated before answering. Of course he agreed. If this job didn't suit him he wouldn't stick it very long.

"Yes," he said firmly, "I agree."

"Good," Mr. McCracken went on; "we seem to agree in principle, I see no reason why we shouldn't agree in practice. First of all, let me tell you a few things you'd better know—if you're willin' to work for me—"

"I've no experience about running a bookshop," Martin admitted.

"I know, I know; I wasn't thinkin' of that," Mr. McCracken said. "You've no experience; and neither have I: so that doesn't matter a hoot. We'll sink or swim together. The few things I want to tell you are about myself."

There was a long pause as Mr. McCracken took a couple of puffs at his cigarette and looked all round the bare shop.

"I'll tell you only the essentials. I'm a married man; I've a wife called Sheila; and we're childless, an' likely to remain so, I fear—nobody's fault, but Nature's; so I'm told. We're both from Glasgow—came to live here during the war. Know why?"

Martin shook his head. He hadn't the slightest notion why the McCrackens had left their native country.

"I'll tell ye why. To escape conscription. I didn't want to fight for m'king an' country. I didn't acknowledge the one, an' I didn't own any o' the ither. So naturally I didn't feel like goin' to fight in Flanders. An' I didn't feel like dyin' there either."

As Mr. McCracken was talking about his past, his accent imperceptibly changed: it became more Scottish.

"Do I shock ye?" he asked, suddenly.

"No."

"Come on, son, tell me if I do shock ye. Ye see, I'm proud o' my war service; I worked hard durin' the war, but only at one thing—tryin' to stop the bloody slaughter. I didn't succeed, of course; that's history, isn't it, but at least I tried—nobody can say, by God, I didn't try."

He paused; and Martin looked at the bookseller's intense face. "You were a conscientious objector?" Martin queried.

"Aye."

Mr. McCracken wrinkled up his eyes as a shaft of sunlight came in through the front window.

"Aye," he repeated; "that's what they called us, when they didn't shorten the words. Bloody conchies—that was it! Bloody conchies! God, we weren't the men that spilt the blood!"

He stubbed out his cigarette with a swift nervous movement of his foot and regarded Martin with a fierce expression on his deeply lined face.

"There's not much more to tell ye. Except that I'm doin' now what I've always wanted to do—start a bookshop; not just an ordinary bookshop, but one with an idea behind it."

He gave one of his long pauses; and Martin waited for him to continue.

"Just a simple idea behind it."

By the expression on his face Martin guessed that the bookseller was anxious to be asked what the simple idea was.

"And what is it?"

Mr. McCracken smoothed out his bushy eyebrows with the fingers of his right hand.

"It's not an original idea of my own; I lay no claim to it; but a good idea's worth borrowing, isn't it?"

Martin agreed, and wondered what the simple idea could be, and he waited for the pronouncement. Was this grey-haired Scotsman, he wondered, a loquacious charlatan? Certainly he liked to talk.

"A good book should be like a bomb," the bookseller said, speaking the words like a clergyman giving out the text of his sermon.

"And I want to sell bombs—books that explode in the minds of men. Ye ken my meaning?"

Martin nodded.

"If I can't change society, I can maybe change the minds of a few individuals."

He gave another of his chuckles as if he were clearing his throat. And his little wrinkled-up eyes glinted as he talked.

The interview lasted more than an hour. At the end of it Martin had accepted the job. Indeed he had already begun it; for during the last quarter of an hour, Mr. McCracken worked as he discoursed, unpacking great parcels of new books and handing over lots for Martin to heap on the counter.

He learnt a lot about the bookseller; learnt, for instance, that his bookshop was really a venture. Mr. McCracken's future didn't entirely depend on its financial success; he had another business—a small, busy hardware shop on the Shankill Road.

"You'll be left a lot on your own, lad. I won't be here to look after you—you'll be in complete charge."

"You'll be taking a risk, Mr. McCracken," Martin said; "I warn you."

"Ach, no risk."

Mrs. McCracken called just after noon; and Martin was introduced to a small white-haired woman who looked slightly older than her husband. She hardly spoke, but when she did speak she invariably said something sensible, to which her husband invariably replied: "Of course, Sheila, you're right. I'll do it."

Martin got the impression that the little bookseller, though not henpecked, would not deliberately cross her.

Mrs. McCracken had brought sandwiches and immediately retired to the room at the back of the shop where there was a gas ring. Out of a cupboard she produced cups and saucers, and in less than ten minutes had a table laid.

"Will ye have a cup, Mr. Connolly?"

He thanked her but refused her offer pleading that he was expected home. Then having washed his hands at a sink in a kind of pantry, he was ready to depart.

"Oh, Mr. Connolly, I forgot to ask you—when can ye start?"

"When do you want me?"

"As soon as you like, my lad. Tomorrow morning, if ye say the word!"

"All right, tomorrow morning. At what time?"

"Nine o'clock. Will that suit ye?"

"Yes."

"See you then, son! I'm dyin' for a cup o'tea! Oh, what about wages! What have ye in mind, lad?"

Martin hadn't thought about wages; he didn't know what to reply, especially with Mrs. McCracken hovering about.

"Ah well, lad, we'll discuss that in the mornin', eh? I'm sure we won't fall out! I won't exploit ye—ye can take m'word for that—I'll do the best I can for ye. But I won't overpay ye either! I can't afford to, mind! But we'll see!"

He put out his hand; they shook hands; and Mrs. McCracken gave him a little nod.

He opened the door and closed it behind him. As he turned he glanced through the bare front window and saw the bookseller standing in the middle of the shop; and they exchanged a wave of the hand by way of farewell greeting.

Fifteen

THE FOLLOWING MORNING, A COUPLE OF minutes before nine o'clock, Martin was outside the new bookshop, ready to start work. But the door was still locked and the place had a forlorn look. He was disappointed; for he had left home at a quarter past eight so that he wouldn't arrive late on his very first morning. As a matter of fact he had reached the city centre so early that he had walked the half-mile to Shaftesbury Square.

He waited.

Mr. McCracken appeared at five past nine, full of apologies, "Sorry, lad, but I missed a tram an' I'd to wait a good quarter of an hour for one to appear. Then God help us, didn't three appear all at once! Two of them empty of course! And the three o' them went down the Shankill like a bloody funeral!"

Still growling at the irregular tram service he unlocked the front door and entered his shop. Martin followed.

"Well, where do we begin?" Mr. McCracken asked. "First, let's come to a decision. Do we officially open up this morning or do we wait till we bring order out of this chaos?"

Martin was all for opening up the shop at once, chaos or no chaos.

"Right, lad, we're open from noon today. Let's get to work till then! Then we'll have a drink—an' I mean one drink, just one—to celebrate the occasion—an' I'll leave ye to carry on on your own!"

They worked hard for the next three hours, putting price-tabs on books, and books on shelves, and arranging the front window; and all the while Mr. McCracken kept up a flow of gossip and comment—about the corruption in the Corporation and the stupidities of the government.

"Imagine a country the size of Ireland with two governments and two civil services! Isn't it ridiculous!"

Martin soon discovered that Mr. McCracken was a monologist; all he needed was a listener who would nod his head either in agreement or disagreement and not interrupt the flow. Martin hadn't the least desire to interrupt. He thought local politics boring though he didn't dare to say so. Still, he found Mr. McCracken's fervour quite impressive.

At twelve o'clock they retired, as Mr. McCracken put it, across the way: their destination a rather dismal pub, almost opposite the shop. Mr. McCracken pushed open the swing door and directed Martin to a pew.

"Scotch or Irish, lad?"

Martin had never tasted whiskey; his only experience of alcohol had been a glass of cider, taken as a dare after a cricket match only three months before. But whiskey! ... Ought he to refuse? Oh, try anything once.

"Are ye a teetotaller, lad?" Mr. McCracken asked, "because if ye are, say so. It's nothin' to be ashamed of. On the contrary."

"I'm not."

"I'm not a drinkin' man, myself, mind," Mr. McCracken added solemnly; "for I believe intoxicating liquor to be one of the many opiates o' the working-class. But there are occasions when a celebration is called for. An' this is an occasion. So if you're not a teetotaller, an' if you're not a bigot—an' I know ye're not, else I wouldn't have ye—then I'll order ye a Scotch—a wee one, mind."

The barman passed over the whiskey; Mr. McCracken added some soda water to his, so Martin followed suit.

"Well lad, here's to success!"

They clinked glasses solemnly and Martin almost choked as the fiery liquid passed down his throat.

He had a sensation of lightness almost at once, accompanied

by a feeling of nausea. The stuff was horrible! Absolutely revolting! He felt his tongue burning at every sip. So this was whiskey! Well, he didn't care for it: it almost turned his stomach. And yet—what was Mr. McCracken burbling about? He looked at his employer more intently than he had ever done before. Yes, it was a most extraordinary face if you examined it very closely. He stared at the eyebrows, brushed up almost like whiskers! At the nose like a prow, with great hairs growing out of it! At the teeth—he hadn't noticed Mr. McCracken's teeth— how white and regular they were! They were beauti ... But, were they his own? Of course they weren't! Look! Look closely! Ah! False! These beauti ...

Suddenly he was aware of Mr. McCracken's voice.

"Are ye listenin' to me, lad?" the beautiful teeth were saying as they clamped and unclamped themselves.

"Yes," Martin answered. His head felt extraordinarily heavy; he didn't hear a word more; and he didn't want to hear anything this ridiculous old man was saying. He felt sick: he wanted to lie down somewhere and sleep. His stomach was queer: his eyes wouldn't focus: everything was blurred, shifting, uncertain. He put his throbbing head in his hands and answered Mr. McCracken in monosyllables, until they left the pub.

It was a near thing he decided; a damn near thing. He had almost disgraced himself; he had almost been sick. But he hadn't been; he hadn't been; and that was the important thing.

Mr. McCracken had left him only ten minutes ago, and already Martin felt the effects of the whiskey begin to die within him. He had seen his boss depart on a tram and had waved at him. And now for something to eat!

He walked down Great Victoria Street. He walked steadily; indeed he was conscious of walking very steadily; and he gulped in great gulps of fresh air as he walked.

His head still felt light. He wondered if he were walking quite straight. Here he was, passing the Great Northern Railway, with the key of a new bookshop in his left trouser pocket. And he felt for it. Yes, it was there. Yes, he'd the key of a new shop entrusted to him.

He felt important. He felt that a great deal of responsibility had been given to him, and that Mr. McCracken was a man in a thousand.

Martin halted in front of a café. It looked familiar to him. Yes, he had brought Claire here once. Claire ...

He wondered if Claire were thinking of him at this very moment. Or had she forgotten him?

An hour later he returned and opened up the shop. He enjoyed the feeling of being in sole charge; and he liked the atmosphere of the shop, now that there were books on display in the front window, and on the shelves round the tiny counter.

Only two people called during the first couple of hours: a man for cigarettes, and a girl for a women's magazine. But from time to time Martin saw people looking at the window display for a few moments before moving on.

The first customer appeared shortly after four o'clock: a tall scholarly looking man in his mid-thirties, with glasses and a slight stoop. He asked for a World's Classics edition of *Jane Eyre*, which was in the window. He went outside and pointed it out; then came in again.

"Just opened?" he asked as he paid.

"Yes, just today."

"Good," the customer replied: "I'm glad to see a bookshop here."

He browsed round for a while, chatting desultorily. He was a schoolmaster, Martin learnt; he taught French and German and suggested that the shop should stock a few foreign books. As he went out another man entered, rather elderly, followed by a young woman. They both made purchases. Then at five o'clock Mr. McCracken appeared.

"Well?"

Martin told him what had happened.

"Not too bad," Mr. McCracken said; then added: "I wouldn't have been in the least surprised if nobody had disturbed ye. Ye can close up the shop yourself, lad, an' take the key home wi' ye. I'll see ye some time the morra morning, about ten, maybe."

With that he was gone.

Martin locked up shortly afterwards and began to walk towards the centre of the city.

Suddenly he felt tired and took a tram. It had been an extraordinary day, he thought, as the tram went swaying along Bedford Street. He felt pleased with the way things had gone; but it had been a near thing with the whiskey, a very near thing.

He decided to say nothing about that when he reached home.

A letter with a foreign postmark was on the mantelpiece. It was from Claire. He put it in his pocket. He could hardly bear to wait until after tea to open it. During and after tea he had to give his mother a full account of his first day at work. She asked him question after question. Finally, however, he was able to escape into the parlour. He tore open the envelope.

Claire had arrived in Bandol, having stayed a night in London and another night in Paris. She wrote:

"How I wish you were here, Martin. That would be truly wonderful, so wonderful that I don't allow myself to think about it; it makes me discontented to do so. And it seems a crime to be discontented in this place. I cannot describe it to you: I have no gift for words as you know—I mean I can't hope to make you see this place. Some day you must come and see it for yourself. Our hotel *Le Beau Rivage* overlooks a bay with a small sandy beach; and beyond the beach there are cliffs. I go to these cliffs most mornings and bathe and lie looking at the Mediterranean. It is blue; but only sometimes. Sometimes it is grey, just like the Irish Sea. And it can be rough too. But usually it is calm, with the water so clear that you see down to the depths. In the harbour the fishermen play boules in the evenings and get so excited as they play. I think I am falling in love with France and only wish I could speak French better than I do. I am too shy to try out any little French I know. If you were here I know you would take all the opportunities to talk to the shopkeepers, the fishermen, the French people staying in the hotel, in fact everybody. As for me, I try to screw up my courage to do so, and am determined to do so—until the last minute when my courage fails me and my determination disappears! You know the kind of person I am: outwardly I appear to have complete confidence in myself, but inwardly I am really all nerves. Just the opposite of you, Martin, dear. You look highly strung and nervous, and I know you are—at least a little—but you seem to conquer your fears so easily and appear full of confidence, and give confidence to people like me who haven't any ... "

The letter then gave a detailed account of the hotel, the other guests staying there, and a trip by the Taylor family to Toulon. The letter ended: *Je t'aime beaucoup*.

Martin spent the entire evening re-reading it and writing his reply.

Each day more and more customers found their way into the shop; and Martin was interested in their behaviour because it varied such a great deal. Some walked out, a little embarrassed, not having bought a book. Martin was often disappointed.

"Let 'em alone," Mr. McCracken warned him. "People are starved of books—though half o' them don't know it—an' if they walk in an' walk out again wi'out buyin' anything, that doesn't matter a hoot! They'll mebbe come back again—always providin' ye don't molest them! So let them be! A bookshop's not like any other shop. Mind that!"

Working for Mr. McCracken was not too exacting; indeed it was very pleasant, better then being at school. And as Mr. McCracken trusted him with the routine of shop business, he felt quite important when ordering new books or consulting catalogues to find if books were out of print, or taking an hour off to go to the wholesale bookseller in Donegall Street. And the shop was doing reasonably well, according to Mr. McCracken; not yet paying its way, of course, but not doing too badly. Mr. McCracken confided in Martin, "The first three months will be the worst. Once we're over them we're over the biggest hurdle. Then I'll be able to give ye a rise in pay."

Martin got thirty shillings a week. It wasn't much, but it was more than he had expected to get. Mr. McCracken had been frank about the wages.

"It's all I can afford ye, lad. Ye'll see that for yourself, from the takings. But if business builds up, ye'll be looked after all right. I'm not a bloody capitalist."

Martin had come to like his employer. Mr. McCracken was surprisingly well-known in the city and had the reputation of being one of the 'characters' in the Labour movement. He was passionately fond of newspapers and socialist pamphlets, but had confessed to Martin that he was neither widely nor deeply read.

"I've dipped into a great number of books," he admitted;

"but I've never had the time—nor indeed the inclination—to systematically study any one great author. Neither William Morris nor John Ruskin, nor Karl Marx, nor William Owen; none o' them. But I've looked into them all, at one time or another, and loved them all too; but ... "

He sighed and lit another cigarette—he was almost a chain smoker—and shut his eyes as he inhaled the smoke. "But," he added, "if ye became a half-timer in the mill, as I did, at the age o' eleven, it's no wonder I'm not a Ruskin or a Marx, is it?"

Sixteen

THE TAYLORS RETURNED FROM FRANCE. TO Martin the few weeks had seemed interminable, despite his being preoccupied with the bookshop. Claire had written him three letters which he had read and re-read. They gave him great comfort. But he longed to see her.

They met as soon as she returned; the first afternoon, in fact, she turned up at the bookshop. He was so taken by surprise that at first he hardly recognised her.

"Claire!"

He was thankful the shop was empty; for he jumped off his stool, ran round the counter, and held both her hands. How brown she was! He'd never seen her looking so well! He wanted to kiss her!

"So this is where you work," she said, looking round the shop. "I tried hard to imagine what the shop would be like."

"Are you disappointed?"

"No."

She appeared uncertain.

"It's very small, isn't it?"

"Yes. Oh yes, it's small," he agreed. "We go in for quality, not quantity. It's the best bookshop in town."

He told her that though it was the smallest bookshop in the

city, it stocked better books and fewer mediocre ones than the other, more respectable bookshops. Still, he didn't want to talk about his job; he had many things to ask her, and was anxious to hear all her news. He was hungry to share all her experiences.

"When can we meet? Are you free tomorrow afternoon, Claire?"

"Yes."

"Where'll we meet then?"

She suggested Shaw's Bridge at a quarter past three. If it was a fine day they could walk along the Lagan; if it was wet they could return to the city by tram. But somehow despite her pleasure at seeing him, she seemed not entirely at ease: something was on her mind. She looked unhappy.

"What's the matter, Claire?"

She appeared a little taken aback by his question; he had spoken suddenly and sharply, just as the thought had come into his head.

"Why?"

Despite herself, she was frowning.

"I've something to tell you," she said in a low voice.

"What is it?"

"I ... "

She was blushing; she looked as if she would burst into tears. He waited for her answer.

"Something's happened," she said at last.

"It must be something pretty dreadful," Martin replied, in an effort to be light-hearted. But he felt far from light-hearted. Claire wasn't easily upset; she was usually very much in control of herself. What could have happened while she was away to upset her? Had she fallen in love with someone else? Impossible! She wouldn't have written her letters; and anyway she would have told him, told him at once. She was perfectly straightforward, and couldn't be otherwise. He waited.

"You remember the night I left, and you came to the boat?"

He nodded. Of course he remembered; he remembered everything that happened that night, the Liverpool boat moving slowly from the quayside until he couldn't see Claire at all, then—

"Yes."

"Ruth saw you."

"That doesn't matter, does it?"

He frowned. Well, what of it? He might have been seeing someone else depart, some friend of his own. Of course that wouldn't be the truth, but if it were absolutely necessary to tell a lie, to invent some story or other, it wouldn't do much harm.

"Does that matter very much?"

"Yes."

He was puzzled.

"How? How does it matter?"

"Ruth asked me if I'd seen you, and I said I had."

"Well?"

"Mother was there."

"Oh, I see. Your mother knows about us?"

"She does."

He took a deep breath. This was serious. If Mrs. Taylor knew that Claire and he were in love and were secretly meeting each other, there could be awkward consequences.

"Well?"

Claire looked down at her gloves, then she raised her head; there were tears in her eyes.

She told him what had happened. Her mother had put two and two together: had asked her a lot of questions. And Claire had answered her mother's questions truly: hadn't concealed anything, but had told about their meetings alone. She couldn't lie, could she? Martin agreed that there was no reason why she should lie. They had nothing to be ashamed of, had they? He asked if Tom had said anything. No, Tom hadn't said a single word. Claire had no idea what her brother thought, whether he approved or disapproved of their friendship; but she suspected he wasn't pleased. And her father? Martin inquired. Her father had taken no part in all this. Then he knew? Martin asked. Yes, he knew: Claire was sure of that.

And now? What was to happen now?

"I'm not allowed to see you," Claire said, "I mean—alone."

"You're not—"

So that was the position!

"Mother asked me to promise—"

"And did you?"

Claire shook her head.

"No, I couldn't promise that, could I?"

She loved him! She had given him proof; she had stood up against her mother! He looked into her face: she was wiping her eyes with a tiny ball of a handkerchief.

"What'll we do?" she asked, her voice now almost a sob.

He felt his heart wrung, seeing the piteous look on her face.

"What'll we do?" he repeated.

He didn't know. What could they do? Why shouldn't they love one another? Why should anybody interfere in their lives? It wasn't right. It was intolerable. He clenched his hands. All right, let anybody—her mother or her father or her brother— just let them try to interfere! He wouldn't stand for it. Why should he? And why should Claire? She loved him. He loved her. Nothing nor nobody could come between them.

Five minutes later Claire left the shop; for a customer had entered. They could no longer talk. But tomorrow was Saturday; they would meet as arranged.

Martin went to the doorway and stood watching her depart. Once she turned and waved—and actually smiled! Martin waved back, then went to the shop to look after the customer, a young man with an open-necked shirt and bicycle-clips round the ends of his trousers. The customer was busy looking round the shelves. Martin returned to his stool.

So he was forbidden to see her! Well it was up to her! As for him, he wouldn't give her up! Why should he? Who did her parents think they were? They hadn't the right to order her life. She had her own life to live. And anyway, he was in love with her. She knew that; he knew it; no one could deny it; no one could prevent it. So let her parents do their worst!

It was of course sheer petty snobbery: no doubt about it! They considered him unsuitable company for their daughter; or rather they were afraid something might happen. Something dreadful, in their eyes, like giving Claire a baby. Then they would have to get married!

Would serve them right if that did happen. But it couldn't happen; she wouldn't allow it. It was against everything she was taught; against her upbringing, her religion, her code of conduct. Yet her parents didn't trust her; or they didn't trust him, that was nearer the truth. He was determined never to enter their house again! Anyway he wouldn't be welcome; that was perfectly obvious. Oh, they might—they certainly would—be polite, as polite as always!

Little Ruth had been the cause of this! The interfering fool! Why didn't she mind her own business! Why couldn't she keep quiet!

The next afternoon they met; and as it was a warm cloudy day they walked towards Edenderry. Few people were out walking along by the river.

The Lagan, for a couple of miles above Shaw's Bridge, was very beautiful, winding between lush meadowland and the hillocks in the valley. The city was no more than a dark smudge across the sky.

They walked slowly: Martin was holding Claire's hand; both looked extremely serious. They had talked for more than an hour; and Martin had learnt that things were even worse than Claire had told him the previous day. She was being sent to England very soon, perhaps within a week, to stay with a cousin of her mother's in Devon; then she would return to school for another year; and then she would be sent to a 'finishing school' in London.

Martin had only the most vague idea of what a 'finishing school' was; and when she explained its purpose he was filled with scorn. How stupid and snobbish the middle class were!

"I don't want to go," Claire said, "There's nothing I want less."

"Then why go?"

"What else can I do?"

Clearly it was a trick to separate them not only for one year or for two years, but for even longer: if possible for ever. He was convinced it was a trick. But Claire insisted that it had always been her parents' intention to complete her education in this way.

"Ridiculous!" Martin cried. "What will it fit you for? Tell me that? It's crazy!"

They were despondent. Silently they walked along the riverbank.

"It just isn't fair," he kept repeating to himself. The Taylors had made no objection to him as a friend of Tom's, no objection whatever; but once he had become friendly with Claire they had immediately clamped down. They were snobs; there was something in what his father and Malachi and Frank McCracken had told him. There were different classes: and you either belonged to one or the other—the working class or the middle class.

He felt he belonged to neither; he had little in common with the people in Chatfield Street—he no longer spoke like them and didn't feel any allegiance to them. He had heard his employer talk about 'working-class solidarity', but such a phrase was meaningless to him. Indeed he hated to categorise people as belonging to any particular class. People were individuals; they were all different; only propagandists like Frank McCracken insisted on labelling people. Martin detested the idea of a label—especially a political label. It was a sort of insult, he felt.

And yet his father wouldn't willingly and knowingly insult anyone; and Frank McCracken reserved his insults for abstractions like 'the capitalists'. Martin was puzzled. Perhaps the explanation of the Taylors' conduct was very simple: that Claire was considered too young to go out with him.

Claire was squeezing his hand affectionately.

"What are you thinking about?" she asked.

"Thinking about?"

She nodded. How could he tell her? Anyway he was really thinking about her. He looked at her. How easily hurt she was! Girls were fragile. Thank goodness he was tough! Though he didn't feel particularly tough just at that moment.

Hand in hand they walked very slowly along the path; then he turned her towards him.

They kissed. And as they were kissing he felt free of all his troubles. And he drew her close against him. He saw her three times more before she left for England. She told him she was having rows with her mother; the tension at home was making her unhappy. She was pale and depressed. Her mother had asked her whether she was seeing Martin, and she had confessed she was.

On the morning of her day for departure she called at the shop for about a quarter of an hour, to say goodbye.

They said little. She told him not to come to the Liverpool boat; then she looked at her watch: it was time to go.

"Goodbye," she murmured; "goodbye, Martin." Her voice was so low he could hardly hear her speak.

She had promised to write: and her letters arrived regularly at first; then after a while they ceased. He wrote and asked why. She explained that writing to him made her so miserable that she thought it better not to go on. It would be far better for them both. And she asked to be forgiven. She hoped they would meet again when she returned, if Martin wanted to see her. But perhaps it would be best if they never met again.

Seventeen

BY DECEMBER MR. MCCRACKEN'S SHOP WAS doing a very brisk business. There was a regular flow of customers, mostly young men, some of them undergraduates, a few of them lecturers at the university. Indeed many people had the habit of calling in for half-an-hour or so; and usually they bought something.

Martin suggested that the shop should run a small lending library; the room at the back, which was used for unpacking books, could very well serve the purpose; and his employer took up the suggestion enthusiastically.

Martin had now a good idea of the kind of books the customers wanted to read, and the library soon began to be successful.

Through his job he was making new friends. One was an Art student called Sam Houston, who usually called on Saturday afternoons to borrow a book from the library—he was interested in modern American literature. Sometimes Sam was in the company of two other young men, Edgar Cochrane and Fred Ross. They used the shop as a rendezvous and often began arguments there, on literature or politics.

Sam Houston invited Martin to his flat: it was on the ground floor of an early Victorian terrace on the Lisburn Road. Sam came from Portrush, where his parents ran a hotel. A squat heavily built fellow, he shared the flat with his two friends. Cochrane was a journalist and Ross a commercial traveller for a confectionery firm.

The flat was usually in a state of disorder, and although the three occupants gave instructions to one another to tidy it up, none of them took any notice. There was often a crate of beer in one corner of the large living-room with its dark-green wallpaper, brown-painted windows, and threadbare carpet. Cochrane, an ungainly fellow with a shock of bright auburn hair, constantly tripped over the carpet.

He was the most talkative of the three. He worked for a conservative newspaper, but his own opinions were radical. He called himself an anarchist, read Kropotkin and Bakunin, and despised the ordinary political parties. Occasionally he expressed admiration for the IRA.

"At least they believe in doing something for their cause," he proclaimed, with a fierce glance at Ross, who professed to be a socialist.

"Have they a philosophy?" Ross asked and, as was his habit, replied to his own question, "Of course they haven't. They haven't either a philosophy or an economic system: all they believe in is a mythical Ireland. Just as your Prince Kropotkin believed in a mythical Russia. Perverted idealists, I'd call them. And I'd call you the same."

"What are your politics?" Sam asked Martin.

"I have none."

"Same here," Sam Houston said. "A lot of bloody claptrap, the whole lot! How any honest, upright, God-fearing man can be taken in by any single politician or political party beats me!"

"I thought you were a socialist," Ross said, trying to open a bottle of stout.

Martin shook his head, and said slowly, "I'm not sure that I am."

"I thought you were," Ross repeated as the cork suddenly popped and the stout spilled.

"I work for one," Martin said, "and my father's a socialist; but I'm nothing as yet."

"Don't you find that position unsatisfactory?"

"Not particularly."

"I'll have to argue it out with you," Ross went on, putting the bottle to his lips; "I don't consider you to be in a state of grace."

"You don't need to hold a confessional now," Houston interrupted, turning up the lid of his gramophone which was the only valuable object in the room. Sam's interest, besides painting, was music; he collected records of chamber music by Haydn and Mozart, and could do without any other music.

"I know I'm prejudiced," he always said; "and I want to be, so what about it?"

"And what about Beethoven?" Martin asked.

"Beethoven, did I hear you say?"

"Yes."

"Did you ever listen to his music?"

"I have."

"And you'd mention his name in the same breath as Mozart!" Sam shook his head sadly. "You've no taste whatsoever! Beethoven had to struggle to write music; Mozart wrote music effortlessly—like an angel!"

Martin, amused at this enthusiasm, made no reply.

"Listen—just listen, my friend."

Sam Houston had the gramophone ready to play; and, with his finger to his lips, he commanded silence.

The sounds of the Mozart Quintet filled the room.

In Sam Houston's company, Martin attended the occasional Art exhibitions held in the city. The one which excited them the most was an exhibition of Rodin's. Martin had never seen any real sculpture before; the strength and vitality of Rodin's figures filled him with admiration, and he returned to the exhibition half-a-dozen times.

"We must go to France," Sam said. "It's absolutely essential for us to see Paris, and stay for three months at least."

His intention was to go during the summer and he wanted Martin to go with him. They could live on very little.

"I couldn't leave the shop for a month, never mind three months."

"Of course you could. Or you could get another job," Sam Houston insisted. "One shouldn't stay too long in any job. That's what's the matter with Cochrane. He's been four years with that bloody newspaper of his! You know what age he is?"

Martin didn't know, but guessed Cochrane would be twenty-one.

"Twenty-three. Two years older than I am. I'm the same age as Ross. What age are you? Nineteen I'd say."

Martin confessed to being only eighteen.

"You look older that that," Sam Houston replied. "You must be engaged in secret debauchery."

"No."

"Then it's the want of it."

"That's more likely."

"Ever had a woman?" Sam suddenly asked, with a sidelong look.

He wondered what had become of Claire. He had never visited the Taylors' again, nor had he seen Tom. He had heard from schoolfriends that Tom was quite happy at Oxford. Anyhow his friendship with Tom had finished: and he was glad. His relationship with Claire was different. He often felt lonely, despite having made new friends. When he was tired of reading at home he often wandered round the streets. The neighbourhood held a curious fascination for him, particularly the street opposite Geary's grocery. It was called William Street, but was always referred to as 'the Gut'. Nearly all the men were unemployed; the few who had jobs were casual labourers.

William Street was squalid. In each house the tiny front kitchen was poorly furnished; there was a scrubbed table, which was covered with a newspaper during mealtimes; a sofa and a couple of chairs; hardly anything else. Sometimes the front windows were broken, and patched with cardboard. The stairs, which were just opposite the front door, were bare. And ragged children played in the tiny hallway or sat on the sill.

At the top of 'the Gut' was the pub: corner boys congregated there and played marbles during most of the year. They did nothing else, except gamble on horses and go to football matches. At weekends they got drunk. One or two had been in jail for petty larceny. Martin was becoming more and more sensitive to the sights and sounds around him. 'There's no room to breathe,' he thought bitterly. 'People like us are jammed together like cattle!'

He hoped to be able to persuade his father to rent a better

house, preferably in the Castlereagh or Cregagh Roads; a house with a garden, and with larger rooms. The family could afford a better house now that Martin had a steady job. But he decided to wait until after the summer holiday before mentioning the matter. In the meantime he led his own life and used his home mainly as a place for sleeping.

Eighteen

SLOWLY HE WAS BECOMING INVOLVED IN the life of the city. He was now anxious to leave home, to lead a more independent life. But he found himself unable to take any decisive step. However, the urgency was now less great. They had left Chatfield Street and now rented a house off the Castlereagh Road. It had a tiny garden—a mere patch of grass—protected by a hedge, both at the back and front; and the privacy was welcome. Also the house had a bathroom, and a boxroom (no larger than a cell) which Martin used as a study. From its window he could look down on the back garden 'backing' onto the corrugated iron paling of a mineral water factory. Beyond the factory he could glimpse the Antrim Hills.

The street was quiet; there were no corner boys, no singing and shouting on Saturday nights, no rowdiness. The removal from Ballymacarrett made life a great deal more pleasant. Even his father agreed to that, though he grumbled a little at having to travel further to the shipyard. And Martin's mother continued to be friendly with her neighbours from Chatfield Street and was constantly visiting them and having them look over her new house. She was very proud of it.

Martin spent more evenings at home; he joined a couple of WEA classes and was studying history and philosophy.

Occasionally he contributed to a monthly Labour paper, *Unity*, edited by a friend of Frank McCracken's called Henry Mason.

Henry Mason, a frequent customer of the shop, was a tall dark haired man in his early fifties. A trade union organiser and a well-known orator, he was a prospective Labour candidate in the forthcoming election. He persuaded Martin to attend a few political meetings.

"What d'you think of Henry?" Frank McCracken asked, after one meeting in the dingy hall in York Street, just past the large Co-operative shop. But Martin wasn't over-impressed with the oratory of the trade union organiser.

"I don't care for tub-thumpers," he said coldly.

"You don't?" Frank McCracken replied, hurt. "What do you care for?"

Martin shrugged his shoulders.

"Henry Mason is the best speaker we've got on our side," McCracken went on. "I've seen him hold a crowd of nearly a thousand at the Custom House steps—hold them in the palm of his hand."

He held out his own hand in a gesture.

"Just like that."

One Saturday evening, accompanied by Edgar Cochrane, he went to a lecture on the Sinn Féin movement. The speaker was a professor from the university, a short pugnacious-looking white-haired man who wore a cloak and a monocle, and who spoke slowly and calmly. He had an air of authority, of a man who wouldn't tolerate contradiction. Martin thought him a little pedantic, a little vain and dogmatic.

"Who is he?"

"Professor R.M. Stevens," Cochrane whispered. "He's the greatest classical scholar in our country."

As the lecture went on Martin was more and more impressed by the small dandaical figure on the platform.

"He knows what he's talking about," he murmured. Cochrane nodded.

"He should," he replied; "he's written the best book on Sinn Féin."

"I'll have to read it."

"The Protestants hate him," Cochrane chuckled.

"He doesn't seem to mind, does he?"

"Not a bit."

Then the lecturer suddenly sat down, acknowledged a brief word of thanks from the chairman, and left the meeting at once, looking straight before him as he passed down the side of the hall and into the street.

From the meeting they went to Cochrane's favourite pub, The Duke of York, down one of the eighteenth-century entries off Donegall Street. It was a small, intimate pub used mostly by journalists. Cochrane was well-known there. Sam stood at the bar, arguing with a couple of men whom Martin had never seen before; they were Dubliners he guessed on hearing their accent. Sam hailed the two newcomers.

"Come and join us."

Sam was now an art teacher, was married, and already had a child nearly a year old. He had given up the flat and was living in a semi-detached house off the Ormeau Road. He had settled down to married life and seldom left home except on a Saturday evening when he would go to The Duke of York to meet his friends. He introduced the four young men. The two strangers were Dublin journalists and both were slightly drunk. One, called Falloon, a small sallow young man, smoking a short pipe, said this was his first visit to the north of Ireland.

"And how do we strike you?" Cochrane asked.

"Ah, all right. Ye're all right. I only wish ye'd sense. That's all that's wrong wi' the North. Ye've bloody little sense, ye admit. Isn't that so?"

Cochrane amiably agreed that it was so.

"Ye're not like us," Falloon added.

"You mean all the sense is down in the South?" Sam cut in.

"No, no, Sam! Ye've got me all wrong. Not all the sense is in the South, but there's bloody little sense up in the north. That's all I'm saying."

"But what do you mean?"

"I mean—ah, God, man, look around ye! What way is this to be carrying on?"

He produced the *Belfast Telegraph* from his pocket and unrolled it slowly. "Look!" he said. "Just take a look at that!"

123

He then read out an account of a shooting incident up the Falls Road in which a Catholic had been killed.

"Bloody disgraceful that, isn't it?"

"Protestants have been shot too. Don't forget that," Sam Houston said.

"Ach, I know—of course they have. Both your side o' the house and our own have their dead—no disputing that, is there? But why? That's what I want to know. Why?"

He turned to Martin.

"Can you tell me why?"

"History," Martin said.

"Ballocks."

Martin shrugged his shoulders, and said, "And what do you suggest?"

"Bloody politicians," Falloon retorted.

An argument started up, a disjointed, incoherent babble of words, which Martin found boring; so, pretending to go to the lavatory, he slipped out into the street.

He took long deep breaths of the night air and walked slowly towards High Street. He thought of his reply to the journalist from Dublin. Because the present became the past he, Martin Connolly, would become a part of history. People were hurrying past him to their homes. He thought of Falloon reading out the newspaper account of a Catholic shot on the Falls Road. He remembered his mother's relative Joe Reynolds who was shot years ago. Joe Reynolds and the dead Catholic were now part of history too.

Scraps of the talk in the pub swirled in and out of his mind. The argument had turned to whether Belfast was an Irish city, like Dublin, or an English city like Liverpool, or a Scottish city like Glasgow. And Cochrane had suddenly said: a city of church bells. He had pronounced the words sardonically, with a mocking ascending intonation, and then had buried his face in the froth of a pint of porter.

Martin had grown to like Cochrane. A lonely, introspective man who drank too much, he had once vehemently confessed to Martin: "I'm a bastard! Does that shock you?"

And Martin had shaken his head and replied, "Why should it?"

"It shocks me, Connolly! Christ, but it shocks me!"

It didn't matter; it shouldn't matter; yet somehow, it did matter. To Cochrane it mattered a lot and explained a lot.

"A city of church bells."

Perhaps it explained his phrase.

Nineteen

HAVING SPENT ALMOST FIVE YEARS IN Frank McCracken's bookshop, Martin began to grow tired of it and considered that the time had come for him to try something else. Both Edgar Cochrane and Fred Ross had jobs which seemed to give them wider experience. So Martin became slightly envious of his two friends; though neither of them apparently got much satisfaction from their work.

Once Cochrane promised to take Martin on a visit to linen factories he was describing in a series of articles.

"You've never seen through a factory?"

"No."

"It's an experience you'll enjoy."

"Why?"

"Oh, I expect you'll feel as I always feel—you'll feel you belong to a privileged class simply because you don't have to endure such conditions."

"Are they so bad?"

"No," Cochrane replied; "they're not supposed to be bad at all; they're supposed in fact to be very good ... "

"But what do you think?"

"I couldn't endure working in them," Cochrane said, with a tone of distaste; then, as an afterthought. "Of course I could. It all depends on what you're used to, doesn't it? Some people can endure anything."

The factory they visited was in a country town, about twenty miles south of Belfast. It was a modern building, and with working conditions, according to Cochrane, far better than average. They spent over an hour walking through the various workrooms; then they had afternoon tea with a director in his office. Martin had been introduced as a freelance journalist who had asked to accompany his companion.

"Well," the director asked, helping his guests to cigarettes, "what are your impressions of our firm?"

"Good," Cochrane replied crisply. "Your workers seem very happy indeed, and the whole atmosphere is one of complete friendliness."

The director purred.

"You journalists can hit the nail on the head first go."

Martin pretended to be correcting his notes while the other two chattered. He was surprised at the confidence shown by Cochrane in dealing with the director.

"You'll send me a copy of your article?" the director requested.

"Of course," Cochrane replied.

"Looking forward to it—and hope to see you again."

They waved their goodbyes and hurried to the railway station.

"Well?"

Cochrane was anxious to hear Martin's verdict.

"Well?" Cochrane repeated. With his rather sly smile he looked at Martin.

"Let's talk about it all later," Martin replied; "do you mind?"

He suddenly felt disinclined to discuss their visit to the factory; after all, he hadn't yet had an opportunity to sort out his impressions. Then he gave a short laugh.

"What's the matter, Martin?"

"I've just thought of how you handled him."

"Who?"

"That director."

"Wasn't he a pompous fool?" Cochrane said. "So many employers are, you know."

"Aren't many workers too?" Martin asked.

127

"Perhaps—but not quite so foolish. Or if they are, they're not so pompous. Their mates won't let them be."

They reached the ill-painted ugly station and waited for their train.

"Degrading, isn't it?" Cochrane said.

Martin paused; at that moment he hadn't been thinking of the factory at all; he had been thinking of an essay on Berkeley he had to write for his WEA class. He must start it at once, tonight, if he were to do it.

"Well, it depends—"

But Cochrane interrupted him. "I don't mean the factory: I mean my own job. Having to be smarmy to that puke."

When they returned to the flat they talked for a while about their visit to the factory: but as Fred Ross was entertaining two dark-haired young women called Betty and Jean Armstrong, the conversation had to be desultory. Both young women were attractive, and well-aware of their attractiveness: Betty was a schoolteacher, her younger sister, Jean, a secretary.

Edgar Cochrane described the factory for the benefit of the young women who politely displayed their interest.

"I've never been actually in a linen factory," Jean said. "Curious isn't it, when you think I've lived in the city all my life."

"People like us don't really know how the workers live," Fred Ross answered.

Fred is like that, Martin thought, always a little sententious.

"No, we don't," the young woman replied, dilating her eyes. She had dark liquid brown eyes, Martin noticed: fine-flashing eyes.

Rather frightening eyes, in fact. He would be a little afraid of Jean, he thought. She was certainly self-possessed. Certainly the more attractive of the two. Her sister Betty didn't somehow interest him; yet she was the one Ross was interested in. Curious. Edgar was obviously interested in neither; for he had gone up to his bedroom and hadn't returned.

Ross, helped by Betty, made tea: so Martin found himself alone with Jean. There was a short silence. Damn! He must speak: say something: anything. He looked at her; she was sitting on a low stool, her long legs crossed. What was she doing? She was half turned from him. Her breasts were

128

outlined against the light from the window. She was fiddling with her handbag. She put it on her knee.

"It won't open," she said, with a frown.

"Maybe I could—?"

"Thanks very much." She gave him a smile.

He took the bag and examined the clasp. He exerted a little pressure on one side of the clasp and it clicked open.

"Very clever of you." She brought out a packet of cigarettes. "You smoke, Mr. Connolly?"

He took one and lit her cigarette, bending over very close to her, noticing her long eyelashes as she inhaled.

"Thanks."

He threw the match on the fire. That was better: he felt relaxed now; in command.

"And what did you really think of that factory?" she asked, her head turned upwards. "Was it really rather horrible?"

He didn't know what to reply: Edgar had said that the factory had depressed both of them.

"It's hard to say." He groped for the words to express what he felt. "I really don't know," he blurted out.

She must regard me as a fool, he thought; what a limp comment to make! Of course he knew! But the fact was he was afraid of displaying his feelings. He was afraid of being thought sentimental and glib. Anyway it was obvious she wasn't really interested in factory conditions: she was merely making polite conversation. How could he state what he thought when the whole experience struck him as utterly lacking in importance, at least so far as he was concerned. Why sentimentalise? The factory girls seemed quite high-spirited and happy. Of course, they were exploited, as Edgar said; but did they feel as if they were? Exploitation was an abstraction, after all: these girls had other things to think about. Immediate things, such as—

"I thought you would have strong feelings about factories," the girl said.

"Why should I have?"

"I don't know why," she replied: "I just thought that you might." She paused. "Perhaps because you're a friend of Edgar's. You are, aren't you?"

He nodded.

"But you don't share his political ideas?"

"Not exactly," Martin said. "Do you?"

She burst out laughing.

"Oh, I've no ideas at all—at least Betty says I haven't. And she should know."

"Why?"

"My sister's a socialist."

Fred Ross entered, carrying a tray, and called to Betty to bring the other things.

"Who's a socialist?"

He addressed the question to Jean.

"Betty is."

"Of course she is. Every intelligent person is. Aren't you, Jean? You're intelligent."

"Not as intelligent as Betty."

"Oh, I know that!" Fred Ross said, teasing. "But you're not completely dumb, are you?"

"I'm a Unionist and a good Conservative," Jean retorted, "if you want to know!"

"Really. Why?"

Ross simulated astonishment mingled with disgust.

"Because my father is. Isn't that a good enough reason?"

She turned to Martin for support.

"Don't you agree?"

"Yes."

"You see. So it's two against two!"

"Martin, you liar! She's only flirting with you!"

Betty had entered with the teapot and a plate.

"Who's been flirting?" she asked pouring tea into her sister's cup.

"Your sister has," Ross replied.

"I'm not surprised," Betty said. "She can never resist a good-looking man."

Martin found himself suddenly blushing as Betty began to pour the tea into his cup.

"I'll tell Tom about you," she said, as she poured.

"Who's Tom?" Martin asked.

"Tom Taylor," Betty said. "That's her beau."

"And how is Tom?" Martin said, trying to control the thumping of his heart.

"D'you know Tom?" Jean said, passing over a plate of sandwiches.

He explained that he had known Tom Taylor at school and that they had been in the same class.

"Did you know his sister's just got engaged?"

His heart seemed to dilate: for a moment he could hardly reply.

"Hasn't he two sisters?" he managed to murmur.

"Oh yes—Ruth and Claire," Jean went on; "I mean Claire, of course—the one in England, that is. D'you know Claire?"

"Yes," he answered, trying to keep his voice calm.

"How interesting," Jean said.

"Where is she?"

"In London. She's a flat in London, you know. I've actually stayed with her. For a week. Last Easter."

"And how is she?"

"Very well. She's going to marry some doctor or other."

Fred Ross sat down last, having seen that everybody was eating.

"And you're going to marry this girl's brother?" he asked, his mouth full of bread. "Is that the idea?"

So Claire was engaged: and doubtless she would soon be married to her doctor. He hardly heard the rest of the conversation and was now anxious for an excuse to leave. The others were discussing a newly-formed drama group: and he had no interest in local plays. Then he noticed that Fred Ross had manoeuvred Betty once more into the scullery, on the pretext of requiring help with the washing-up.

"I'll tell Tom I met you," Jean was saying, as soon as they were left alone again.

"Please do; and give him my regards."

"He's come down from Oxford now, you know."

"Is he still keen on the Law?" Martin asked, with as much interest as he could muster.

"Oh yes. He's with Cowan and Barr—the solicitors."

"I thought he wanted to be an advocate."

"Oh, he's changed his mind."

"I see."

He lapsed into silence again. He didn't care how many times Tom Taylor changed his mind! If the truth were told he didn't consider that Tom had a mind to change! He wondered if Oxford had at all altered Tom's outlook. "I bet it hasn't," he thought. "Tom won't change much now. Oxford won't be able to stir him up." He felt superior to the Taylor family. And he felt bitter towards them.

Half-an-hour later he left the flat, on the pretext that he had to call on a friend.

He kept thinking of what he had heard; he found it difficult to imagine Claire engaged to anyone else. It was incredible: how could she forget him so soon? He refused to believe that she had. Who was this doctor to whom she had become engaged? Doubtless some glib Englishman whose looks and manners had impressed her, and who had doubtless flattered her? Yes, she could be flattered, he decided: she couldn't resist flattery. That was the only explanation possible. He felt bitterly towards this unknown young doctor who had won her.

It was ridiculous: and it was unjust. A girl like Claire snapped up by some Englishman, somebody not worth a damn! But what could be done? Nothing. He would have to accept the fact of her engagement; he would have to accept the fact of her marriage. He was helpless.

Or was he? Could he not make a fight? At least he could write to her. He could do that much. He could write and tell her that he had heard about her engagement. He would write to her at once. This girl Armstrong—Jean Armstrong—would have her address. He must get it at once!

Two days later his letter to Claire was posted. He had written and re-written it, and finally had sent it off. As soon as he had posted it he regretted having written it. After all, what good could it possibly do? He had made a fool of himself by sending it. He had even made a fool of himself by getting Claire's address; for he had to ask Fred Ross where Jean Armstrong worked; then he had to telephone her office; and finally he had to ask, after suffering from embarrassment, for Claire's address. Luckily Jean was able to remember it; and luckily she had made things easy for him. She seemed to think it was the most natural thing in the world for him to get in touch with Claire. In fact, she had actually said, "Please give her my love, won't you, and tell her I'll be writing to her soon."

What did he hope to achieve by writing to Claire? Did he expect her to break off her engagement on reading his letter? He refused to believe that Claire would willingly give herself to this Englishman. He only wished he had written her a more persuasive letter; but he knew his letter was completely inadequate.

He had tried to tell how he felt on hearing of her engagement and he had succeeded in writing commonplaces. Some of the sentences he had written were so trite that he blushed on recalling them. "I heard quite by chance that you are engaged," he had written, "and I felt that I must tell you I shall never forget you, and I hope you will never forget me. Perhaps you will reply to this, perhaps not. I hardly hope for a reply."

Within the week he received her reply. Her letter was brief and very courteous. She told him she was glad to have his letter, and she told him that she often thought of him. She was sorry to have caused him pain and hoped that he would remember her kindly. She would be getting married in six months' time, in Belfast, but thought that they shouldn't try to see one another: a meeting wouldn't do either of them any good. After her marriage she would be settling down again to live in Surrey with her fiancé who worked as a surgeon in a London hospital. Perhaps some day in the future they would meet and be friends but in the meantime—

Her letter was dignified, far more dignified than his had been; and he read it many times before tearing it up.

He felt calm now that he had her reply.

Martin began to spend his weekends at the flat on the Lisburn Road. Both Cochrane and Ross enjoyed his company and made him welcome.

"You keep us from fighting," Cochrane admitted, and Ross, with a shake of his head, agreed.

So Martin took over one of the two attics belonging to the flat; the back attic, which contained an old-fashioned iron bed, a battered wardrobe and a single chair.

"I must pay you rent for it," Martin said.

"Why?" Edgar asked frowning.

"Because I'd rather."

"But the place isn't being used; we don't need your money."

"I'd rather pay for it all the same."

"How much?" Fred said. "How much do you want to pay us?"

"Hell, Fred, you're not going to—"

Edgar was indignant that Fred should be willing to take any money: for after all the attic was damp and lay unused, so why shouldn't Martin have it free?

"He *wants* to pay, Edgar. Don't you?" Ross said, appealing to Martin.

"Yes, I do."

They argued for a while and finally settled on a pound a month, much to Edgar's disgust.

Martin was pleased with the arrangement; it gave him the freedom he had long wanted. He at last had a room to which he could retire when he wanted to be by himself; he had the use of the sitting-room to entertain his friends; and he had also the company of Edgar Cochrane and Fred Ross when he wanted company. However he was seldom short of company: he now made friends quite readily.

An extraordinary assortment of people called into the shop; many of then engaged Martin in long conversations. A bookshop was somehow quite different from any other kind of shop. People seemed to want to talk not only about books but about themselves. Martin often found himself asked to give advice on the personal problems of customers.

His work was far from being arduous; indeed, Frank McCracken became worried about the future of the shop. There was too much unemployment in the city for such a bookshop to flourish. He warned Martin that the shop might have to close in six months' time.

The thought that the shop might have to be closed perturbed Martin. What could he do? He would like similar work: therefore he should find out whether he could get a job in one of the libraries. In the meantime he would work for Frank McCracken, and stay as long as the shop remained open.

One Monday morning Frank appeared in the shop with a bandage round his head.

"What's happened?" Martin inquired as soon as his employer removed his cap. "Did you have an accident?"

"Ye could call it that, I suppose, only it was done on purpose."

"How did it happen?"

"I was hit with a stone. I might have been killed. Just feel that lump."

He took Martin's hand and placed it on the wound above the right ear.

"It was a glancing blow—lucky for me. Else I wouldn't be here; I'd be—"

He turned up his eyes and caressed the bandage; then explained what had happened.

He had been addressing a meeting on Sunday afternoon at the Custom House steps. There had been interruptions from the crowd. The meeting had broken up in disorder, after some stone throwing. Getting down from the platform, he had been hit by one of the stones and knocked almost unconscious.

"The wife nearly passed out when they brought me home," he added. "She thought they'd shot me."

"They would," Martin said with conviction.

"I know they would," Frank McCracken agreed. "They'd make a corpse of me, and be glad to do it!"

Frank McCracken became dispirited, especially after an election in the autumn. He had worked hard on behalf of Henry Mason; but the result of the election had been disastrous for his candidate.

"The wife wants me to go back to Glasgow," he told Martin, "and I think I'll go. We don't belong here, anyway—and it's time for us to go home; we're both gettin' on in years."

The bookshop would have to be closed, and the ironmonger's shop on the Shankill Road would have to be sold. Mrs. McCracken had made up her mind; she wouldn't allow her husband to risk his life again.

"This is no city for people like us," she told Martin on one of her visits to the shop.

"I saw the factory-girls—hundreds of them—on Election Day, shouting their slogans at us. Ye know, Martin, what I felt like doing? I felt like cryin'. Yes, that's what I felt like—cryin'. I tell ye the tears were in my eyes, just to see that sight o' them girls, wi' their arms linked together, shouting daft things at us. Ack, well ... " she said resignedly.

Book Two

Twenty

THE CLOSING OF FRANK MCCRACKEN'S BOOKSHOP was symbolic of what was happening to the city. The shipyard had no orders; the great slips were empty; and thousands of the workers were walking the streets in idleness. Among them was Martin's father, who was unemployed for over two years.

The linen factories were also closing down, one after the other. And among the firms which fell into bankruptcy was Mr. Taylor's—one of the smaller firms. And the city from time to time underwent spasms of violence. Citizens—both Protestants and Catholics—were shot in raids. And a curfew was imposed in the troubled areas where Catholics and Protestants lived.

For three months Martin was without a job after the closing of the bookshop and Frank McCracken's departure for Scotland. But he had actually plenty to do: he was attending an evening class for shorthand and typing; and he was also doing a little freelance journalism.

At the weekends there were occasional parties at the flat, usually spontaneous affairs, with half-a-dozen people casually calling in for a chat; someone would go for stout and beer, and sandwiches would be hastily made; the gramophone would be played and the sitting-room cleared for dancing.

Both Ross and Cochrane had a large circle of acquaintances in the district, including some teachers, medical students, and youngish professionals and businessmen and their girlfriends. The flat was a convenient meeting place for anyone who liked company and who enjoyed talking politics and literature and art.

"The trouble with us," Edgar grumbled, "is that we talk a hell of a lot; but we do bloody little—about anything."

"What should we do, Edgar?" asked one of the guests, a little Englishman called Green, who taught history in a secondary school.

"Fight. We only talk. There's a hell of a lot to fight for just now."

"I prefer to live," replied the Englishman, showing his large protruding teeth.

"Call this living?" shouted Fred Ross, who was on his knees lighting the fire.

"It's time you were married," Edgar retorted.

"That's the trouble with all of us," Green added, giving his toothy smile.

"You mean—sex?" Edgar asked.

"Is that your trouble?"

"I suppose so."

"God, this fire!" cried Fred, getting up from his knees and looking at his blackened hands.

"Won't it light?" Edgar asked.

"You try it," Fred replied, vexed with himself—he hated to be thwarted in anything he undertook.

"No fear."

Edgar didn't move, but lay sprawled on the large lumpy armchair near the window. He was smoking his pipe and giving half his attention to the newspaper on his lap.

"We should be helping with this strike," he said, lifting the newspaper. The railwaymen had come out on strike at the weekend and the paper had an editorial about the irresponsibility of the men and their leaders.

"Just listen to this."

He read an extract in his deep voice, emphasising the inflated language, the muted note of hysteria.

"Did you ever hear such drivel?" Edgar added, throwing down the paper in disgust.

"We should be helping the workers," Fred remarked, once again on his knees in front of the fire.

"We should be on the picket-line," Edgar retorted.

The Englishman crossed the room and picked up the paper. He had little interest in politics, especially local politics, and had often been warned not to meddle in Irish controversy.

"I see that some students—" he began.

"Yes, I know," Edgar said. "That's what happened during the General Strike in England, isn't it? Bloody blacklegs!"

At last the fire was lit. Fred Ross got off his knees and watched the flames leaping up the chimney. Then, smoking a cigarette triumphantly, he took a chair near the bookcase.

"Have we any bread in?" he asked, looking at Edgar, then at Martin.

"I don't think so," Edgar said.

"Didn't you say you'd get bread?" Fred asked.

"Did I? I don't remember."

Fred Ross hated inefficiency; and he regarded Edgar Cochrane as inefficient. He frowned.

What a nuisance! Somebody would have to go and fetch bread. This was Saturday: and they had all Sunday before them. The shops were shut on Sundays of course. How could they exist without bread?

"I'll go," Martin said, in a mollifying tone.

"Why should you?" Fred asked, looking at Edgar, who had lifted a book from the floor. Edgar succeeded quite easily in ignoring the look.

Martin rose. He felt the need of fresh air. The flat was stuffy: the atmosphere of the living-room smoke-laden.

"I won't be long," he said, "back in about twenty minutes."

He walked down the Lisburn Road, past the Deaf and Dumb Institute, a mock-Renaissance building which was almost a replica of the University building a couple of hundred yards away. He passed the City Hospital; through the gates streamed a crowd of people carrying flowers and parcels of food and fruit.

He glanced at the faces of the passers-by: they looked care-worn as they hurried through the gates towards the wards.

He went into a grocer's near the hospital, made his purchases and turned to go out.

"Hello!"

It was Jean Armstrong. She had been standing behind him; he hadn't noticed her. She was smiling; he was conscious of her full lips.

"How are you?"

He returned her greeting and looked at her.

She was hatless and wearing a loose fawn coat and her black hair, brushed straight back from her face, was gleaming.

"Did you get in touch with Claire?" she asked, still smiling.

"Oh, yes," Martin murmured. "Thank you very much."

"Is she well? I haven't written to her for ages ... "

The grocer approached them, ready to take the young woman's order.

"Oh, dear, what do I want? Let me see ... "

She gave her order; he waited; and they struck up a conversation. Then, as they walked out of the shop together, Martin offered to carry her basket.

"Haven't you enough to carry?" she retorted. "You should have a basket. But I suppose you wouldn't carry one." He nodded and told her he hated shopping. They walked along the Lisburn Road and he offered to accompany her as far as the University where she would catch her tram. They chatted about Claire Taylor and the forthcoming marriage.

"You were in love with her," she said suddenly.

Martin was taken aback at the directness of the statement. He flushed slightly. He had been quite unprepared for such a remark. Impossible for him to make any reply on the spur of the moment.

"Oh, I shouldn't have said that, should I?"

He was silent.

"I'm sorry. Are you offended?"

No, he wasn't offended. Not in the least.

"Yes, I was," he said, after a pause.

"You mean you were offended?"

"No, no. Not at all."

"Oh, you mean—the other."

"Yes."

They walked along in silence. Martin felt at first slightly embarrassed at the thought of this young woman's sharing his secret. But his embarrassment soon changed to a feeling of

142

intimacy. He looked at her: she was smiling as if the situation were really a ridiculous one. He resented her apparent levity. At last she spoke.

"I know how you feel."

Her voice was low; and he wondered what she meant. Was she, in fact, trying to be sympathetic? He didn't want her sympathy.

"Do you?"

He paused. He looked at her: she had a fine profile, he thought; he was enjoying her company. She walked well, with a swing of her hips, her head proudly held.

"Yes," she said. "Yes, I certainly know how you feel. I feel like you."

"What d' you mean?"

"Tom and I ... "

She shrugged her shoulders. Martin waited for her to continue.

"It's all over between us."

There was no tram in sight when they reached University Road, so they decided to walk a bit up the Malone Road. She seemed to be glad to have someone to talk to.

"All over?"

"Yes; it didn't work out. Just as well, isn't it, that we found out before it was too late?"

Jean gave one of her sidelong glances. Her eyes were remarkable, Martin decided; dark and large and humorous. She was, in fact, an extraordinary person. She seemed to take it for granted that Martin should be interested in her affairs, and that she had a right to be interested in his.

"What actually happened?" he found himself asking.

She invited his curiosity.

"Oh, we got tired of each other. That's all. It was just as simple as that."

Jean wrinkled up her nose.

"I don't think I like the family either—except Claire. She's the only one I like and the only one that liked me. She's different from the others, of course. Isn't that so?"

He agreed. Yes, Claire was certainly different from the other members of her family.

143

They discussed the Taylor family, doling out merits and demerits to the various members. Martin learnt that the Taylors no longer lived in the style to which they had been accustomed. They had given up their seaside house; they had sold their own house on the Malone Road and were living now in a much smaller one on the same road.

"Isn't Tom doing well at the law?"

Jean shook her head.

"I think that's the trouble. Mr. Taylor's business collapsed, Tom isn't earning much yet, and Ruth does nothing except keep on the lookout for someone to marry."

They halted at a tram stop. Martin looked at his watch.

"I'm afraid I've taken you out of your way," she was saying.

But he wasn't listening. He wanted to see her again—and soon.

"What are you doing tonight?"

He waited for her reply. He looked at her. Her face was expressionless. This was the moment of decision. She might make an excuse; or else she might have some engagement. But in the few seconds before she replied, he was on edge.

"Nothing in particular," she said.

"Couldn't we meet somewhere?"

"If you like."

"Where?"

"Where do you suggest? Not at our flat. My sister might be there. Anyway it's too nice an evening to stay in, isn't it?"

They decided to meet at the front gates of the University.

Twenty-One

THEY WERE TO MEET AT EIGHT o'clock. Martin turned up at five to eight and walked up and down University Road. She was late. Perhaps she wouldn't turn up at all. If she didn't come, well—but he hoped she would turn up. He hated walking up and down aimlessly.

He glanced at the University. It intimidated him, the actual building itself, dark red and remote looking. It looked withdrawn from the city, as if it didn't quite belong there.

He halted at the front gates. It was twelve minutes past eight. He glanced along the road and saw Jean walking towards him.

He went to meet her.

"Hello," she said, "Sorry I'm late."

"It doesn't matter."

"Have you been waiting long?"

"No."

He had been waiting over a quarter of an hour. But it hadn't seemed long. Jean had turned up in a bright blue coat and a black hat, tilted to one side; she looked smart, he thought, and he wished he had paid more attention to his own appearance.

"Well," she said, "what next?"

They walked towards the centre of the city. Martin

suggested a film. The evening was cool, with rain threatening; so she agreed to his suggestion and they entered the stale darkness of a cinema.

Groping his way to their seats he took her hand, the better to guide her. "Sorry," he murmured, stumbling over legs in the aisle.

Then the usherette illuminated their seats with her torch: they sat down and tried to follow the story.

It was, he soon discovered, an incredibly stupid historical film about the French Revolution, and he found himself unable to concentrate on it, the characters were so stilted, the situations so absurd. He glanced at Jean.

"Rotten, isn't it?"

She nodded.

"Shall we go?"

But just then the hero escaped from the prison in which he had been languishing, and the film suddenly caught Jean's interest.

"In a moment," she whispered, restraining Martin with a half-conscious movement of her hand. She surrendered her hand to him and they sat through the film to its inevitable happy ending.

After supper in a café near the cinema they walked towards her home. She lived in an avenue not far from the University. He led her along a dark pathway leading to a tennis-club pavilion.

"What time is it?" she asked.

"A quarter to eleven," he replied, looking at his watch. "Quite early."

He took her hand and led her further along the narrow path.

"Where are you taking me?"

He made no answer but halted under a tree and drew her towards him. They kissed. She put her arms round him, pressing herself close.

"Is that what you want?" she whispered.

He pressed her closer and he could feel her whole body against him. She lay tense in his arms, waiting for him to kiss her again. Her eyes were closed as he put his mouth to hers, hungrily, and his hands explored the warmth of her body.

"I must go."

Slowly she broke from his grasp. He caressed her face,

146

gently, with the tips of his fingers. How smooth a woman's face was to touch!

His hand slipped to her breasts.

"What time is it?"

It was twenty past eleven.

"Then I must go."

She buttoned up her coat, took a comb from her handbag, and tidied her hair.

They left the darkness of the pathway for the lighted avenue. Jean halted underneath a lamp post.

"Do I look a sight?"

"No."

"I feel as if I've been pulled through a hedge backwards."

She laughed and smoothed her rumpled coat, took Martin by the hand, and walked slowly towards her house. They halted.

"When shall I see you?" he asked.

"Do you want to?"

"Of course I do. Tomorrow evening?"

She reflected a moment: then shook her head.

"No, not tomorrow, I'm afraid."

She explained that on Sunday evenings she usually visited one of her friends.

Yes, she was free on Monday.

They met on Monday, and again on Wednesday, and again on Friday.

On Friday evening they returned to the flat: Jean knew that her sister was in Portrush for the weekend; and Martin was sure that Edgar wouldn't be back till eleven.

"Are you really sure?" Jean asked.

"Of course I am."

He shut the front door and they entered the dining room. It was a room almost without character: the furniture bits and pieces of Victorian junk. Jean looked around it, critically.

"Bit of a mess, isn't it?"

"Yes, it is."

She crossed to the mantelpiece, rubbed her hand along it. It was dusty.

"I thought a woman cleaned it once a week."

"She does."

Jean laughed, wiping her hand with her handkerchief.

"She doesn't! She doesn't half-do it."

"Better wash your hands; you know where the bathroom is."

She left the room. Now that he was alone he felt he must act at once. He was nervous; he could hear his heart thumping. He wanted to take her to bed. Should he just ask her, bluntly? No, he couldn't; he couldn't possibly. But he would have to say something, to make his intentions clear. Weren't they already clear to her? He was inexperienced: that was really his trouble; he had never yet had a girl. He had made feeble attempts to make love to girls whom he'd met casually at dances. Make love? Lust. And what was this? Did he feel anything for Jean other than lust? She certainly attracted him physically. Yes, her body excited him.

She excited him physically more than Claire ever had. But he had never had such an opportunity as this with Claire.

Jean returned to the room. She was smoking a cigarette.

"Well—" he said.

She sat down on the armchair. He went towards her, took her left hand in both his hands, raised her to her feet.

"Yes?"

Her voice was quizzical: neither encouraging nor discouraging.

"Won't you come to my room?"

She hesitated.

"Please—"

She looked at him: a long silence.

"If you want me to."

Putting his arm round her waist he brought her to his room. He turned out the light at once. But the bedroom was half-lit by a lamp-post on the opposite pavement.

They went to bed. He tried to conceal his shyness as best he could by pretending to be casual as he undressed. Jean appeared to be in much more control of the situation, taking off her clothes quickly, but turning her back to him as she did so.

"Oh, it's cold," she whispered, shivering slightly.

"I'll soon warm you."

Her skin was soft to his touch. He trembled slightly as he felt her body by his side. She lay very close to him.

It was what he had longed for, this intimacy with a girl's body. And he caressed her slowly, slowly in the semi-darkness, his hands going forth on their voyage of discovery. And then he felt her hands on his body, gently, ever so gently.

An hour later they got up and dressed. They spoke little.

"We must hurry," Jean whispered.

He nodded his agreement.

"Kiss me," Jean suddenly said, facing him.

He took her in his arms and she sighed as they kissed.

"I wish you could stay here all night," he said.

"I couldn't."

She held him tightly in her arms: then suddenly released him.

"Let's go."

They left the flat and walked towards the Malone Road. Neither referred to what had happened; they had been intimate and the warmth of their intimacy still glowed in their bodies; they had explored each other's bodies and had enjoyed the exploration. Now it was over they acknowledged their new relationship with a squeeze of the hand. They walked slowly along, as if not quite in the present.

Martin left Jean to the front gate of her house.

"When shall I see you again?"

She looked into his face as if trying to guess what was in his mind.

"Should we see each other again?" she asked.

"Why not?"

He was insistent that they should meet again the following evening. She agreed, smiling.

He kissed her goodnight: her lips were warm and moist.

"Goodnight."

"Goodnight."

She turned and ran up the path.

That night he had the feeling of having entered into manhood, of having realised himself as a male capable of satisfying a woman; though whether he had really satisfied this particular young woman he was far from certain. He had been tentative, completely lacking in confidence. She had had to guide him. He was certain she had been in bed before with a man. Was it Tom Taylor? She might have given herself to Tom, and possibly to other men as well. She was quite experienced: of that he was perfectly certain: she had made no attempt to simulate innocence. Indeed she seemed to be secretly proud of her knowledge; and at the time he had been grateful for it.

His feelings towards her were surprisingly complex and contradictory; and he could not refrain from admiring her assurance. And yet she had little cause for confidence in herself. For hadn't Tom Taylor recently jilted her? She must have been Tom's mistress.

Twenty-Two

HE SAW HER THE FOLLOWING EVENING, as arranged. They met at Shaftesbury Square, on the left-hand side, at the tram stop; and she was ten minutes late. He didn't mind. He didn't mind in the least waiting for her. As she got off the tram she greeted him.

"Hello."

Her greeting was surprisingly casual, even offhand; his greeting, on the contrary, was extremely self-conscious. He felt himself blushing.

"Well, how are you?" she said as they walked along Bedford Street.

He muttered in reply that he was all right; but in truth he felt uncomfortable. How was he going to cope with this young woman? He hardly knew her, in one sense at least: she was merely a friendly young woman, with good looks and a certain amount of charm, whom he had met casually and had become involved with, just as casually.

And now she was walking by his side, looking very smart in a dark-green costume and a triangular-shaped hat which looked slightly ridiculous to him.

He certainly admired her aplomb. Here she was, a respectable middle-class young woman, who had been in bed with him and who regarded the incident as not worth mentioning! At any rate, she made no attempt to mention it. Perhaps she wanted to forget the incident; perhaps she didn't consider it important. He hardly knew a single thing about this young woman—except that she was remarkably compliant.

"Where shall we go?"

She shrugged her shoulders; she said she didn't mind how they spent the evening. He knew exactly how he would have liked to spend it, but didn't dare suggest going to the flat again. Perhaps he should say what was in his mind; perhaps that was what she wanted; but somehow he felt he must suggest something else.

"Would you like a drink?"

She paused and looked at him.

"I don't know," she said. "Perhaps I shouldn't. I can't make up my mind. Make it up for me, will you? I'll do what you want me to do."

That was the kind·of remark that left Martin without a rejoinder. This girl was so pliable that she seemed to be ready for anything. He just couldn't understand her.

"Let's go in here?"

They went into the pub. It had a brightly-lit room at the back which they had to themselves. They gave their order to the barman; Jean wanted a gin and tonic, Martin a whiskey; the barman brought the drinks and disappeared into the front bar.

"I don't really like going into pubs," Jean said, "just in case you think I do."

"But, why—?"

"It's just that they're so sordid, aren't they? They're just drinking dens. And that barman! He almost gave me the creeps!"

"I hardly noticed him."

"He'd a wet mouth—and a leer. I felt he was wanting to— ugh! Never mind!"

Martin leant forward and took Jean's hand, caressing it gently. As he did so he looked at her face. She was certainly a fine-looking girl: her features beautifully moulded, her nose straight and narrow, her lips full, her eyes dark, almond-shaped.

"Well, what are you thinking?" she asked, releasing her hand and sipping her drink.

"I'm just admiring you," Martin replied. "That's all."

"You're not the first," she replied pertly.

"Oh, I know that."

She lifted her glass again. Martin was at once conscious that their last words were ambiguous and that they had both been immediately aware of the different meanings. She said nothing. She stared into her glass.

"What do you think of me?"

"I've told you, haven't I?"

"You haven't told me anything. Do you think I'm a slut?"

"Of course I don't!" He raised his voice at the imputation that he should make such a judgement. Still, he was blushing slightly.

"I suppose I am," she went on, in a calm, matter-of-fact voice. "And I shouldn't be, the way I was brought up."

She finished her drink and said that it was her turn to stand: she wouldn't listen to his protest.

"I can afford it: and you can't; so let's have no more argument."

Martin rose and called the barman from the front bar.

They stayed in the pub nearly two hours. And they talked; they talked about each other, about their lives at home and their families. The time passed quickly; and the other customers came into the back bar and left again, hardly noticed; and Martin listened to what Jean had to tell him about her background.

It was not an exceptional upbringing. Her father had been a cashier in a bank but had retired at the age of fifty after a heart attack, and her mother now nursed him; they were not very well-off—her father's pension was small.

"We appear to live better than we actually do," she explained. "I don't know what'll happen when Betty gets married—you know she's marrying Fred next Spring?"

"Yes."

"I hope it works out all right."

"It should."

"Yes, it should, shouldn't it? But you can never tell with marriage, can you? It never seems to work out right, does it?"

"I suppose not."

"I remember my mother and father used to have rows, and they wouldn't speak for days, sometimes for weeks; and I thought we were the only unhappy family in the world. I really did. But now I think we aren't so bad—better than most families, I think."

She paused. Though she had taken only two gins, Martin had the impression that she was slightly drunk, but not unpleasantly so; perhaps he was slightly drunk himself; anyhow, he felt warm towards this girl, who was now looking at him with her head on one side, like a small child about to ask the teacher a puzzling question. Suddenly she gave a little giggle.

"What is it?" Martin inquired.

"Oh, nothing."

"It must be something."

"Shall I tell you? No, I couldn't. No, I couldn't."

"Go on, do."

Their glasses were empty; there was no-one in the back bar except themselves. She was certainly attractive, he thought, as he watched her fingering her glass, caressing it, turning it round and round. Her mood seemed to have changed. She looked serious; abstracted; as if she had forgotten where she was. Her thoughts seemed to be elsewhere; she appeared to be quite oblivious to his presence. He waited. She had something to say to him: and he was curious to know what. This young woman filled him with curiosity. And yet, somehow, he was not in love with her. There was something missing in their relationship. She attracted him; attracted him very much: her body was soft, yielding, her breasts beautifully moulded.

He became conscious of the fact that she had been silent for what appeared to be a long time; it was, perhaps, five minutes; and her head was still bowed.

"What's the matter, Jean?"

Momentarily she had the appearance of a much older woman. What was the matter with her? She had made no attempt to answer him. Was she sick? Perhaps the drink had disagreed with her.

Or perhaps—

"Nothing," she murmured at last.

"Yes, there's something!"

His voice was insistent. He would bully this girl if necessary;

she was keeping something back from him, something that might concern him. It was all very curious. And when his curiosity was aroused he wanted it to be satisfied.

"Yes," he repeated, "yes, there's something! I know there is!"

She fumbled for her handkerchief.

He suddenly saw that she was crying, crying bitterly, and nothing he could do would comfort her. Gradually her sobbing ceased.

"I'll tell you in a minute," she whispered.

He waited for her. She was pale and distraught; and looking at her fixedly he was sorry for her, and puzzled; but above all he was inquisitive. He wanted her confidence; so he waited for her to become calm.

"I don't know whether I can tell you—" she began, sniffing.

"You must. Please—"

"I'll try." But she was unable to go on.

He waited; he was becoming irritated by her mystifying behaviour.

"Yes?"

She looked him full in the face.

"I'm pregnant."

She blurted out the words; and Martin stared at her, incredulously.

"You're—"

"Yes, I am."

"But—how could you be?"

She nodded in affirmation, staring at the glass in her hand.

"Oh, it wasn't you. I only wish it was. I let you have me last night because—Oh, I don't know why! Only you wanted me, didn't you?"

Martin nodded. His mouth felt dry.

"I knew you could do me no harm, the way I was. So I let you—"

From the other bar came a raucous voice amid the low chatter of customers.

"Time, gentlemen ... "

Jean rose. Her scarf fell on the floor; Martin picked it up and handed it to her. She wrapped it round her and quickly buttoned up her coat.

He followed her outside.

They went out into the ill-lit street. All sorts of wild thoughts were passing through his mind as he stood on the pavement for a moment, undecided what to do next. The girl beside him seemed bereft of willpower. She stood beside him, her face pale and expressionless, as if drained of all feeling.

"Let's go to a café," he said.

They walked down a dingy side street which led to Great Victoria Street, almost opposite the gaunt grey façade of the Great Northern railway.

They had hardly spoken since leaving the pub; Jean seemed to be almost unaware of where she was and what she was doing. Martin took her by the arm and gave it a sympathetic squeeze. She made no response.

They entered a café near the railway and ordered tea and biscuits. By now Jean seemed to be completely enveloped in her misery. What could he do? How could he help her? He didn't even know what to say to her now. She sat sipping her tea, miserable looking, with the marks of her tears still apparent; she hadn't bothered to powder her face again. Then at last she said: "I'm sorry I told you about this, Martin. It's got nothing to do with you."

"Oh, yes, it has."

"No."

"I'll help you all I can."

"How can you help me? Nobody can."

He didn't know what help he could give her; for he felt quite helpless. He was wondering who was responsible for her pregnancy. It must be Tom Taylor, he decided, though it was hard to imagine Tom in the part of a seducer. But if it wasn't Tom, then who could it be?

"What can I do?"

She was appealing for his help. He couldn't refuse her: he felt involved in her life now, as if he were responsible for her condition.

"I don't know yet," he answered.

She must tell him who the man was; she must confide in him; only then could he help her.

"Well ... " he began. He hesitated before blurting out the question he wanted to ask her. "Who was it? You'll have to tell me."

Twenty-Three

HE WAITED FOR HER ANSWER. BUT she remained silent, her eyes lowered, her hands clasped together as if she were praying. He wondered momentarily if she was indeed praying. He looked at her hands. How shapely they were: how long and narrow her fingers: how beautiful even her fingernails. Still he waited: still she remained silent.

"Was it Tom Taylor?" he murmured at last.

She made no rely; and he knew now for certain that it was Tom who had made her pregnant.

"Have you told him what he's done?"

She nodded.

"And he won't help you?"

"No."

He waited for her to confide in him: but she remained silent. How could he help her if she wouldn't give him her confidence?

"I'll do something," he said firmly.

"What can you do?" she said, her voice drained of emotion.

"I can see Tom Taylor—"

"I don't want you to see him."

"But he's responsible—"

"That doesn't matter."

Her voice was suddenly filled with passionate hatred. Martin was startled; and afraid that she would burst into angry tears.

"I don't want anything more to do with him—or with his child!"

She looked up at Martin, her eyes liquid with tears of anger and pity.

"I won't have it!" she cried. "I'll get rid of it!"

Martin left her to her home along the deserted suburban avenue which now appeared slightly eerie under the ill-lit street lamps.

She had finally agreed to allow him to see Tom Taylor, though she was certain no good could come from the meeting. She had repeated that she had now no desire to marry Tom, even if he wanted her to; and she was perfectly sure he didn't want to. And she'd confessed too that she'd been in love with Tom: very much in love.

"Curious, isn't it, what's happened to both of us," she said.

He nodded his agreement. He supposed she was referring to what had happened between Claire and himself. Yes, it was indeed curious that Claire had left him and that Tom had left her.

He looked at his watch. Twenty minutes to twelve! He had missed the last tram and would have to walk back to the flat.

"Don't worry," he said, squeezing her hand.

He glanced at her face in the semi-darkness. She was extremely pale and forlorn-looking. It wasn't fair, he thought, to make anyone suffer like this. He would see what Tom Taylor had to say!

Tenderly he kissed her.

"Goodnight, Martin," she said.

"Goodnight, Jean."

Three days later Martin met Tom Taylor, at six o'clock; their meeting place was a pub in Chichester Street, not far from Taylor's office.

Martin had never before been in this particular pub which was frequented mostly by business and professional men. He had arrived first, a few minutes early, and had sat down at a corner table.

He was feeling nervous. It seemed a long time since he'd

been on friendly terms with Tom; and a longer time since his life had centred on Claire. As he waited he wondered whether Tom had changed much; he also wondered exactly how he'd introduce the subject of Jean. On the telephone the previous evening he had given Tom no explanation but merely said that he was anxious to arrange a meeting as soon as possible. Tom had been quite friendly and had suggested the rendezvous.

"Hello—nice to see you again," he greeted Martin, shaking hands. "Hope I haven't kept you waiting long?"

"You haven't. I've just arrived."

"What'll you have?"

Martin ordered a beer, Tom a sherry.

"Well, it seems years since we've met!" Tom said as they raised glasses. "What on earth have you been doing with yourself?"

Martin replied that he was doing very little, except occasional freelance journalism, but that he had a chance of joining the staff of one of the provincial papers. He had in fact written a letter to an editor only three days previously; and the editor, a friend of Edgar Cochrane's, had replied that he had received Martin's application and would soon be coming to a decision.

"I expect you like journalism?" Tom asked.

Martin admitted that he did and asked whether Tom liked the law.

"It's all right, I suppose," Tom replied, "but I'm keener on politics. You'll hardly approve of me—I'm a Tory. I may be a candidate in the next election, with a bit of luck."

Martin said nothing; he had no desire to talk politics, so he quickly changed the subject and inquired about Tom's parents.

They were well, Tom said, a little brusquely, without offering any further information about his family.

Suddenly Martin felt his heart thumping: he was anxious to know all about Claire; he wanted to know everything about her, everything; he was hungry for any tiny scrap of knowledge. But Tom avoided mentioning his sister.

The conversation flagged as Martin ordered the drinks, and Tom looked up at the clock. There was a silence. Martin realised that he must soon explain why he had asked Tom to meet him. The barman returned with the drinks.

"Thanks," Martin said, placing a ten-shilling note on the tray and feeling rather grand.

They lifted their glasses saying, "Cheers!"

The moment for explanation had come.

"I wanted to see you about a personal matter—" Martin began.

"Oh, I'd hoped it was professional," Tom interrupted, with a laugh. "But go on—it sounds more interesting, the way you put it."

"This doesn't really concern me at all," Martin self-consciously added. But as soon as he spoke he felt he'd made the wrong remark.

If this matter didn't concern him, if it really didn't, then he was leaving himself open to be told to mind his own business.

Tom raised his eyebrows, made no comment, and waited for Martin to continue.

"You know Jean Armstrong?"

"Yes, I know Jean."

"She's a friend of mine too."

"Is that so?"

Feeling his mouth dry, Martin gulped down his drink. "It's about Jean I want to see you."

"Is that so?" Tom repeated.

"Yes. She's in trouble."

Martin noticed that Tom Taylor's face had gone stiff: had become mask-like; his voice explosive in tone. He waited for Tom to say something in reply, but Tom was playing this cautiously, like a lawyer. So Martin repeated his remark.

"She's in serious trouble."

"Well?"

There was another pause; Martin looked at Tom a little contemptuously, then added, "I'd like to help her, wouldn't you?"

Tom shrugged his shoulders.

"She's only herself to blame, you know—I'm not responsible for her condition. Did she tell you I was?"

"Yes."

"And you believe her?"

Martin nodded.

"Well, believe me, I'm not responsible. Are you?"

Martin flushed and Tom laughed.

"Oh, don't look so guilty. I don't believe you're responsible either, but you've been screwing her too, I expect. She likes it, doesn't she?"

Tom reached for his drink, drained the glass, and, while waiting for Martin's reply, signalled to the barman.

"I don't know what to say—" Martin began. "It's all a bit of a mess." He was perplexed, and frowning.

"She likes to play around," Tom said, "and I hope you aren't too heavily involved."

Martin shook his head. No, he liked her of course—he was very fond of her. But that was all.

"Well now, let's get this clear," Tom said. "I've screwed Jean and so have you; but we didn't make her pregnant. There's been others before us, and there'll be others after us. She's in trouble because she's promiscuous. It just doesn't pay a girl to be promiscuous."

"She should know that."

"She wouldn't admit it, would she?"

"I never asked her."

"Don't. She's a bit of a fool, but you'd hardly expect her to admit that too."

Tom Taylor looked at his watch. Nearly seven o'clock. He explained that he had an appointment and would have to go soon. He hastily finished his drink and got up.

"What should she do?" Martin said.

"What does she want to do?"

"Get rid of it, I think."

"That shouldn't be too difficult," Tom replied. "Have you a pencil?"

Martin wrote the doctor's name and address on the back of an envelope.

"Well," Tom began as they reached the bottom of the stairs, "it's been nice seeing you again. Give me a ring sometime soon, and we'll spend an evening somewhere."

They shook hands.

"My sister—Ruth, I mean—saw you in Castle Street the other day. Said you mustn't have seen her. You passed her by."

"Oh, I'm sorry. But I'd hardly know her, it's so long—"

He felt his heart thumping with excitement. He was thinking

of Claire and wondering whether he'd have the courage to mention her name. He coughed, nervously.

"And how is Claire?"

He tried to make his voice as impersonal as possible.

"Oh, Claire!" Tom exclaimed. "Haven't you heard about her?"

Martin shook his head.

"She's just married. Last month, in fact. She's just back from her honeymoon. They went to Italy—to Venice, as a matter of fact."

"Really."

It was all Martin could say in reply. His mouth felt so dry he could scarcely speak.

"Yes, she married Bill Mansell—he's a doctor, you know ... They've got a very nice house in Richmond."

But Martin was no longer listening.

"Well, cheerio ... " Tom said, and with a wave of the hand was gone.

Martin stood alone on the pavement for a moment; then walked slowly in the opposite direction.

Twenty-Four

HE WALKED HOME AS IF IN a daze. He had tried to forget Claire; he had tried to push her out of his thoughts, out of his life, to be free of her image, the sound of her voice.

He had imagined he had won his freedom from her. But, no; he was wrong; he was still bound to her. He had felt sick when he had learnt that Claire was married, that she now belonged to another.

He breathed in the damp air. So she had made another life for herself, across the water. She had found someone to cherish; she had made her home in another country, with someone he'd never met and was never likely to meet. He couldn't believe it. It was unjust, the whole crazy scheme of things. Bitterly he thought of her in another's arms; and he thought of her all evening—as he was walking to his mother's, as he was having supper, as he replied to his mother's questions, as he tried in vain to finish a book.

In despair he went up to his bedroom at a quarter past nine.

"Are you feeling all right, son?" his mother inquired.

"Yes, I'm all right," he snapped, unable to control himself. She looked at him full of concern. But he ignored her; it was as if he had rejected her.

And he had. He had also rejected his home, wilfully, without consideration. He had been unable to do otherwise. He had had to hurt his parents. And yet he deeply cared for them, for both of them, in his brusque, undemonstrative way.

Mutely they accepted his growing away from them; accepted with little protest, as if realising that what was to be would be. There was a strong streak of fatalism in Martin's parents, as in so many working-class people.

Sometimes he looked at them as if they were strangers, as if he were really not their son. They were growing old, he noticed; particularly his mother. She had grown stouter, her step was slower, and she had become more and more devout. She clung to her church as if for support against the drabness, the lack of colour, in her everyday existence.

She looked forward to Sundays, to dressing up in her best clothes, and to the morning and evening church services. The singing and the sermons appeared to give her a kind of peace; they helped her to overcome the loneliness of her middle age.

Martin neither explained nor excused himself to his parents. He was conscious of having failed them.

His father was employed again, after a lay-off of two years. But the future of the shipyards was uncertain.

He had lost his enthusiasm for the political struggle: all the fight had been knocked out of him. The months of unemployment, the backwardness of his fellow-workers, the atmosphere of political obscurantism and bigotry had finally defeated him. It was this acceptance of defeat that had demoralised him. He had given up the struggle and was ashamed of himself. More and more he talked to his mates about football or horses, always a little cynically, as if he didn't really care what team or horse won. And he didn't.

He advised Martin to leave the country—to go to Canada or Australia where there might be a future for the young.

"This country's done: it'll never get on its feet again. You should get out."

Martin refused to argue: he had discovered that argument on such matters was futile and only bred bitterness between them.

"I'll maybe have to go," he admitted.

But he entertained any such notions reluctantly. He had still sufficient belief in his own ability to win a decent life for himself at home. And yet—could he?

He felt himself outside the most vital life of the city: for he believed now that this was in the factories and in the shipyards. Here the most important work was done: here the strongest social links were forged. His father still participated in this life; and Martin was convinced that his father had been enriched by his long communal experience.

Mr. Connolly always read Martin's journalism carefully and critically: testing the value of the words as if they were tools. He had been very critical of Martin's last article—an impressionistic account of the launching of a ship.

It was Martin's first experience of a launching. He had found it as moving as a great play in which the theme transcended and transformed the people portrayed. The ceremony really had resembled a drama, with the workers as the heroes; it seemed to him that the building of a great ship was indeed heroic, and the launching magnificent. The whole experience struck him as aesthetic.

So he was quite pleased with his article: he felt he had put into the writing of it some of his own feelings about the shipyard. He had enjoyed the whole spectacle: especially the sight of workmen standing high on the deck of the ship itself— on wooden platforms; on gantries; on cranes; all of them proud of the towering beauty of their ship.

Then came the moment of release: the high metallic voice of the female personage saying—"I name this ship." Then the pause; then the movement, almost imperceptible at first, of the ship in motion; and then the cheers as she slid slowly, and then quickly gathered speed on her way to the water.

"Workers don't see a launch the way you do, son," Mr. Connolly said firmly.

"I know that," Martin replied. "But they should."

"How could they?" his father replied, bitterly. "It's not their ship, is it? It doesn't belong to them. And it should. It should be theirs by rights. But it's the bosses'! An' when a ship's launched and finished an' done her tricks, off she goes—an' that's the end o' her! An empty ship means—ye should know what it means!"

They argued. Mr. Connolly felt strongly about the launching of any ship. It was a kind of death as well as a birth; to be seen in the light of practical consequences and not in the light of poetic impressions.

"It's a big occasion for the bosses an' their womenfolk, all right. They take the cake, the head 'uns! You'd think they'd built the ship—to see them paradin' about, all dressed up! All they do is the junketin'—the eatin' an' drinkin' and' talkin'!"

Martin was silent, a little surprised at his father's vehemence.

"Did ye know, son, that at that launch there was an accident?"

"No."

"Well, there was! A worker got a leg broken; an' another fella in the same gang got a broken arm. Just before she went down the slip it happened."

"What actually happened?"

"They were knockin' away the stays an' they lost their footin' when a plank collapsed. That's all. But nobody bothered much about that, did they? It wasn't in the headlines in the paper. No, it wasn't important enough. Workers are two-a-penny, anyway."

"But I didn't know about the accident—"

"No, son, of course you didn't know. But I'm tellin' you what happened. There's more than one way a' lookin' at anything—that's all I'm trying to say ... "

Twenty-Five

A WEEK PASSED BEFORE HE SAW Jean again.
    He met her in a café and told her he'd spoken to Tom Taylor. She looked tired and pale.

"Well?"

Martin gave a shrug.

"I don't know what to say, Jean. Honestly I don't—"

"I suppose he denies he'd anything to do with me?"

"Not exactly."

"I want to forget about him. You shouldn't have seen him anyway—I didn't want you to. He's a—"

Jean shook her head; she was near to tears but managed to keep control of herself.

He took the bit of paper from his pocket and gave it to her.

"Thanks."

She folded it up and put it in her pocket.

"You'll come with me?"

She looked at him, defenceless and dependent; and he nodded.

"Yes, of course," he added, "you'll be all right."

But he was unable to give the remark a ring of sincerity. He wasn't at all sure she would be all right. The idea of her body being mutilated in the hands of some shifty, unscrupulous doctor made him shiver.

"You'll fix an appointment for me?"

"Yes, Jean."

"When?"

"Whenever suits you. D'you want me to make it now?"

"The sooner the better."

They decided that if the doctor could give her the abortion on a Friday she could arrange to stay with a girlfriend who had a little bungalow near Bangor; she could stay for the weekend—or longer, if necessary.

They left the café and took a tram across the city: the doctor lived near the Holywood Arches. They didn't talk much as the tram lurched along the Newtownards Road; Jean looked out of the window most of the time; this was, for her, an unfamiliar part of the city. Martin assured her they were going in the right direction.

"I know Ballymacarrett backwards," he said. "Better than anywhere else on earth."

"I forgot you live in this part of the city. I hardly know it at all."

They got off at the Arches: and a train puffed past overhead, throwing wreaths of white smoke into the night sky.

Martin found the doctor's house without any difficulty: the end house of a Victorian terrace of dark-red brick. It looked shabby from the outside, with its tiny front garden protected by a dusty privet hedge, and on the iron gate a nameplate which badly needed to be polished.

"I'm nervous, Martin."

He squeezed her hand; but she made no response.

Then he rang the bell. A middle-aged woman wearing an untidy apron answered.

"Is the doctor in?"

She nodded and brought them into the sitting-room and asked them to wait for a few minutes. They crossed the room and took a couple of chairs near the window. The woman put down the blinds and left them alone, she hadn't spoken a single word to them while they were in the room.

The waiting room had the usual dingy furniture—a hard sofa, a row of battered chairs, a scratched table with a pile of out-of-date, well-thumbed popular magazines. The air was as over-used as the furniture; the whole atmosphere oppressive and stale.

Everything in the room exuded a slight stench.

The door opened and the caretaker poked her head inside the room.

"Yez can go up now."

Martin and Jean rose together.

"Is it the both o' ye?"

Martin hesitated and looked at Jean, but before he could speak, the caretaker said, "Ye can wait here, mister. The doctor can see ye afterwards—that is, if ye want to see him."

Jean nodded her agreement and crossed the room; and Martin dropped his gaze as she passed in front of him.

He hadn't long to wait—no more than a quarter of an hour—when he heard a man's husky voice in the hall; then Jean's voice saying, "Yes, all right." And the door of the waiting room opened.

"Good evening," the doctor said, giving Martin a mechanical smile.

Martin rose and made his way into the hallway. He looked at Jean: she was staring at the glass-frosted front door, her face completely drained of colour. Her hand, which she'd raised to fix her hat, was tremulous.

"Until next Friday ... " the doctor was saying. He was a man of about forty, with spiky black hair; a pale, mottled face with dry-looking skin; his teeth were stained with smoking. He stretched out his hand and said goodbye to Jean, and Martin noted the nicotine on the fingers.

"There's no need to worry ... " he was saying. Then he gave his attention to Martin.

"No need to worry at all," he said, "she'll be in safe hands."

Martin said nothing and Jean nervously fingered her handbag. Then the door opened and they both heard the doctor's throaty voice bid them goodnight and they were out in the cold night air.

Martin took Jean's arm as they walked back towards the Holywood Arches. He felt her shivering. "I'll be all right in a moment," she said, "I feel cold, that's all."

"Are you sure?"

"Yes, I'll be all right."

They walked quickly towards the centre of the city.

It was all fixed up, Jean told him; and she thanked him for accompanying her.

"I couldn't have done it on my own," she said.

"D'you think that doctor's competent?" Martin asked.

"I can hardly choose, can I?"

Martin was silent as they waited for a tram to bring them back to the Castle Junction. What a sordid and sickening affair! And he wondered how Jean could endure it. And yet she had to go through with it. She had no choice—except to have a child she didn't want. That would be even more sordid: it would involve another human being.

Could a four-month foetus be described as that? He had once seen a reproduction of a foetus: a tiny human being, perfect and at peace, like an inhabitant from another world, curled up asleep.

The night had turned out cold and wet, and Martin had little to say; anyhow Jean hardly bothered to reply to his few half-hearted attempts at conversation. She looked exhausted, as if she wanted to be alone, to cry herself asleep, like a child.

He brought her to her home; she had refused to have a drink: and she had also refused his offer to go with her the following Friday evening when the operation would take place. She told him that she had confided in one of her girlfriends, who had promised to look after her.

"I'll write to you, Martin, when it's all over." Suddenly she kissed him and ran up the garden; she opened the front door, waved to him, and was gone.

During the next month he often thought about her, wondering what had happened. No letter came.

She had just disappeared; and he couldn't get in touch with her. But he didn't very much want to see her again. Still, he was curious to know what had happened to her, and imagined she had stayed the month in Bangor, at her friend's bungalow.

The spring came. He felt tired of the city; tired of his home; tired of the life he was leading. He wanted to be free.

One Monday morning, six weeks later, Jean's letter arrived. Eagerly he read it.

Dear Martin,

I meant to have written to you sooner but somehow I just

couldn't. I don't know why. I only know that I didn't want to write to anybody, I didn't want to see anybody either. That's why I didn't give you my address. I expect you didn't want to see me either.

Anyway the whole thing was awful. That is all I can tell you, all I ever want to tell anybody. I'll never forget these last few months. I felt I wanted to die. If I had I wouldn't have cared. My life is useless anyway.

I enclose my address in Bangor if you want to see me, but I won't be surprised if you don't answer this.

And I am grateful to you for helping me the way you did.

Jean

He replied at once, saying he would go by train on the Wednesday afternoon and to expect him about three.

At the County Down Station he bought a third-class ticket to Bangor. He found an empty compartment and put his feet up on the worn yellow-plush seat opposite and lazily looked out of the window. It was a slow train, stopping at a station every couple of miles. He was glad to be able to relax and watch the mean backyards of the city on his right; and to catch glimpses of the lough on his left. And then after Holywood the scenery became well-wooded, fresh and green; the houses large and prosperous-looking.

It was strange, he thought, his coming to see Jean in Bangor, the town where he'd spent part of his early childhood. He'd been back there only a few times, yet he'd retained an affection for the grey, slightly bleak town.

The train puffed into Bangor station. Martin got out, asked the way of the ticket-collector, and was directed towards Ballyholme bay.

"It'll only take ye about half-an-hour," the ticket-collector said. "It's a nice day for a walk, isn't it?"

Martin agreed that it was; and walked briskly out of the station.

He saw Jean immediately he reached the bungalow: she was sitting at the window, reading. He waved. She turned her head towards him, raised her hand in greeting, and came to the door.

"Sorry, I'm a bit late. I hope I haven't kept you waiting."

171

She shook her head and smiled.

"No, you haven't. Do sit down, Martin."

She had tea ready and for the next few moments busied herself with the tray; so he'd a chance of observing her.

She was thinner and paler, and her hair, brushed straight back, had lost its sheen. She was wearing a green tweed jumper and skirt which certainly suited her, but which gave her a more mature look. He asked her how she was and she said she was feeling well; but it was quite obvious that she didn't want to talk about herself. Instead she asked him questions about his own activities; she had read a couple of his articles in the local newspapers.

"You should become a journalist," she said.

"You think so?" he asked, genuinely unsure of himself.

"Oh yes. Don't you want to?"

"I really don't know what I want to do."

But he admitted that he enjoyed journalism: and thought it a pleasant enough way of earning money.

"It's not really work," he said, "not really hard work. At any rate it comes fairly easily to me."

He then told her that he had applied for a reporting job in a town forty miles from Belfast.

"I hope you get it," Jean said; "I mean—if you want the job, of course."

"It's about time I left home."

After a while their conversation flagged; Jean suggested a walk along the seafront.

She locked the door of the bungalow, having told Martin that the owner would be back in about an hour's time.

"Dorothy's been very good to me; I don't know what I'd have done without her—"

As they walked along the sea wall Martin took Jean's arm, squeezing it affectionately, and feeling the warm response of her body.

"I thought I'd never, never want to see a man again," she said, looking up into his face.

The wind, which had suddenly sprung up, had whipped colour into her cheeks. She gazed out to sea, to the low hills, misty-soft, on the other side of the lough. The sea had turned choppy and a collier was nosing its way out to sea, towards England.

"I'm trying to forget what happened—" she added, "shouldn't I?"

"Of course you should."

"I don't think I'll ever be able to. It was like ... like some awful nightmare. It was a nightmare."

"Forget it," Martin whispered.

He told her to forget all about her experience. Why should she suffer any more? It was all over, something to be forgotten. But she wanted to confide in him.

"My mother's got to know," she continued.

"How did that happen?"

"I don't know. She said she guessed; but I think someone told her."

Jean had been frightened of what her mother would do. But her mother had quickly accepted the situation and had given her money to stay in Bangor for another two months.

At the end of the bay they turned and walked towards the bungalow; Martin left her to the garden gate.

"You'll come and see me again?" she asked.

"Oh yes."

"Soon?"

"As soon as I can."

He glanced around; no-one was in view. He took her in his arms. She turned her cheek to him; then slowly she twisted her head and gave him her mouth, gently, without passion.

Twenty-Six

A FORTNIGHT LATER MARTIN RECEIVED A letter about the reporter's job: he was to have an interview with the editor, William Watson, on the following Saturday morning at eleven-thirty, if convenient.

"You'll have to find lodgings, son—if you get this job," his mother said.

"Yes I know that."

"I wonder what the wages'll be like."

"They won't be much—just enough to live on, I expect."

"I hope they don't expect you to work for a starvation wage," his father said.

"I'll take what I can get," Martin replied, irritably.

He arrived punctually at the office of the *South Sentinel*, having spent three-quarters of an hour roaming around the streets.

Situated near the border, the country town had an air of slow decay; most of the buildings—some with the elegance of the eighteenth century—were neglected-looking; and the unused canal lay ill-smelling and stagnant. Only a few shops and banks in the main street were busy.

He entered the newspaper office and was ushered up a winding narrow stairway to the editor's office. He knocked, and a voice called, "Come in," and he found, on opening the door, that he was in the presence of an enormously fat man wearing glasses and in his shirtsleeves.

"Good morning," the fat man rumbled, looking up from an untidy table and taking off his glasses.

"I've come to see Mr. Watson."

"That's me. You're Mr. Connolly?"

Martin nodded, and Mr. Watson heaved himself very slowly and ponderously to his feet, grasping the table for support as he did so. He stretched forward a large fleshy hand, gave a loud groan, then introduced himself more formally. He sat down again, with more groaning, and invited Martin to take a chair on the opposite side of the table.

"What age are you, Mr. Connolly?"

"Twenty-two."

"You've never actually worked for a newspaper?"

"No."

"But you've had some articles published?"

"Yes."

"How many?"

"About a dozen."

He named the paper where his work had appeared.

"Can you write quickly?"

"Yes."

Then followed questions on general education, ability in shorthand and typing, outside interests. Finally, with a cough, Mr. Watson turned to the question of salary.

"As you haven't any experience, Mr. Connolly, you'll be really learning this job. Isn't that so?"

Martin nodded.

"We could only afford ... let me see ... two pounds fifteen ... no ... I'll make it three ... Three pounds a week ... for six days a week, of course. But you'll have a weekend off every month ... yes ... well, the job's yours—if you want it."

Martin pretended to reflect for a moment: but he had no notion of refusing. He accepted the offer and they shook hands.

It was arranged that he should turn up on Monday week, in nine days' time, and that in the meantime he should find himself lodgings. To do so shouldn't be difficult, Mr. Watson assured him; he himself knew two or three good houses.

"I don't know what kind of place you'd like best. Or how much you'd be willing to pay—" He paused for a moment or two, put on his spectacles, and looked at Martin quizzically.

"I think you'd be like myself—"

He took off his spectacles and polished them with a not very clean handkerchief, "—you'd be willing to pay a little extra to have your home comforts."

He put on the spectacles again. "—I'd say Miss Louise Garland would be your best bet. She'd only take in somebody she'd like, y'know. P.G's in fact. And she's a lovely house—just outside the town. A lovely house. You'd be comfortable with her ... a home from home, in fact. I don't know, exactly, what she'd charge you, but it wouldn't be ... well ... it wouldn't be exorbitant ... What'd you say? Please yourself, Mr. Connolly!"

Martin decided that he might as well try Miss Garland— provided Miss Garland was willing to have him.

"I'll give her a ring now if you like. Get it all fixed up. She's an old friend of mine. Plays bridge y'know. D'you play, Mr. Connolly?"

"No, I don't."

"Pity," Mr. Watson said, the telephone to his ear.

"Hullo, Louise—" he began, "How are you this morning? ... Have you five minutes to spare ... ?"

Mr. Watson put the phone down. "Well, there you are," he said, automatically lighting a cigarette, and just as automatically looking through the dust-stained window of his office to the passers-by on the opposite pavement. He sighed. It was obvious to Martin that a decision had been made. Miss Garland was willing to give him board and lodging: he had given his assent to the arrangement and Mr. Watson had already turned his mind to more pressing matters.

"Better go and see Miss Garland, hadn't you?" he suggested, as an afterthought, and rose from his chair and stood staring out into the street. Martin got up as well, eagerly assenting to the suggestion, and glad that the interview was over.

"Well, that's that," said Mr. Watson with another sigh, and with an air of something vital achieved. "I'd better tell you how to get to Miss Garland's house ... "

Taking an old yellow duster out of a drawer on the left of his table, he carefully wiped the window and called Martin over.

"This is the Main Street, as you know; you go up to the top, turn right, go past the Technical College, then go along by the canal for say five hundred yards; then take the first road to the right, go straight up the hill, turn left and Louise's house is the first on the right. It sounds a bit complicated but it really isn't. She lives in an old grey house, with elm trees all round it. You can't miss it really. If you do, ask for Miss Garland. Everyone hereabouts knows Louise."

It was clear to Martin that Mr. Watson certainly knew Miss Garland and her house very well indeed.

"Well, goodbye now."

They shook hands, Mr. Watson going as far as his office door; then Martin quickly walked downstairs, with a hasty glance into the front office of the *South Sentinel* where he saw a middle-aged woman selling something to a couple of small boys.

Without much difficulty he found Miss Garland's house. It was on the edge of the town, about a quarter of a mile outside the boundary.

He liked the house at once. On three sides it was surrounded by tall trees; on the fourth side by a wall of granite. He guessed the house to be about a hundred and fifty years old and it was a little decayed-looking. It needed painting; the green curtains were faded and the path needed weeding. The lawn in front of the house dropped down to a tennis court which appeared not to be used at all—the net hanging limp and rotting.

The front door lay open, and Martin could see part of a large untidy hallway littered with walking sticks, old golf clubs, coats and hats, a few gardening tools; and a full shopping basket lay on the rather threadbare mat.

He rang. The bell sounded somewhere in the distance and reverberated through the house. He waited. No-one appeared for a full two minutes. Then mysteriously a maid appeared from somewhere under the staircase.

"Did you ring, sir?"

Martin admitted he had, and asked if Miss Garland was at home.

"I don't know whether she's in or out, sir. I've been in the kitchen, an' I never noticed her comin' in. But then I never noticed her goin' out, an' I know she was out."

The maid picked up the shopping basket as she spoke; and as she did so, a grey-haired ruddy-faced woman came downstairs.

"Hello, Mr. Connolly," she exclaimed. "Do come in. Mary, get us a cup o'tea, like a good girl. We'll be in the drawing room."

She shook hands warmly and led Martin into a large room on the right of the hall.

"Sorry for keeping you—I was at the back of the house and didn't hear the bell. I must get a new one anyway. What's the use of a doorbell if you can't hear it no matter where you are in the house, eh?"

They chatted in the drawing room until the maid brought in the tea.

Then after tea Miss Garland suggested that Martin might like to see his bedroom. He followed her upstairs, along a corridor, and into a bedroom at the side of the house. It was a beautifully proportioned room with a high embossed ceiling; old-fashioned highly polished furniture; and a low window jutting into the side garden.

From this window he could see the elm trees along the drive and, beyond, the hills of Armagh.

"You'll have the run of the whole house, of course," Miss Garland was saying. "I've only one other guest—Mr. Flack—who's a bank cashier. And there's my brother Arthur; but there's plenty of room for four of us, isn't there?"

There certainly was plenty of room; but what surprised Martin was that the owner of Elm Grove should be obliged to take lodgers—or 'guests' as they were called; it seemed incongruous somehow. However, Miss Garland seemed very friendly and pleasant. He judged her to be in her mid-forties, perhaps fifty. She was quite good-looking but dressed rather carelessly, and he noticed that her hands were large and red, like the hands of a manual worker.

It was arranged that he should arrive the following Saturday. So they shook hands and he walked down the sloping drive.

A week later he was installed in Elm Grove house. He felt like an impostor, as if he had obtained entry by false pretences.

After all he was only a poorly paid reporter on a small provincial paper—and here he was living in a great mansion in its own grounds, with a spacious bedroom to himself, and with a maid to bring him tea on a silver tray. He felt completely out of place; it was incredible, indeed a bit ludicrous.

It was all the more ludicrous in that Elm Grove contrasted so much with the office of the *South Sentinel* which was drably poky and chaotic; for Mr. Watson made no attempt to give his premises an air of dignity, nor even an air of cleanliness. The nondescript building which gave birth to the *South Sentinel* twice a week fronted the main street and was divided into three parts: a front shop which sold office equipment and took in the advertisements; an editorial office in which Martin had a desk facing Mr. Watson; and, at the back, the printing-presses, which, when they were in motion, made the entire building shudder and shake as if it were enduring birth pangs.

Martin discovered that the work on the *Sentinel* suited him quite well. And within three months Mr. Watson gave him so much responsibility that he was virtually running the paper. The editor was content to give a quick glance at the gallery sheets and then usually disappear into Halliday's hotel in the square.

The *Sentinel* was a ramshackle concern; the paper itself was mostly made up of advertisements, reports of local meetings, of councils, churches, societies, courts; no item seemed too unimportant for inclusion.

Martin found that though his working hours were long he had quite a lot of leisure time, especially at weekends. He returned to Belfast once a month; and while he was at home his father and mother bombarded him with questions. His mother was particularly curious about the meals provided at Elm Grove; but when she was given details of his fare she was not in the least impressed—or so she pretended.

"Is that all you get for breakfast—an orange, a slice of toast, and a boiled egg? It's not much, if you ask me—it's not much when you think of what she's chargin' you. I wouldn't like to set a breakfast like that down to your father. He'd look at me ... "

Lightheartedly, Martin agreed; he was anxious not to hurt her feelings. He knew his mother was impressed with the idea of his being socially equal to middle-class folk. And she was more and more proud of him, and sure he was destined for great things.

But his father's attitude was different: his genuine pride was mixed with not a little scorn.

"It's very nice—the way middle-class people live," he remarked. "They know what's good for themselves—and what's good for the workers."

"Don't be envious, Bob!" Mrs. Connolly replied.

"Shouldn't I be?"

"No, you shouldn't!"

"What should I be then?"

"You should be pleased that Martin has done so well for himself."

"But I am, I am," Mr. Connolly insisted, a little irritated, and frowning. Martin looked at his father and said:

"I know what you think."

Mr. Connolly looked at his son, a quizzical expression on his face.

"Do you, son?"

"I do."

"Tell me then."

"You think I'm changing—"

"You've certainly changed your life, haven't you?"

"So you think I'll change my allegiance?"

"How do I know that, Martin?"

Twenty-Seven

MARTIN QUICKLY SETTLED DOWN TO LIFE in Elm Grove. He loved to return to the house after a busy day in the office or in the town picking up items of news. After six months Mr. Watson gave him a rise of ten shillings a week. He was grateful for the extra money: he needed all his salary to live. Now he should be able to save a few pounds. Occasionally he bought his father tobacco, or his mother a trinket for the home. It was all either of them wanted—a token of his feelings for them. And it was little enough to give. He had pangs of conscience when he thought of himself in the evenings at Elm Grove and his parents sitting in their small sitting-room.

He had become acclimatised to his new surroundings; and though he had to work long hours for the *Sentinel* he was enjoying himself. Reporting was giving him the variety of experience he wanted. He loved to meet new people; and he loved to attend the various meetings in the town, to listen to the gossip, to be recognised as the *Sentinel* reporter, and to be regarded as somebody of importance in the local community.

At Elm Grove he kept a good deal to himself. Sometimes he had a chat with Miss Garland at breakfast or supper; and sometimes he met her in the garden. She was fond of gardening and frequently helped her gardener with the weeding.

One June evening she was fixing up the tennis net as Martin came out with a rug and a book under his arm.

"I need a new net," she remarked.

He went over to join her and saw that the cording was rotten: Miss Garland was vainly trying to make it fit for a game.

"I think I'll have to buy a new one for the tournament," she said. "It's had its day. Do you play tennis, Mr. Connolly?"

"I'm not much good."

"But you play a little?"

"Oh yes."

"Would you play in my tournament next Saturday?"

He hesitated; he had no tennis things with him; but Miss Garland insisted that she would like him included among her guests.

"Oh, I can beg or borrow things for you," she exclaimed. "We don't have a real tournament, of course—"

"I hope you don't," Martin said.

"It's just a Saturday afternoon's fun. Only about a dozen or so people I know. Now don't forget, turn up at three o'clock."

He took his rug to a secluded part of the garden and lay down, his hands pillowing the back of his head. He gazed up at the sky. There was hardly a cloud: the sky was clear azure, except on the horizon to the east, where he could see a few wisps of cloud. The sun was setting over the Armagh hills, the whole countryside bathed in its glow. Everything was peaceful—the trees in the drive and the flowers in the garden; not a breath of wind.

He felt tired; the book he had brought with him—Zola's *Germinal*—lay unopened by his side. For the moment he luxuriated in the immediate world of his senses—the faint perfumes of the garden, the evening sky glowing like a furnace, the still elm trees along the drive. It was pure sensuous joy merely to breathe.

He reflected on the happenings of the morning and afternoon. In the morning he had been confined to the office; and in the afternoon he had attended the prize distribution at the Grammar School.

He had been bored by the speeches—the address by the chairman of the Board of Governors had been the usual stringing together of platitudes; and the Headmaster's report had been little better. But when at the end of the proceedings the school choir had sung three songs by Schubert, the whole atmosphere of the ceremony had been transformed. It was as if at last some true emotions were given release, and the musty sentiments of the personages on the platform blown away.

He reflected that he had intended to teach himself German but had given up after a few half-hearted lessons. It was a language he must conquer. Without a knowledge of it he felt handicapped. He reflected that he mustn't become lazy; give himself over to self-indulgence, slide into easy acceptance of a not-too-exacting job. He mustn't lose his nerve, his gusto for living. To enjoy life he must remain in some degree detached from this community into which he had been thrown.

He lay and looked up at the sky. The air was now becoming colder. The sun had disappeared below the horizon of the Armagh hills. He shivered slightly and decided to go indoors.

Lying in his armchair he watched the dying light; the evening clouds gathered. His bedroom was now bathed in the twilight. He thought of the dialect word 'dayligone' which had always struck him as beautifully expressive. He repeated it to himself, silently at first, then he spoke it softly. It was a good word: and he regretted that it had been lost.

He got up and switched on the light; put *Germinal* on the table at the side of his bed; sat down again in the armchair; lit a cigarette.

Below him, beyond the trees, lay the town. He remembered that he had to attend the petty sessions in the morning. He liked court work. It was strange, observing the behaviour of people in the courts, and fascinating.

He stubbed out his cigarette. The melody of 'Roselied' came into his head, and reminded him of the school art exhibition.

The art master had shown him round the drawings and paintings. They were extraordinarily good, Martin thought, not in the least stiff or conventional.

The children must have been encouraged to express themselves so boldly and so freely. Looking at the work he recalled with distaste his own efforts at drawing and painting. He remembered the endless drawing of an ugly bucket he had been condemned to copy. It was criminal, the way he had been taught.

This exhibition had been really wonderful. He decided that he must give it a special article. Yes, that would be worth doing. Perhaps he should interview the art master—he couldn't remember the man's name—and make a splash of the whole thing. He would get up early and write a decent report on this exhibition. He would get up at seven. An hour's work would do it.

He took the crumpled catalogue from the inside pocket of his coat and laid it on his table; yes, that would give him pleasure, first thing in the morning.

He woke at a quarter to seven and got up at once. The house, at this hour, was preternaturally quiet. He looked out into the garden, the lawn wet with the morning dew. He went to his table and wrote quickly for the next hour and then took a short walk before breakfast. The article had been easy to write and he hoped Mr. Watson would like it. Anyhow, whether the editor liked it or not, it had been worth doing.

It was five minutes to eight when he went into the dining room. He rang the little copper bell on the sideboard and in a couple of minutes Mary appeared. She was a very shy girl, a Catholic, who seldom uttered a word beyond 'good morning, sir' or 'good evening, sir'.

Halfway through breakfast Miss Garland entered the dining room, followed by her brother Arthur. (Mr. Flack seldom appeared at breakfast, Mary usually brought his up at a quarter to nine.)

"You were up early this morning," Miss Garland said.

"Yes—before seven."

"Really! You must have a bad conscience!"

"I suppose I must have."

"It's a beautiful morning," Arthur said, in a low voice, as he tapped his boiled egg with his spoon.

Miss Garland and her brother were very unlike each other: she was cheery and talkative; he silent and morose. Martin had heard from his editor that Miss Garland held her brother in contempt.

"If she could get rid of him, she would," Mr. Watson had said. "He's a bit of a jenny-jo."

"Is he married?" Martin had asked.

"Married! Arthur! He wouldn't go near a woman!"

"What does he do?"

"He inherited his father's hardware shop; he preaches in some hall or other; but the only thing he succeeds in doing is annoying Louise."

Martin sat watching brother and sister. Yes, it was true—hardly a word did pass between them. Arthur seemed to eat little, and what he ate he ate quickly, almost surreptitiously; he then excused himself and slipped out of the room. His sister glanced after him, then turned her attention to Martin.

"I heard you were at the prize distribution yesterday."

"Yes."

"I usually get along, but yesterday I'd a friend to tea; so I didn't get. Pity; I like going every year."

"There was some good singing by the choir."

"I'm sure. Miss Magee's a very good teacher—very good indeed."

"And there was an art exhibition—it was excellent, I thought."

"That would be Mr. Furness' classes. Did you meet him?"

"Yes, I'd a chat with him about the exhibition."

"He'll be coming to my tournament on Saturday."

"Does he play tennis?"

"No, he doesn't. But his wife plays. Did you meet her?"

"No, I don't think so."

"She's French. They've been married only a couple of years. They're certainly a very likely pair—especially George. He's something of a painter, you know—he's had an exhibition in Dublin. Oh, and he'd talk the hind legs off a donkey if you'd let him!"

"I'm writing an article on the school exhibition."

"For the *Sentinel*?"

"Yes."

"Oh, George'll be delighted. He doesn't get much credit, you know, for what he does."

"Doesn't he?"

"He certainly doesn't. And he's not too popular with some parents."

"Why not?"

"Oh, the busybodies in this town wouldn't let anybody see

daylight if they could help it. But George Furness does exactly what he pleases."

"Good for him."

"That's what I say."

They chatted on about the prize-giving ceremony the previous afternoon; and Martin discovered that Miss Garland had a particular interest in the school: she had once taught domestic economy there.

"I was only a temporary teacher—and part-time—and it was a long time ago. The year after I came back from Edinburgh, in fact. Have you ever been there?"

"Never."

"It's a lovely city. I often wish I was back; I've some very good friends there."

Martin learnt that Miss Garland had studied domestic economy in Edinburgh and had subsequently worked in a hospital there. Then when her father died she had come home to help keep house for her brother. She'd been home seven or eight years now; but she still hankered to be away.

"This town doesn't suit me," she declared, getting up from the table. "It never did, and it never will. Yet I was born here."

Martin also rose, wondering exactly why Miss Garland's native town didn't suit her.

On Saturday the weather was showery: and it looked as if Miss Garland's tournament might have to be postponed. So Martin imagined as he walked up the hill to Elm Grove. But when he asked Miss Garland she pooh-poohed such an idea.

"Tennis or no tennis, let's have a party!" she exclaimed. "Anyhow, a shower of rain won't do anybody any harm. We're neither sugar nor salt."

Miss Garland had no trace of the genteelness which Martin associated with people of her class. He found her refreshing: he even thought her a little unconventional. She was completely lacking in stuffiness. She seemed to go her own way about the town, dress as she pleased, have all sorts of friends, and altogether was rather daring. It was known, for instance, that she liked a glass of gin or whiskey, and that she smoked heavily—even while out shopping. Also she was often seen in the company of married men. Martin learnt that Mr. Watson was one of her closest friends. Both were passionately fond of bridge, and played in an upstairs room in the main hotel two or three times a week. So her activities created a good deal of gossip.

But she didn't seem to mind what was said behind her back.

Martin was curious to know who had been invited to Elm Grove, and wondered if brother Arthur would put in an appearance.

The first guest to arrive was Mr. Watson, who drove up in his car. Dressed in white flannels and a grey jacket he looked surprisingly spruce, almost youthful; for although he was bulky he was quite quick in his movements.

"Hello, young fella," he greeted Martin who had just finished mowing part of the garden. "Are you Wimbledon standard or a rabbit?"

"A rabbit."

"Then we'd better avoid each other. I haven't played a set for years. And I refuse to play unless I get a drink beforehand. Where's Louise anyway? She should be here to receive the guests!"

At this moment Miss Garland appeared at the front door. She was wearing a white dress and cardigan, and her hair was brushed straight back.

"Follow me if you want a drink, or two!" she called and disappeared into the dining room.

They followed her. The drinks were ceremoniously laid out on a table, and she ordered them to help themselves.

"Mary's too busy in the kitchen to be here; and I've too many other duties to attend to."

She disappeared again, only to reappear as the other guests arrived. Martin knew some by sight: there were three or four teachers, including Miss Magee, the music teacher, and Mr. Furness, the art teacher and his French wife; some bank officials, including Mr. Flack; a few sons and daughters of local business people. In all about twenty guests. Most of the younger people were dressed for tennis.

They had only about an hour's tennis; for at four o'clock the sky suddenly became overcast and a steady drizzle began to fall. But nobody minded very much and they went indoors and began chatting and eating and drinking.

Martin found himself next to the art teacher and his wife; and Miss Garland introduced him.

"I'm glad to meet you again," the art teacher said. "I've read your article in the *Sentinel*. Very good of you to give us a write-up. I need an ally in this place, believe you me."

"What do you mean?"

"How long have you been here?"

"Three months."

"Why did you come?"

"I wanted a job."

"Well, leave as soon as you can."

"I intend to."

"I intended to, but I've stayed—too long. Four years too long. What do you think of this mob?"

"George!"

Mrs. Furness frowned as soon as her husband asked the question, squeezing his arm by way of reprimand.

"Have I said anything wrong?" her husband asked, feigning surprise. "Have I?"

"Not to me," Martin said.

"Please, George," Mrs. Furness said in a low voice, with a trace of a foreign accent.

"Why did we come here? Answer me that."

"We're friends of Miss Garland," Mrs. Furness said.

"Acquaintances," her husband corrected. "The only friend Louise Garland has in this town is Willie Watson; and that's because she's a good fuck."

"George!"

"Well, she is a good friend of his, isn't she?" the art teacher continued, with a sly smile and a reassuring pat on his wife's shoulder. "I'm all for it, myself: but I'm not allowed to say so. It never did anybody any harm except those who don't get it. D'you agree?"

Martin nodded his agreement.

"Are you being polite?"

"No."

"You are the first ally I've had in this town!" the art teacher exclaimed. "Let me shake you by the hand."

At six o'clock the guests began to drift away; the Furness couple was among the last to go. Before they left George

Furness came over to Martin and invited him to his house, which was about three miles from the town.

"It's a cottage, really; but it's got a view. I'll drop you a note next week. All right?"

Martin replied that he would be glad to come. As they left him, he told himself that he had at last met someone who spoke the same language as himself.

Twenty-Eight

ON THE WEDNESDAY THE FOLLOWING WEEK Martin received the promised letter from the art teacher. It read:

> Bedlam
>
> Dear Connolly, My classroom is as above, as it is the last period of the day. Thank God. I have a headache. Come on Friday evening, any time, if you're free. If you're not free you're a slave. Which I don't believe.
>
> No reply necessary to this.
>
> George Furness
>
> P.S. On the other side of this I've drawn a map to guide you to our abode.

Though a bus would have taken him within a hundred yards of the cottage, Martin decided to walk. It would take him little more than an hour, he reckoned; and the evening was pleasantly cool for walking. The road out was dusty; the end of the town ugly, with a newly-erected Catholic chapel, and, a little further, the dreary green-coloured gasworks, overlooking a row of red-brick houses. He hurried into the countryside. The road now ran along a river and a couple of miles off lay the foothills of the Mournes.

He arrived just after eight. The bus had passed him on the way, so his arrival was a bit unexpected.

"I'd given up hope of you," Furness cried, "when I saw nobody off the bus."

The art teacher was wearing a black high-necked fisherman's jersey and a pair of old flannels; his wife a bright-red blouse and tweed skirt. To Martin both looked romantic: the man with his squat figure, sandy hair and beard, and his sudden smiles, like an animal baring its teeth; the woman with her dark hair, rather pale complexion, and steady grey eyes that seemed to look at him coolly, appraisingly. Her manner was extremely quiet as she moved about the room unobtrusively preparing the food. At once her husband showed Martin through the cottage; it was small, with only four rooms—two tiny bedrooms, a living-room and the fourth room a studio. Everything was neat, the rooms freshly painted in bright colours. Then the three walked into the back garden and looked at the view.

"That's why we came here, isn't it, Elise?"

His wife nodded. They could see the foothills of the Mournes and beyond, the grey mountains themselves, looping towards the sea.

"Lovely," Martin murmured.

Later a couple of bottles of French wine were opened in Martin's honour.

"We were in Paris at Easter," Furness said. "Only for ten days, but it was just what I needed—ten days of France!"

"Have you been?" Elise asked.

"No."

"You haven't?"

Furness pretended astonishment: extraordinary that Martin, a fully grown man with an interest in painting, had not yet visited Paris.

"What's the matter with you? Are you absolutely broke? Because if you are that's no excuse. We're broke; but we went to Paris last summer and this Easter."

"How did you do it?"

Furness turned to his wife.

"How did we do it?"

Together they explained how they saved up enough money

to go abroad. The husband remembered that he gave up smoking for a while; refused to buy Christmas presents (a custom he heartily disapproved of); used the bicycle instead of the bus to and from school.

"And I starve myself—and Elise," he cried, laughing heartily, and showing his slightly discoloured teeth.

"You don't look starved—either of you," Martin replied.

"Oh, and I leave off the booze."

At this remark Elise registered complete disbelief.

They talked about France for a long time. Martin learnt that Elise's home was in Rouen. Her husband had met her there when he was an art student. They had corresponded for a while, then got married after having known each other for less than a year. Elise's father had worked on the railway; he had died suddenly from a stroke the year before she started school. So she hardly remembered him. All this Martin learnt from the husband; but occasionally Elise corrected something her husband said. As for Furness himself, he explained that his father, a designer, originally came from Yorkshire and had settled in Belfast on the eve of the First World War.

"I consider myself a Yorkshireman," Furness remarked, "though I've lived the most of my life in Ireland. My roots are here, I feel—though I'm certainly no Celt!"

Martin looked at his watch. It was, surprisingly, a quarter past eleven. He would have to go—he wouldn't be back at Elm Grove until after midnight. He rose with reluctance; Furness had begun to talk about Ancient Celtic Art.

"What's the hurry, man?"

"Well, it's getting late!"

"Late! It's not even midnight! What the hell's the matter, man? Aren't you enjoying yourself? I thought you were?"

"I am—very much."

"Then stay! Stay a while longer; stay the night. Yes, stay the night! I haven't shown you my work yet; and I want you to see it."

"I'd like to very much."

"Like to what? Stay? Good man!"

"But —"

"Oh come on, we've a perfectly good bed, haven't we, Elise? You can leave first thing in the morning—if you want to. I tell you what: we'll both catch the morning bus. It comes at eight and another at half-past ten. We'll catch the half-ten one. Agreed?"

Martin agreed.

It was the most exhilarating evening of talk he had had for months.

During the weeks to come he got to know George and Elise Furness extremely well: they became his closest friends, and hardly a week passed without his visiting their cottage.

He admired the art master's painting—particularly the landscapes: Furness could see a field of grass or barley as if he'd seen a vision; and paint it in rich, glowing colours, wonderfully dark greens and browns. He was a boldly romantic painter, constantly struggling to find himself. Clearly he had talent, Martin thought, perhaps more than talent; but it was difficult to assess such a painter's work, too difficult for someone like himself with only a superficial knowledge of art. One thing, however, was certain: he found Furness' company amusing and his talk stimulating.

"I must give up teaching," Furness constantly said; "it saps my energies."

"But you can't live on air," Martin said.

"Painters before me have done so."

"How?"

"Miracles happen. Isn't the creation of art itself a kind of a miracle? Why do we have to do it? Yes, we have to do it. The impulse comes from within and without; from God—or what you will—and from society. It's both an isolation and a communion; a deepening of myself and of others."

Furness loved to theorise; he also loved to look at paintings— not only his own but reproductions of French and Italian masters; and he worshipped Cezanne and Giotto above all.

But he was frightened of the influence of such painters on his own work and told Martin: "The Mediterranean landscape isn't mine; and their light isn't mine. God help me not to see through their eyes, but give me power to use my own."

His voice was deep, almost a growl; and when he was angry his growl became a bark. His pupils feared his voice; they feared his dark shaggy eyebrows and his long thin lips which when opened revealed his stained neglected teeth. He was certainly not attractive, physically.

His wife was. Yet she made little impression on Martin. She seemed unsure of herself; and she was given to long silences that made her appear rather morose. He found her perfectly pleasant, of course; and he thought that she might have latent charm as well as obvious good looks. She gave the impression of being completely indifferent to what people thought of her. So far as Martin could see she was completely wrapped up in her husband. Her eyes followed him as he walked about the room; she obeyed his slightest requests; she tried to anticipate his needs. And because Martin had been accepted by her husband as a friend, she accepted him as well, unquestioningly.

Twenty-Nine

ENCOURAGED BY GEORGE FURNESS, MARTIN planned to go abroad that summer: he wanted to spend a fortnight in Paris, to explore the great city and savour the experience by himself. He felt ashamed to be twenty-five years old and yet had never been outside his native country. He felt himself to be provincial in manner and immature in mind: altogether lacking in confidence, in initiative, in spirit.

Shortly before he was to leave for France he got a letter from home; it was from his mother; she told him that his father was ill.

The doctor had advised Mr. Connolly to take things easy for a while, and had made him leave off work. Martin's mother ended her letter: "Your father isn't as strong as he thinks he is, and when you come home you'll find him failed. Dr. Harper told me that his heart isn't really strong and that he will just have to look after himself better. Not to rush round doing things that he needn't do at all ... "

So Martin took a day off and went home to Belfast.

His father was alone in the house when he arrived.

"Your mother's out doing her messages," Mr. Connolly said. "It's a wonder you didn't run into her—she's just out this minute."

"How are you, father?"

His father gave a slight shrug of the shoulders and led the way through the sitting-room and kitchen to the tiny back garden.

"Bring out another chair, son," he called. "It's nice an' warm here when the sun's out."

His father looked ill—his complexion an unhealthy yellow. His movements, too, had become slower.

"What yarn did your mother spin you?" he asked Martin.

"She wrote and told me you were off work ill."

"Aye."

"Do you feel groggy?"

"I've felt better," his father replied, reluctantly; at once adding, "How are things with you, son?"

"Fine."

His father nodded and raised his head to enjoy a glint of sunshine that had pierced the high billowing clouds; his eyes were closed; and Martin looked at him closely.

His father had aged all of a sudden, his hair had become completely grey now, his skin had wizened, his hands were those of an old man—thin, wrinkled, and blotchy.

"When d'you set off for France?" his father asked, opening his eyes.

"In a fortnight's time."

"You're staying in Paris, aren't you?"

"Yes, father. You never got there, did you?"

"No, never."

His father's memories of France were of cold and mud and lice: most of all, of cold grey rain. But the old man now sat in silence, keeping his memories to himself.

"You still like your job?" he asked.

Martin nodded and picked up the newspaper his father had dropped on the grass.

"There's nothing in that paper," his father said, "I've read it through from front to back and found nothing in it worth five minutes' thought."

Mrs. Connolly appeared round the side of the house. Her eyes lit up on seeing her son.

"Hello, mother."

"We didn't really expect you till the weekend, Martin."

"I was able to get the day off."

"Well, there he is," his mother said, looking at her husband. "What d'you think of him?"

"He needs a rest," Martin said.

"I'll not let him put a foot in that shipyard till he's fit for it," Mrs. Connolly said. "He's already talkin' about startin' on Monday next. Did you ever hear such nonsense?"

Mrs. Connolly brought cups of tea and the three sat in the patch of garden, talking. The afternoon kept up fine; sometimes the sun was really hot; his father shielded his head with the newspaper. Martin always enjoyed being at home for a day or two. He enjoyed the city—seeing people he knew, drinking and talking in The Duke of York. But when at home he realised most clearly that he had certainly changed his life; he was rapidly becoming accustomed to middle-class standards.

He was becoming accustomed to the spaciousness of Elm Grove, with its well-proportioned rooms and large protecting garden. His own home seemed to him intolerably cramped; even the garden, which he had once been grateful for, now appeared pathetically small. He looked across the privet hedge to the rusting corrugated iron paling of the mineral water factory at the back of the house. He could hear the shouts of the workers, the peals of laughter of girls, the clanking of cans and bottles. From his bedroom window he had often seen the men and girls at work, wearing thick red rubber aprons and heavy gumboots; their raucous shouts and loud singing had often interrupted his reading.

"What are you thinking about, Martin?" his mother asked.

"Why?"

"You weren't listening to what I was saying."

"Sorry."

"Well, what were you thinking about?"

"How nice it is to be at home," he answered, smiling.

"Then you should come more often," his mother replied.

It was a reproach. He looked at his mother. She wasn't angry; she wasn't seriously reproaching him; but he knew she'd have liked him to spend more of his weekends at home.

"Have you a girl to see?"

She was quizzing him now; she was profoundly curious about everything that happened to him.

Martin shook his head.

"Oh, you haven't?"

She seemed unsure whether to believe him.

"No, I haven't," he repeated, so emphatically that she was convinced.

His mother occasionally questioned him about girls, but always he evaded her questionings. He believed in keeping his life private; so he resented his mother's natural curiosity.

He was ready and anxious for marriage. And he believed that some day he would indeed marry. He couldn't imagine himself as a middle-aged bachelor. He certainly needed a wife and a home and children. He must marry: of that he was sure. But he couldn't afford to marry yet—his wage was still scarcely a living wage; he had with difficulty saved the few pounds he needed for his holiday. Anyhow what sort of girl would want to marry him? He'd met no-one in his own class to attract him: his interests simply weren't theirs—to deny that was foolish. He accused himself of snobbery.

Certainly he preferred the company of girls with tastes similar to his own; and that ruled out nearly every working-class girl he'd met. It was a miserable condition to be in. His accent was no longer working-class; neither were his clothes nor his manners. And yet—and yet he felt no desire to be middle-class. He belonged emotionally to the working-class; he felt rooted there; was at ease with workers. But he had been acquiring middle-class standards ever since he had won a scholarship and now, living at Elm Grove, he felt that the living conditions of his parents were intolerable. The street, rooms, furniture, everything appeared to him tawdry and cheap.

He left home shortly after seven o'clock, promising to come again on Saturday for the weekend.

Immediately the train moved out of Belfast he felt glad. He lay back in his corner seat and looked out as the line of backyards was gradually replaced by suburban gardens and then by small fields. In the distance he could see the gentle slopes of the Antrim hills.

An hour and a half later he left the train and made his way through the town to Elm Grove. Opening the front door he went at once to his bedroom. From somewhere in the house a clock struck nine.

He washed and returned to his room with the intention of

reading for the rest of the evening. Somehow his mood was too restless for reading; so he rose, took a cigarette from a drawer, and walked about the room, smoking. He then stood at the window, looking out into the garden. The flowers and trees were still; and there was a stillness in the house itself.

Suddenly he saw a figure appear in the drive, between the tall trees. It was George Furness. He was carrying a small suitcase in one hand; from his other hand a mackintosh trailed along the path. As he walked towards the porch he was swaying, his head sunk in his chest. Martin pushed up the window and called out.

"George!"

George Furness halted; looked round puzzled to see where the voice came from; then finally caught sight of Martin.

"Come here, man!" he called back, with a violent gesture.

Martin ran downstairs, across the hall, opened the door, and approached Furness, who had fallen full-stretch in the garden, his legs and arms apart.

"What's the matter, George?"

Furness lay back as if nailed to the ground, his eyes closed, his face pale, all expression drained from it. Then he opened one eye.

"Nothing's the matter!"

It was clear that Furness was drunk.

"Where on earth have you been, George?"

"Dublin."

"Dublin? What were you doing there?"

Furness sat up and yawned.

"On a blinder. Should a' been back last night."

"And you've only arrived now?"

Furness nodded.

"What about your wife?"

Furness shrugged his shoulders and turned his long mouth down as if to say that what had been done was irreparable: there was nothing to be said about it.

"She'll be very worried about you. You'd better get home soon. I'll look up the bus timetable and find out when the next one leaves."

"All right."

Furness made no effort to move.

"You can't sit there, George."

"Why not?"

"Why not? You want people to see you drunk, do you?" Furness looked at Martin, belched; then burst into a roar of uncontrollable laughter, lying back on the wet grass and howling drunkenly. At last he sat up, still breaking out into spasms of laughing.

"I know I'm drunk. I like being drunk. I want you to be drunk too, Martin. That's your trouble you know. You're too sober. You never let yourself go. You should let yourself go, like me. Just let yourself go. Just forget yourself and become—"

He paused and belched, again.

"Become what?" Martin asked.

"One with the cosmos," he hiccupped.

Martin bent over his companion and helped him to his feet; together they made their way up the steps of the house and into the dining room.

"I'll get you some coffee," Martin said.

"Why?"

"To sober you up, man!"

"Who wants sobered up?" Furness replied, truculently.

"Just a minute, George."

Martin left the dining room and knocked at the kitchen door. Mary appeared.

"Yes, sir?"

"I wonder, Mary, would you make some coffee for me—and for a friend of mine?"

"Certainly, Mr. Connolly."

"Thank you very much."

"Anything to eat, Mr. Connolly?"

"No, no—nothing. If you leave the tray here—" Martin indicated a small table that stood on one side of the hall, "I'll collect it myself."

"Very good, sir."

Martin returned to the dining room to find his companion slumped over the table.

"George—"

"What ya want?"

"I want you sobered up."

"Aw, Christ, let me alone! Let's go outa this!"

"I'm getting you some coffee—"

"For Christ's sake! Who wants coffee?"

Martin persuaded Furness to remain in the dining room. And while they were waiting for the coffee Furness began to ramble on about his trip to Dublin. He had tried to arrange an autumn exhibition of his paintings but the dealer had been evasive, insisting that the gallery was booked right up to Christmas and beyond.

"He's a bloody liar," Furness kept on repeating. "He's a dirty bloody liar."

At the memory of the dealer's evasiveness he became enraged and thumped the table viciously. Martin had never before seen the art teacher drunk, and the sight of him sprawled out was disgusting. He wanted rid of the drunken man; and after a while went for the coffee and brought it in. Half-an-hour later he put Furness onto the last bus.

Thirty

AFTER SCHOOL THE FOLLOWING AFTERNOON FURNESS called at the *Sentinel* office. Martin was out at the time but appeared just as Furness was leaving.

They met on the pavement in front of the office.

"I left a note for you with the boss," Furness explained, looking a bit ashamed. Then went on: "I owe you an apology, Martin—"

"What for?"

"The state I was in last night. I don't know why I called up at Elm Grove. I must have looked stupid."

"You looked tired."

"I was tired."

"How are you feeling now?"

"Oh, all right, thanks. Would you've time for a coffee?" Furness added with a smile.

"Thanks. I'll call in at the office first. I won't be two minutes."

"I'll be in the café at the corner—I've to meet Elise there, but—" Furness put his forefinger to his mouth, "not a word to the wife."

"Of course not."

There was nothing urgent to do in the office so Martin went

at once to the café. Furness was alone and remarked that his wife was shopping somewhere in the town. He explained in detail why he had got drunk the previous evening. Coming back by train from Dublin and being depressed after the interview with his dealer, he had met a friend from his art school days, a commercial artist.

"He was having a bad spell too. So—we drowned our sorrows. But a good feed o'drink once in a while does you no harm, does it?"

"No harm."

"All the same you're a bloody careful man yourself," Furness added with a chuckle.

"I suppose I am."

Just at that moment Martin saw Elise Furness enter through the swing doors of the café. She was wearing a light grey coat, which she had thrown open because of the heat of the June afternoon. She had no hat and her jet-black hair shone in the sunlight. As she walked up the café she smiled and half-raised her left hand by way of greeting.

"Here's Elise now," Martin said to Furness, whose back was towards his wife. "Remember—not a word about last night."

The two men rose; Elise shook hands with Martin. As she did so he was for the first time aware of her beauty. Under the impression that she was late she had rushed along the main street, and her colour was heightened.

"I'm out of breath."

"A cup of coffee, Elise darling?"

"Please."

They began to advise Martin about his holiday. Unfortunately they were going to France in August, else they would have invited him to join them.

"I think it's better to go alone," Martin said.

"Why?" Elise asked, her eyes portraying her puzzlement.

"Because—" Martin suddenly felt embarrassed; he realised that their invitation was attractive; certainly he would enjoy her company.

He said: "I think the first time you go to a new country you should see it through your own eyes. And you should do exactly what you like—without thinking of anybody else."

Elise nodded her head slightly: "Yes. Yes, I agree."

Some commotion in the street attracted the notice of the people in the café, and George Furness rose and looked out of the window. The wheel of a country cart had grazed the mudguard of a car; and a little knot of bystanders surrounded the two vehicles. The traffic of the main street was blocked and into the café came the honks of impatient motorists. George watched the scene with amusement; but Elise and Martin ignored the commotion outside.

"I understand your father is ill," Elise was saying.

"Yes."

"Is it serious?"

"We're not quite sure yet."

"I'm sorry."

It seemed to Martin that her simple conventional expression of grief was somehow neither simple nor conventional.

"You've heard about George's visit to Dublin?"

"Yes," Martin replied, "he was telling me about it."

Elise was frowning a little—a frown of annoyance and bewilderment.

"George was very annoyed," she said.

"I'm sure he was."

Elise glanced at her husband who suddenly called out across the café: "A bobby has arrived now—notebook and all—and there's a hell of an argument goin' on—I only hope he knows shorthand!"

Elise gave a slight shrug as if to say that her husband was a law unto himself.

"This is a pleasant little café," Martin remarked, to change the conversation.

Elise nodded and said, "Do you come here often?"

"Oh yes—well, it's according to what you mean by 'often'—I suppose I drop in once or twice a week."

"I've never seen you here before."

"I'm seldom here at this time of day."

"No, I suppose not."

As she was making these banal replies, Martin felt himself unable to repress a tingling of excitement: it was as if his whole body had suddenly become electrically charged; her words, apparently harmless, were detonating inside him; and the feelings they generated were outside his will.

It was as if each syllable invited him to know her more intimately. Indeed it seemed to him that she actually wanted to arrange a meeting with him here, in the café, and the sooner the better. But the expression on her face gave him no hint of her feelings. She appeared to be quite calm, even a little bored, as if anxious for her husband's return to their table. And within a couple of minutes George crossed from the window and sat down, saying, "That was a bit of a fracas. My coffee's cold! How about another cup before we go?"

"Have we time?" Elise asked.

"Oh yes, plenty of time." And, turning to Martin, said: "It was the faces they were pulling. Like this—"

And he gave a demonstration of mimicry which made people in the neighbouring tables burst out laughing.

"George, behave yourself," Elise said, softly, quite unable to control her own amusement.

"I should have had my notebook with me. There was an old farmer—"

And George went on to give a detailed account of the whole affair. But Martin wasn't listening though he was trying to pretend he was.

As for Elise, she was apparently giving her husband her whole attention.

Thirty-One

MARTIN SPENT THE WEEKEND IN BELFAST at home. He thought a good deal of the incident in the café. Had he really received an invitation from Elise Furness? He was almost sure, at the time, that he had; but as the hours passed he became less and less sure. But of one thing he was quite certain now: she attracted him physically; and the attraction disturbed him. He found himself thinking about her constantly, in spite of himself.

His father's health was slightly better; at least his mother was less anxious, largely because the doctor had again visited the house and had assured her that there was no immediate cause for anxiety so long as her husband was very careful. It was, of course, out of the question that he should return to work for at least six weeks.

Martin suggested that his parents should go to the seaside for a while. The sea air would do his father good, would put colour into his cheeks.

"What do you say to that, Bob?" Mrs. Connolly inquired.

"Maybe later in the summer," Mr. Connolly replied, a little impatiently. "Every place'll be too crowded this month."

"Would you go to Newcastle or Donaghadee in September?"

"I might."

But he didn't want to go to the seaside, even for a week. He was content, for the time being, to stay where he was. A chair in the back garden and a book to read were all he wanted for the present.

Martin spent his Saturday evening wandering round the city streets. A couple of French naval ships were in the port; and the sailors were strolling about in their uniforms and white red-tasselled caps. As he passed groups of them Martin could hear their vivacious speech, but only occasionally could he catch a word or a phrase. He had a drink and a sandwich in Mooney's at the Cornmarket and then wandered out into the street, aimlessly following the Saturday night crowds. It was the custom to go 'into town' on a Saturday for shopping and sightseeing, and the streets were packed. He found himself in front of the Empire and thought he might go to the first house. He looked at the bill and photographs outside the ticket-office: the usual variety acts, headed by a Scottish comedian. He entered and took a seat in the back.

The show had begun and a couple of Japanese acrobats had just started their act; then came an Irish tenor, followed by a troupe of dancers. The audience, out for full-blooded entertainment, got it. Martin liked this theatre, it had an atmosphere and tradition of its own—Edwardian and rather raucous.

At the interval he strolled into the bar, looked for a while at the yellowing theatre bills with their forgotten stars of thirty and forty years before, then returned to his seat.

About nine o'clock he boarded a tram at the Markets. His mother asked where he had been.

"The first house of the Empire," he replied, a little brusquely.

"Oh."

She was surprised at his visiting a variety theatre, and gave him a glance of disapproval. "Did you really enjoy it, Martin?"

"Yes, I did. I felt really in the mood for the Empire."

"You felt—?"

His mother shook her head.

"Yes, I felt in the mood for a little fun," he said, tartly enough.

The trouble with his parents, he reflected, was that they

didn't know the kind of person he really was. Their Puritanism was deeply ingrained: and he detested it—it was so joyless and so bleak.   ✗

He left home on the Sunday evening train. At nine o'clock he was back at Elm Grove, and thought that in ten days' time he would be out of Ireland for the first time in his life and wondered whether he would see Elise before he left.

He did see her; he saw her two days later; and not quite by chance. On Monday he had called into the café at half-past four, looked round the tables for her, and then hurried downstairs again, disappointed. But on Tuesday, when he had called at the same time, she was there, alone, at a corner table. He pretended surprise and greeted her with a wave of the hand. Then he crossed the café towards her.

"Hello."

"How are you?" she said, smiling.

"Are you alone?"

"Yes, I've been shopping. Do sit down."

He took a seat beside her. It was curious, he thought, that she seemed to avoid using his Christian name. Why should it be so? Did he use her Christian name? Certainly he thought of her as 'Elise'.

"Has George finished school yet?" he asked.

"I don't know."

"Aren't you meeting him?"

"Oh, I'll probably meet him at the bus. He doesn't know I'm in town this afternoon. I didn't know myself I was coming, but I just came."

"For no reason?"

"Oh, I had a reason."

Martin waited. Would she give him the reason he imagined to be true, that she came to see him?

"I felt bored at home," she said at last. "Do you ever feel bored?"

"Sometimes—not too often."

"You're lucky."

"I've so many things I want to do," he said, "and I never seem to have the time for anything. My life just rushes past—it frightens me."

She nodded, and gave him an odd look. "Sometimes I'm frightened too."

They sat in silence for a while, sipping their coffee. The café was almost deserted and sitting together in the corner gave them a feeling of intimacy; and they spoke almost in whispers. Suddenly Elise said softly, "What do you think of my husband?"

Martin looked at Elise: her face was a little flushed.

"What do I think—?" he began, but she interrupted him.

"I want to ask you that question. Perhaps I shouldn't have. But you needn't answer if you don't wish to."

Martin paused; the directness of the question had disconcerted him. He had never tried to analyse the character of George Furness but had accepted him as someone with interests like his own.

"I shouldn't have asked you that question—"

"No, no," he murmured. "I'm only trying to think of an answer that'll satisfy you."

"I want you to tell me the truth."

"But—" he laughed, a little nervously, "I—I don't know the truth. I like George—very much indeed."

"Do you, really?"

"Yes."

What did she want him to say? She hardly wanted him to confess that at the moment he hadn't the least desire to discuss her husband—he wished in fact that there was no husband to be discussed.

Was she still in love with George? That was the kind of question he wanted to ask her. But what would be her answer? Her face appeared so calm, so enigmatic that it was impossible to guess her thoughts. She certainly had the gift of silence: and yet her silence had a most disturbing effect on him. He waited. She sat with her face immobile, as if carved, and he envied her such poise. There was a silence which he found almost unendurable. What game was she playing? She had laid her hand on the table and was playing with a knife. A long shapely hand, browned a little by the sun, the nails beautifully shaped and well cared for.

"I don't understand my husband," he heard her saying. "Does that surprise you?"

He looked at her. "Yes."

She drew in her breath slightly, Martin looked at her breasts and wanted to caress them.

"I wonder why I'm talking to you like this," she went on, looking along the café where a waitress was tidying one of the tables. "I've never talked to anyone before about George. You believe that, don't you?"

Martin nodded.

"I can talk to you quite freely about my husband and I don't feel in the least ashamed. Yet I hardly know you; and I've never talked to you alone before, have I?"

"No."

She was still concentrating her gaze on the middle-aged waitress at the other end of the café; and at the same time she was drawing circles with her knife on the rumpled tablecloth. Martin slowly stretched out his hand and took the knife from her; and she smiled at him and said: "You're not very encouraging, are you?"

"I'm trying to be."

"This is foolish of me."

"No, it's not. Please say anything you like."

"You're being polite."

"I'm trying to be truthful."

She looked at him: her eyes were suddenly clouded and troubled.

"Can I be truthful too?"

"I hope so," he answered gravely.

"I don't love my husband." Her voice was so low that he could hardly hear the words.

She turned her face away from him, her eyes brimming with tears.

"Please excuse me," she said. "I'm making a fool of myself. Forget what I've just said, won't you? I had to tell somebody."

"I'm glad you told me."

"You've been very kind."

He shook his head. He glanced at her, full of compassion for her in her distress. But what could he do to help? She looked so miserable now that she had confessed her secret, and he took her hand.

"I'm sorry," he murmured.

Just then he caught the eye of the grey-haired waitress and ordered more coffee.

After a while Elise began to talk and Martin felt he could ask her questions. She told him she was miserable because her husband was drinking regularly and leaving her a good deal to herself. And she was lonely, out in the countryside, all day by herself; she had made no friends, and she was homesick. She thought she would leave her husband.

"You never suspected we were unhappy?" she asked.

He shook his head. No, the idea had never crossed his mind. Of course he suspected that George might not be an easy person to live with; he was moody and irritable; and frustrated, too, in his work. His painting hadn't gained the recognition it deserved.

Suddenly Elise looked at her watch and rose.

"I must go."

Martin also rose and made to accompany her out of the café.

"No," she said. "I'll go alone."

They shook hands.

"Have a good holiday," she said, "I hope you enjoy France."

"I hope so."

"You'll tell me all about it when you come back?"

"Of course. I'll tell you everything."

"*Au revoir*."

"*Au revoir*."

He returned to the office almost at once. He had still some work to do—a report to type—but he paid hardly any attention to its contents. It was nearly six o'clock, and he was astonished to learn that he had been talking to Elise for over an hour; he had imagined they had been together less than half that time.

He thought of what she had told him; it was a great deal, the few short remarks she had given him in confidence. He felt sympathy for her; and he felt pity. He would like to have taken her in his arms and comforted her. He would like to have caressed her. And he had no doubt that she would have allowed him to—though she was married, and married to his friend. Then for the first time he thought of Elise's religion; she was probably a Catholic, though he had never thought of her as a Catholic. Certainly she had never referred to her religion in his presence. Would Elise's religion prevent—? He hesitated for a moment. The door of the office opened and Mr. Watson entered.

"I thought you'd gone off home," he said.

"I'd a job I wanted to finish."

"Good man."

Mr. Watson was in a breezy mood, and added: "Come and have a drink."

"Thanks."

"You look as if you need one," he said, slamming Martin's shoulder. "Anything on your mind?"

"On my mind?" Martin replied, echoing the phrase. "No, there's nothing at all on my mind—nothing at all."

He rose from his table, whipped the sheet of paper from his typewriter, put it alongside some others, and followed his employer out of the room.

Thirty-Two

IT WAS EARLY IN SEPTEMBER; GEORGE Furness had just returned to school after the holidays; and one Friday afternoon he called at the *Sentinel* and left a message inviting Martin to spend the weekend at the cottage. On the Saturday Martin took a bus which swung its way noisily up the hills. He found the front door wide open; and knocked.

"Come in," called George, "I'm working."

Martin entered the room.

"Just one minute, please."

George was painting a landscape. Martin sat down and watched him at work. George never looked happier than when he had a brush in his hand. He worked quickly and deftly, dabbing blobs of colour on the canvas, and stepping back to observe the result. Martin liked to watch him at work; liked even to listen to his out-of-tune singing of snatches from operas.

"There! Finished."

He stood back to admire his canvas.

"I believe this one might be good," he said, "Don't you?"

Martin nodded: he thought the landscape—small, dark—green fields and almost black rocks, geometrical in form—had originality and intensity.

"I want to forget it now! I need fresh air!" George exclaimed. "And I want to hear all your news!"

They went along the hall and into the front garden. Martin wondered where Elise was; she hadn't appeared yet. George at once threw himself among the long, neglected grass, burying his face in its greenness and rubbing his hands along the stalks.

"I like grass to grow like this!" he cried; "you should be able to feel and smell the stuff! Have you a cigarette?"

Martin took out his packet and threw him a cigarette which he caught and put in his mouth.

"A match?"

Martin threw over a box of matches.

"You may begin now."

"Where?"

"Wherever you like."

Martin laughed and said that he could talk all night about what he had seen and done in London and Paris.

"We've all night to talk," George said, adding, "Oh, I forgot to ask you—are you hungry? Shall I get you something to eat? Elise is still with her parents—she's staying on in France for another month. I'm looking after myself."

As Martin wasn't hungry George suggested they walk to the village and go to the pub for a drink. So they spent most of the evening in the pub—a squalid building in the middle of the neglected-looking village. And Martin talked about his experiences in London and Paris. He had explored both cities, going to the obvious places—the National Gallery and the Louvre, Hyde Park and the Bois de Boulogne, Covent Garden and the Opera—but most of all he had enjoyed wandering about the streets, content to watch the endless streams of passers-by. He had enjoyed a walk from the Place Pigalle to the Sacré Coeur: and he had enjoyed a couple of evenings in Soho. He had picked up a few acquaintances—a tall pretty girl from Boston studying modern languages at the university of London, and a swarthy Italian schoolmaster holidaying in Paris. The Italian, Alberto Masi, had impressed Martin with his knowledge of politics, painting, and literature. "He was so enthusiastic about everything," Martin said. "He was a good socialist, he told me, and a good Catholic as well. I've got his address—he lives in Milan—and I've promised to write to him."

As the evening wore on, Martin noticed that George became more and more silent; and at closing-time he had obviously lost interest in Martin's experiences. Of his own holiday abroad he had hardly spoken, except to confess that he had painted very little in France, certainly not as much as he had hoped to. After a long silence he suddenly remarked, "You didn't tell me much about that American girl you met."

"Oh, I met her in the Haymarket theatre; she was sitting beside me, in the upper circle. It was a dreadful play—meant to be a comedy."

"Did you do her?"

Martin laughed at his companion's question. "No, I didn't. I took her to supper in Greek Street, then left her to the tube. I found her a bit disappointing to talk to."

"But you shouldn't have wasted your time talking to her. That's not what she wanted."

"How do you know?"

"I know what women want."

"All of them? All the time?"

"No, most of them; most of the time."

They walked very slowly back to the cottage, a distance of about two miles, and George was a bit drunk; occasionally he reeled across the road. He was in a mood for talking about women, and said that he regretted having married while he was under thirty.

"A mistake," he repeated. "You're a wise man, Martin boy."

"I don't know that I am."

"Well, I know, I've had more experience of women than you have." He paused. "I shouldn't have married Elise, you know. It was a mistake—it's always a mistake to marry a foreigner. They just don't understand you; and you just don't understand them—no matter how you try. And after a while you give up. It's a curious thing, marriage—very curious."

He halted in the middle of the road, shook his head, and then continued, "You once told me you weren't a virgin."

"I'm not," Martin quickly insisted.

"Oh I believe you—I believe you."

George then took a few steps backwards as if involuntarily, and regarded his companion.

"But you're not a Don Juan by nature either, are you?"

"I suppose I'm not. Sometimes I wish I were."

They walked up a long hill, and then the cottage came into view. It was a clear September night, the stars very dim, and a light wind blowing.

"Tell me this," George went on, "just tell me this. What kind of a person are you—inside yourself?"

Martin hesitated.

"You don't know, do you?" George said.

"I just don't know what the question means," Martin replied, drawing the palm of his hand across his brow in a gesture of perplexity. He often felt that he lacked solidity: was too easily influenced by people he met or by books he read.

"I let things happen to me—I know that—and it's feeble."

"Of course it's feeble. Are you really a feeble person by nature?"

"Why talk about me?" Martin protested. "Why not talk about you?"

"Talk about me?" George now stood at the top of the hill, and crossed to lean over an iron gate flanked by two white-washed conical-tipped circular pillars. He pointed first at one pillar, then at the other.

"Beautifully cared for, aren't they?"

"You mean—the pillars?"

"Yes. We're a phallic people, you know." He hiccupped and caressed the pillars.

"You're drunk, George."

"I may be drunk, but I know what I am."

"And what are you?"

"A hedonist. I take it, Martin boy, when I can get it. Always take what you can get and enjoy it. That's my motto."

"It's a philosophy *comme un autre*."

"An ancient one."

"Not a satisfactory one."

"It suits an artist!"

"But I'm not an artist."

"You're certainly not a hedonist! More likely a bloody Puritan!"

They talked until dawn. When, at last, each went to bed, Martin found his throat hoarse from smoking and talking too much. It had been a long day and he felt exhausted. He wondered what George Furness, in the other room, was thinking of; Martin could hear him coughing; then after a while heard him snoring.

Despite his tiredness Martin couldn't fall asleep for a long time. Both Elise and George Furness had confessed to him that their marriage had been a mistake. What had happened during the summer holidays? Had Elise decided to leave her husband? Was George telling the truth when he said his wife was staying in France for another month?

On the Sunday it was almost noon by the time they had breakfast. It was a cool grey morning, so George suggested a cycle trip to Newcastle; Martin could have Elise's bicycle. George wanted to do some sketches of the quarries in the Mourne mountains or of the woods near the town. If the afternoon turned out warm they might swim.

"I've no bathing things with me," Martin said.

"We'll go along by the sand dunes—we can go in there in our pelts. Nobody'll see us."

Martin looked slightly surprised at the notion they could bathe naked so near Newcastle; but George said that few people walked along by the dunes.

"We can leave the bikes at the railway station. That's what I do when Elise comes with me. We often go in naked."

"Isn't Elise afraid of being seen?"

George gave a short laugh.

"She is, yes," he replied, "but like any woman she can be persuaded to do a lot of things she didn't like at first."

He looked at the expression on Martin's face.

"Can I still shock you?"

"You can."

"I wonder why. You must have a guilt complex somewhere."

Martin found himself blushing.

"I expect I have."

"It's about time, then, you got over it. Sex isn't very important, you know—not as important as it's made out to be. A little of it goes a long way. I've been married nearly five years: so I ought to know."

"You really don't think sex is important?" Martin asked.

217

"Of course not. Do you?"

"Yes."

"Well—"

George hesitated: then gave one of his gruff laughs like a clearing of phlegm from his throat.

"The act itself isn't very important, is it? Sometimes when I'm doing it I want to laugh. And I do. Makes Elise very angry. She says I'm laughing at her. But I'm only laughing at myself."

"Or at both of you."

"Yes, that's the truth, Martin. I'm really laughing at the both of us. It is funny, you know."

He appeared, at that moment, to recall something, for he burst out into his obscene-sounding laugh.

"I remember once, when I was in the first position—" He paused. "Oh, but you don't want to hear about it."

Martin made no reply, and George took out a packet of cigarettes and rolled a one between his fingers: it was one of his mannerisms. He enjoyed the feel and texture of the cigarette; and from time to time he liked to smell the tobacco before lighting up.

"You're a funny bloody man, Martin. You should a' been a clergyman or something."

"I don't think so."

"You know, I haven't an idea what goes on in that mind of yours. Don't you ever feel lascivious?"

George spoke the word with emphatic relish.

"Quite often."

"Then why not get rid of your lewdness—at least verbally."

"I do sometimes."

"Not often enough. Not when you're with me. What's the matter with you is you don't get enough sex. And you know what's the matter with me?"

Martin shook his head.

"I'm tired of it. I want a change. I need another woman. I've my eye on one—a sandy-haired games-mistress that's just joined the staff. Looks exciting. Have you seen her about?"

"Yes."

"What do you think of her?"

"She's not unattractive."

"She's the athletic type—the type I like."

The afternoon had turned out cold and the Mourne mountains became clouded over. The sea was grey and choppy.

They decided to return to Newcastle and have a drink in the hotel overlooking the golf links.

After a couple of whiskies George again mentioned his wife.

"You know, somehow I think she'll leave me," he said, morosely.

"Why should she?"

"I believe she already has."

"You mean—?"

"I mean I don't think she'll come back to me."

"Are you serious?"

"Of course I'm serious. And d'you know what I'm goin' to tell you? It makes no difference to me whether she comes back or whether she doesn't. I'll survive, no matter what happens."

On the way back to his cottage George talked a good deal more about his wife. What had gone wrong in their marriage was something he found hard to analyse; perhaps there were too many differences—of nationality, of religion, of language—between them; all the same he was fond of Elise: he was even, at times, devoted to her.

But he no longer desired her very much; he felt dead emotionally. And so his painting suffered.

By now he had talked himself into a gloomy mood.

"I don't know why I tell you my troubles. I'm sure you've plenty of your own."

"They're not the same as yours."

"You're not thinking of getting married, are you?"

"I hope I will—some day."

"Don't be in a hurry. You've plenty of time."

They were silent for a time and then George gave a deep sigh.

"I feel bloody sad, as if life—"

He threw up his hands in a gesture of hopelessness.

"What's the use of anything?"

Soon afterwards they parted, Martin promising to spend an evening at the cottage towards the end of the week.

Thirty-Three

HE KEPT HIS PROMISE. NEXT FRIDAY evening, having dropped George Furness a note, Martin walked out to the cottage; only to find it deserted.

A neighbour, a grey-haired woman, who saw him standing at the door, called out that Mr. Furness hadn't returned from school—she had seen him leaving in the morning and thought that he might have gone away for the weekend.

"He sometimes goes to Dublin," she added, a trifle acidly.

Martin thanked her and walked towards the town, dispirited, wondering what had happened.

He arrived back at Elm Grove just after eleven. He felt tired; he would go to bed at once, after having the biscuit and glass of milk left for him on the dining room table.

He entered the room. On the tray was a note in Miss Garland's handwriting. It read: "Mr. Connolly, would you please ring the Belfast number below as soon as you can?"

He went to the telephone and got through at once.

"Hello. This is Martin Connolly—"

"Oh, yes," came the answer, a man's voice which Martin didn't recognise.

"I was asked to ring this number."

220

"Were you? Oh yes. Yes, of course. Just hold on a moment, please ... "

There was a silence. Then suddenly Martin heard a woman's voice.

"Hello—"

He recognised Elise's voice immediately.

"Martin Connolly speaking," he replied, trying to keep his voice natural. He felt himself flushing.

"Were you ringing me, Elise?"

"Yes, I wanted to speak to you, please. I'm sorry to bother you."

Her voice sounded somehow unnatural too; her accent more pronounced than normal—or so he imagined.

"No bother. Where are you?"

"In Belfast."

"But where—exactly?"

"In a small hotel."

"Is George with you?"

There was a short pause; and in a lowered voice, almost a whisper, Elise replied, "No."

"I thought he might have been."

"He is not." Elise's reply was firm: then she said: "Will you help me?"

"Of course—if I can."

There was a pause: then in a low voice she said: "Thank you, Martin."

On him the words had almost the effect of a caress.

"What can I do?" he asked, eager now.

Did his voice betray his feelings? He felt tremulous, as if about to embark on a strange journey into the unknown.

"Can you see me?"

"Where? When?"

He was committed now.

"Here, please."

"What's the name of your hotel?"

She gave it. A rather dingy place near Shaftesbury Square.

"Are you all right?" he inquired.

"Oh yes, thank you."

"Good."

He hoped his tone of voice was reassuring; he felt, as he

spoke, more confident of himself. He had, after all, embarked on this. And he felt almost protective now.

"When can you come here?"

"Tomorrow."

"Thank you."

"Not in the morning—I've to go to the office."

"Of course."

"Some time in the afternoon. Will that do? Say about three or four."

"Thank you very much."

A pause.

"Are you sure you want to come?"

He hesitated.

"I want to help you if I can."

"Thank you," she replied, after a pause. Then: "Goodnight."

"Goodnight."

He put down the receiver and walked slowly upstairs; and when he reached the top of the stairs he suddenly remembered his supper. But hunger had now left him.

Saturday morning in the *Sentinel* office was the slackest period of the week. The paper went to press on Tuesdays and Fridays and so on Saturday mornings business was almost at a standstill. Very often Mr. Watson didn't turn up at all; and if he did, he stayed for less than half-an-hour.

So Martin usually found himself in control of the editorial office.

There was little work to be done. The advertisements, which were handed in to Miss Hamill, the assistant at the stationery counter, were lodged in her great black ledger, given their code number, then brought upstairs by Joe Stuart, the message boy. Sometimes Miss Hamill—or Alice, as she was called by Mr. Watson and Martin—wearily climbed the bare worn stairs to the editor's office with an inquiry from a customer, or with the morning cup of tea.

"Here's your tea."

Martin thanked her; but his acknowledgement of her deed—and her bulky presence—was so perfunctory that she went downstairs muttering to herself in a half huff.

He looked after her bulky back, covered with a hand-knitted

brown cardigan. Usually he chatted with her for a minute or two, for she relished a bit of gossip, and some of her gossip he found useful as 'pars'. But this Saturday morning he was hardly aware of her. He sipped the hot over-sweet tea (he must tell Alice once more that he liked one teaspoonful of sugar, not three), lit a cigarette, and sat comfortably back in Mr. Watson's chair.

He then wandered along towards the printing office, which was reached by a wide entry at the side of the shop; Alice made a point of ignoring him as he was passing the counter. She had buried her head in the pages of the *Sentinel*, which being now twenty-four hours old she must have known almost by heart.

"Not speaking to anybody?" he called out.

"Why should I?" she retorted, not looking up.

But by her tone he knew she had recovered from her feeling of pique.

He looked at his watch: quarter past eleven. The morning was going very slowly.

He passed through the printing office and went up a flight of rickety wooden stairs to the composing room. At the far end stood the two lino-type machines; and all round were the benches with their trays of type. In the middle of the room stood the stone on which rested the formes ready to receive the columns of type.

He reached the desk where he did most of his work. It was littered with copy that had been left lying round, and he swept it into a newspaper basket.

Mr. Watson appeared at the door.

"Did you get that story yesterday about the closing of the abattoir?"

"Yes."

"It's worth a column."

"I'll write it up."

Mr. Watson nodded his agreement and said:

"Head it something like this: ABATTOIR TO CLOSE AT END OF MONTH. SURPRISING DECISION. HEALTH COMMITTEE DECLINES TO INTERFERE."

Martin made a note in his jotter. Then Mr. Watson disappeared as quickly as he had appeared. Irritated, Martin stared at the door through which the proprietor of the *Sentinel* had come and gone. Blast him! And blast the mouldy county abattoir!

He was tired of reporting trivialities in which he couldn't summon up the least interest—the petty session courts; the rural district meetings; the urban council, the education committee, the health committee, the minutiae of this, that and the other committee.

An eternal round of parochialism! And he was thoroughly tired of it! He must get out: and the sooner the better. He was being stifled. A life of slow asphyxiation. He must liberate himself, or be smothered.

In a mood of querulousness and irritability he put on his coat and walked through the shop and out into the street, his expression one of unusual sternness. He never glanced at Miss Hamill on his way out. And as for Mr. Watson, he didn't care what the proprietor of the *Sentinel* thought. Just let him object if he dared!

Thirty-Four

FOUR HOURS LATER HE WAS WALKING along Great Victoria Street in Belfast, his mood entirely different. The *Sentinel* office already seemed remote and insignificant: the affairs of the paper contemptible—not worth his attention. He was now remote from them, altogether above and beyond them. He felt nervous and apprehensive. Was he a fool? Yes, he was a fool. Else why should he choose to get entangled with a married woman? It didn't make sense.

He slowed down; stopped at a shop window; lit a cigarette; and breathed heavily. He was becoming frightened of the possible consequences of his actions. He puffed nervously at the cigarette and stood looking at the shop window. A hardware shop full of useful domestic everyday tools, it might as well have been empty. He drew his hand across his forehead and down his face—an unconscious gesture betraying his anxiety.

Then, stubbing out his cigarette, he made up his mind. For suddenly his moment of indecision had passed: he had no choice now. Walking firmly to the dingy hotel he opened the rusty front gate, took the few steps along the litter-laden garden with its almost obliterated privet hedge, and rang the bell.

Almost immediately the door opened: and Elise stood before him. She was wearing a dark grey dress that somehow didn't suit her; and she looked drab, careworn, and unhappy. Then, with a shadow of a smile, she greeted him. "Won't you come in?"

He followed her up the hallway.

She went upstairs, along a narrow corridor at the end of which stood a low table with a tall potted plant. As he passed it he knocked against the table and had to grasp hold of the plant. He steadied it; and it was safe.

Elise turned round.

"I nearly upset it," he said, relieved.

She smiled at his embarrassment but said nothing; and he followed her along the corridor.

He looked at her figure as she walked: she carried herself proudly, her head held high, her arms gracefully swinging. Her body looked slim and strong. She halted; opened a door with a key which had lain hidden in her hand; entered a room. He followed.

It was her bedroom.

He took a quick glance round. The room was small and dark. He was vaguely aware of the single bed, a faded pink coverlet, a cheap and worn dressing table near the dusty window. He stood in the middle of the room, embarrassed; his hands felt sticky, his forehead damp.

"Stuffy, isn't it?" Elise said. "I tried to open the window, but it wouldn't open."

"Let me try," Martin offered, glad to be doing something. He crossed the room and tugged at the window. It didn't budge an inch.

"This hasn't been opened for years," he muttered, irritated at his defeat. He tugged again; but without success.

"Please don't bother," Elise said.

He was slightly out of breath with his efforts and annoyed at his failure. He stood rubbing the grime off his hands.

"Do you want to wash your hands?"

Following her glance he noticed the washhand basin at the far side of the bed.

"No, thanks."

Elise had sat down on the only chair in the room.

"I'm afraid—"

"I'll sit here," Martin interrupted, sitting on the bed opposite her. Then for the first time since he had entered the room he had the courage to look at her.

Almost at once she blushed under his gaze; then smoothed back her hair.

"I'm sorry," she said, "I shouldn't have asked you to see me here."

"Why not?"

"It's wrong."

"Is it?" She nodded her head, almost imperceptibly.

"I think I must be mad," she said in such a low tone he could hardly make out the words.

"Why?"

"I ... "

Her eyes were brimming with tears. He acutely felt her distress. Looking profoundly unhappy, she took out a pathetic little wisp of a handkerchief and dabbed her eyes.

She had all his sympathy now, she looked so alone.

"I must be mad."

"No."

"Yes, I must be."

"But why?"

"I don't know what to do," she said, her voice tremulous, her whole body quivering. "I want to leave my husband. I don't want to go back to him—ever. I don't love him any more!"

The tears were running down her cheeks and she seemed unconscious of them: she had, for Martin, entirely thrown off her womanhood, had become, pitifully, a forlorn girl. With bent head she spoke to him, her voice charged with emotion. "I love you! I must be mad, Martin! What can I do? Tell me please—tell me what I can do?"

He bent over her and touched her hair. He gave her his large handkerchief—her own pathetic little rag had become a useless damp ball in her hands—and he touched her forehead, gently.

She sobbed, her shoulders rising and falling. He bent over her, to console her, his hands caressing her neck, her shoulders, her arms. And slowly, she appeared to get control of herself; and her sobbing ceased; and she became calm.

"What can I do for you?" he asked.

She looked straight into his eyes: a look of trust as if she had thrown herself at his feet. He could help her, and he must help

227

her. She had surrendered to him her dignity, her pride: the meaning of her glance was crystal-clear to him. She was his, for the asking. She was waiting for him to put his arms round her.

He held both her hands and drew her to her feet. She stood before him, her face streaked with tears, her hair dishevelled.

Releasing her hands he crossed the room and locked the door.

Then he turned to her and kissed her; but her lips were cold and unresponsive: it was as if she were dead.

"Don't be unhappy," he murmured, kissing her wet cheeks, her neck, her mouth.

He felt her arms, which had lain inert by her side, touch him; ever so tentatively he kissed her again and began to caress her body. Slowly he felt her body become warmed, more responsive to his touch; and now she too began to caress him; and he felt that his senses were swooning. Dimly he was aware that her clothes were loose about her and that she was responding uncontrollably to his caresses. Her body no longer seemed her own, but an instrument of his.

They were on the bed now, their arms round each other; and he could smell her hair and feel the surprising toughness of its texture. He was kissing her, with long deep kisses and she was returning his kisses.

With groping hands he pressed her body to his and whispered to her that he wanted her. And she said yes, yes, if he really wanted her. She wanted him, she whispered, but please be gentle, please be gentle, and she closed her eyes and lay waiting for him to come into her.

He looked at his wristwatch. Ten minutes to seven. Elise lay beside him, her head half buried in the bedclothes: she was still asleep. He wanted to move his legs—they felt cramped—but he refrained from making any movement.

She seemed to him beautiful, her face pale, her expression peaceful: and the thought struck him that if she were dead she would be like this. She seemed scarcely to be breathing. Suddenly she moaned a little in her sleep and her lips opened slightly and she gave a sigh.

He looked at her: he could see the tiny dark hairs in her nose, the beads of sweat along her upper lip, the dark brown mole on her left cheek. Her black hair lay across the rumpled pillow.

Her moan in sleep had recalled her moaning when he had come into her, a moaning of ecstasy that contained and encompassed pain.

He had thought that he had hurt her and had asked her; but she had at once shaken her head wildly in denial—no, no, he hadn't hurt her, he hadn't. He had been gentle, had been good, and she was grateful.

She wanted his love—she had asked for his love in a few whispered words and he had told her yes and had held her tighter and had caressed and possessed her; and after making love he had become drowsy and they had both fallen asleep.

She opened her eyes slowly and looked at him; then she turned on her back and stared at the ceiling as if she were alone. He stretched out his right hand and caressed her breasts; she put her left hand in his hand and held it: and she lay still, staring.

At last she spoke.

"What can I do with myself?"

He had no answer. What could he say in reply? Elise wanted his advice; but what advice could he give her? Did she really want to leave her husband for good? She was willing to let Martin make up her mind for her. It was ridiculous—she would have to make up her own mind! Immediately he despised himself for his evasiveness and was annoyed that Elise had made him feel so mean. He had no wish to be responsible for her future; she would have to make her own choice, and surely she should return to George Furness. What else could she do?

"Let's talk about it."

With a movement sideways he got up from the bed. He dressed quickly and arranged to meet her in the dining room downstairs.

"What's the food like here?"

Elise made a gesture of disgust.

"Very bad."

"Then let's go somewhere else. I'll wait downstairs for you."

He thought it best they shouldn't leave the bedroom together: but Elise didn't mind; no-one would see them.

"The hotel is almost empty."

"No wonder," Martin replied, looking round at the bedroom

with its chipped chairs, its decaying wallpaper, its yellowing curtains.

"Why did you come here?" he asked.

She shrugged her shoulders: it was the first hotel she had tried; it was near the railway station, and anyway she had been in despair—it didn't matter to her where she slept.

"I think you should go somewhere else. This hotel is pretty awful, isn't it?"

"I suppose so."

"You could get something better."

It offended him that she should stay in such a place: he had imagined her to be fastidious.

"I don't care," she murmured.

"Well, you must."

He told her she was being silly, not caring about where she stayed or what she did with herself.

"Oh, let's clear out of this!" he said.

"Where can I go?"

"I'll find somewhere for you."

"But—"

He wouldn't allow her to argue, so cut short her protest. The dinginess of the hotel depressed him, and he told her that if she needed money he could give her enough for a day or two.

"Let's clear out," he repeated.

He put her suitcase on top of the bed and told her he would wait for her downstairs. In an hour's time he was certain he could find a much more comfortable hotel; and when that was done she would be able to think straight.

She obeyed him. It was clear she wanted to be taken care of, to be told what to do. She seemed entirely indifferent to her surroundings.

A quarter of an hour later she appeared at the top of the stairs; and he ran up to carry her suitcase.

"I have to pay my bill," she said.

Martin offered to pay it but she refused his offer. She rang the bell on the hall table. The proprietress—a fat blonde in her fifties—came through a door at the back of the hall, and Elise explained that she wished to leave.

"You'll have to pay for tonight," the woman began, her voice grating, her tone aggressive.

"Of course," Martin interrupted.

The woman disappeared, leaving a smell of cooking behind her.

"I wish she would close that door," Martin said. "You could cut that smell with a knife."

The woman reappeared; Martin held out his hand for the account. She gave it to him. It came to a couple of pounds, and Elise let him pay it.

"Thanks, but you must—" she began.

"Let's get fresh air," Martin said as they walked down the hall into the street.

Outside a fine rain was falling. Great Victoria Street was wreathed in the grey evening light. At the Great Northern station Martin hailed a taxi and gave the driver the name of a hotel near St. Anne's Cathedral.

"I've never stayed in it, but it looks quite comfortable," he told Elise, taking her hand and pressing it gently, as if for comfort.

"You're cold," he whispered, "aren't you?"

"Yes."

"Everything'll turn out all right."

The taxi stopped in front of the hotel: a solid-looking mid-Victorian building. Martin, having paid the driver, picked up Elise's suitcase from the pavement.

"Martin ... "

"Yes?"

"Will you—" Elise hesitated. "Will you stay with me tonight?"

It was his turn to hesitate. He had been half-expecting such an invitation, but he hadn't made up his mind whether or not to accept it. He'd never spent an entire night with a woman: and it was the experience he had yearned for—the long nocturnal hours of sensuality. He glanced at Elise: she looked away, a little embarrassed now by her proposal.

"I shouldn't have asked you," she said.

"Yes, you should."

He had suddenly made up his mind: it was as if he had no choice.

"I want to stay," he said, decisively, taking her by the arm.

231

Thirty-Five

MARTIN WAS AWARE OF PEOPLE STREAMING into the unfinished Cathedral. He walked slowly, with Elise beside him, into Royal Avenue. He had forgotten it was Sunday morning.

The city had its shuttered Sunday appearance: no shops open: little traffic about the main streets. The everyday bustle was absent, and the passers-by seemed to have a more relaxed look; they walked more leisurely, the expressions on their faces were less worried. And, of course, at this time of the morning most of the people had on their Sunday clothes and were obeying the church bells calling them from all parts of the city to weekly worship.

Martin was conscious of the atmosphere of piety and religiosity that pervaded the city on this one morning of the week. He resented it—his resentment springing from his sense of alienation. He felt he had deliberately cut himself off from sharing the most fundamental feelings of this community; and he obscurely experienced a feeling of deprivation and guilt.

He wondered what Elise was thinking of as she walked along by his side. She carried herself well, with a slight swing of her hips. He noticed, too, that she walked slightly apart from him: not like a wife or a fiancée but more a stranger.

She had a withdrawn look as if she were only half aware of her surroundings.

He had suggested taking her to Bellevue—it was a good morning for a tram ride outside the city and a climb up the hillside. She had never been to Bellevue, though George had once promised to take her. But he had forgotten about his promise: she said he was careless about his promises, sometimes.

During the night she had talked a good deal about her marriage, confessing to Martin that he was the only person in the world to whom she could talk so freely. She had never before told anyone her feelings towards her husband. She had tried hard to be faithful to him. And until last night she had been faithful: she asked Martin to believe her. As a Catholic she had been brought up too strictly to be promiscuous; and her marriage vows had meant a great deal to her. But she had been unable to go on being married to George Furness; he had neglected her, in every way. And when they quarrelled he beat her.

The tram swayed up the Antrim Road. To the right lay the lough, like a shield, in the grey morning. They saw a collier on the horizon, steaming out across the Irish Sea. And ahead stood the war memorial on Knockagh, breaking the line of hill and sky. They climbed the steps of Bellevue and took a winding path into the woods. Below them, through a clearing, lay the smudge of the city, arched by a crescent of hills. Walking slowly, they reached the top of the plateau.

Since they had left the hotel an hour ago, they had talked very little; but before that they had discussed Elise's marriage for hours. She was willing to leave her husband: she told Martin that she trusted him; she would do anything he wanted her to do. She abased herself before him: she was his—body and soul—to do with as he desired.

He couldn't marry her—even if she were free—and he had told her so, brutally. She didn't mind: she was willing to live with him anywhere, without marriage. They could go to England, somewhere, anywhere. She was half-crazed with desire for him; she needed him; she didn't know how she could exist without him.

The intensity of her desire astonished him: he had never imagined a woman would give herself like this. It filled him with wonder that it could be so. His own emotions, compared

233

with hers, were so thin that he felt ashamed of them. And now, after the night's sensuality, he felt drained of emotion.

They lay down on the tufty heather and looked at the city beneath and Martin took her in his arms without passion to comfort her. They lay still. Above them broken masses of soft white cloud moved steadily across the blue of the sky.

"Let's go down," Martin said, helping Elise to her feet. "Are you cold?"

"Yes."

He kissed her.

"You won't leave me, Martin?"

She turned her pale face to his and he kissed her again.

"No," he said.

She was comforted.

In the early afternoon they parted. Martin waved her goodbye as she disappeared through the barrier at the Great Northern station. Reluctantly she was returning to her husband and Martin had promised to see her the following Wednesday. They had arranged to meet in the café near the *Sentinel* office.

Thoughtfully he left the draughty railway station with its smell of stale air and crossed Great Victoria Street where two middle-aged prostitutes stood anxiously looking for custom. He passed them.

"Anything on your mind, dear?" one called after him, and he heard their hoarse laughter.

He walked across Bedford Street in the direction of the fruit markets. He had decided to walk home by the Albert Bridge, past the slaughterhouse and the electric station. He had often walked through these streets on his way from school. A dreary part of the city—especially on Sundays, when the deserted warehouses stood as silent as morgues. He reached the Catholic quarter of narrow streets backing the markets. Two streams of people were going in and out of the forbidding Byzantine-looking Roman Catholic church. He had a momentary feeling of compassion: to such people his sympathy most freely flowed.

Then his thoughts turned to Elise. Perhaps George would forgive her for staying away from him. She might be forgiven, and they might be reconciled. And that was what he hoped.

He had committed adultery with Elise; and he was ashamed

and guilt-ridden. He had encouraged a married woman to commit adultery; and he wouldn't bear the consequences of his act. He had no real, deep feelings for her. He had enjoyed her body; and her admission that she was in love with him flattered his vanity. He could so easily yield to flattery; and as easily to sensuality. He found women almost irresistible: not only their beauty of face or symmetry of body, but even their defects—a mole on the cheek, or a blemish on arm or leg. He could be equally attracted by the smell of a woman's hair or the subtle odours of her body. He was becoming more and more sensual.

He opened the door with his latch key and his mother called out at once.

"Martin!"

"Yes, Mother ... "

Her voice came from upstairs.

While he was hanging up his coat in the hall stand she came down the stairs. As soon as Martin saw her he knew something was wrong.

"Where were you? I've been trying to get you. I rang your office—"

He said nothing in reply, unable to explain his disappearance.

"Why, Mother, what's up?"

"Your father's had a stroke ... "

Martin's first thought was that his father was lying upstairs in the front bedroom, dead.

"Where is he? Is he—?"

"He's in the hospital. Oh, your poor father ... "

His mother began crying, piteously, into her rough apron: she was unable to control her grief now that Martin was home. She sat on the old worn horsehair sofa, her head bent over her apron, and wept. Martin stood helplessly by her side.

In the evening they went to the hospital. By now his mother was more in control of herself. She spoke very little, all the way across the city.

He entered the ward where his father lay. The screened-off bed was at the far end of the ward. He followed the ward sister and his mother along the polished floor, their steps echoing along the ward. There were two rows of beds, and as he passed he glanced at the patients, mostly old and middle-aged men. The ward was very quiet. Most of the patients had their eyes closed, but one old man raised a skinny arm in greeting and smiled.

The ward-sister pushed the red screens to one side and Martin saw his father lying unconscious, his grey-black hair parted differently, making his face look different. He lay on his back, breathing gently. The ward-sister said something and Martin nodded, though he didn't catch what she said.

He looked at his father's face and knew that his father was going to die.

On Monday morning he telephoned the *Sentinel* and told Mr. Watson what had happened and that he wouldn't return to the office until Tuesday, if that was convenient.

"Don't worry, Martin—take Tuesday if you want to—I can manage all right."

"Thanks."

"I hope it's not so bad as it sounds. I'm very sorry to hear about your trouble ... I'll tell Miss Garland if you haven't already done so."

"I haven't."

"Then don't bother to. I'll do it this minute."

"Thank you very much, Mr. Watson."

It was decent of the boss to help. People could be very helpful at such a time. Two or three of the neighbours had been good to his mother, giving her the sympathy she needed and running a few messages for her.

By now Martin had heard his mother's story. On Saturday afternoon, just before two o'clock, his father had collapsed in the bedroom while changing out of his working clothes. Mrs. Connolly, wondering what was keeping her husband so long, had called up to him several times. Then she had gone upstairs and found him unconscious across the bed. She had thought him dead. Somehow she had made her way out of the house, to call a neighbour.

She suddenly asked: "Where were you on Saturday, Martin?"

"I had to go to Armagh."

"Mr. Watson didn't know where you were when Mrs. McGrath from up the street got through on the telephone."

236

But to his relief his mother asked no more questions.

On Monday morning Martin visited the Royal Victoria Hospital again; this time he had persuaded his mother to stay at home. She could go in the afternoon; he had promised to take her then.

He spoke to the doctor in charge of the ward. It was as Martin feared—his father had had a very severe stroke—it was not hopeless, of course, but—well, it was difficult to tell what would be the outcome. The doctor said that in the meantime all that could be done was being done. Martin thanked him and left.

In the afternoon he went with his mother and again watched his father's silent struggle for life. After a few minutes he whispered that they should go. Mrs. Connolly shook her head.

"We can do no good, Mother."

The words appeared to him, after he had spoken them, as casual and unfeeling. But his mother paid no heed to him. She stood watching the face of her husband.

As last Martin took her arm and she allowed him to lead her away. As she left the ward she said quietly, "He'll get better—your father won't give up."

On the way home they talked about Martin's work and she seemed content to listen to stories about the various sorts of people who called in at the *Sentinel* office to insert advertisements. Once he succeeded in making her laugh.

"Your father will get well again," she said firmly, as they entered the house.

Martin made no reply, pretending to look for his handkerchief in his overcoat.

"You'll go again tonight, won't you?"

"Yes, I'll go."

She was satisfied at that. And after tea Martin left her in the company of two neighbours. He was glad to be out of the house.

When he arrived at the hospital, the ward-sister, who was sitting at a table writing, stood up quickly when she saw him.

"Mr. Connolly ... "

She came up to him and spoke gently. "Mr. Connolly, I am very sorry but I've bad news for you—"

His father was dead.

Thirty-Six

HE LEFT THE HOSPITAL AND STOOD for a moment outside the gates, undecided what to do next. He'd have to go home and tell his mother. But no need to hurry. He lit a cigarette and decided to walk down the Grosvenor Road. There were few people about at this time of the evening. He looked at his watch. Twenty to eight. He would reach the Hippodrome in about twenty minutes if he took his time; and he began to walk slowly towards the centre of the city.

He had found his father lying in the morgue. They had put the corpse in a long narrow metal drawer, a kind of temporary coffin; and he had looked at his father's face for a minute or so and then the drawer had been closed. It had all happened quickly and now he found himself almost bereft of feeling.

He had been fond of his father: but the affection he had felt he had never once really shown. Emotional display had never been encouraged in their family; had always been regarded as unbecoming and unnecessary. And now Martin was for the first time aware of the love that had bound him to the dead man. And now his father's life was over.

His mother was working in the kitchen when he came home. She looked up and, seeing his face, said: "He's dead, isn't he?"

The day after the funeral he returned to the *Sentinel* office, glad to be back at work. The last couple of days had been like a phantasmagoria—the preparations for the funeral, the visits of relatives whose names he could hardly remember, the reiteration of condolences, the long drawn-out routine of bereavement. The whole rigmarole he ironically viewed as a mockery, which he knew his father would have hated; his father had always hated fuss, and in particular funeral fuss. But now it was all over. His mother had borne up surprisingly well. She had accompanied all the relatives in their ritualistic viewing of the corpse lying in the parlour in its bright yellow coffin; she had sometimes wept a little into her handkerchief; and she had discussed, calmly enough, her husband's good qualities. Indeed her air of composure had amazed Martin: he had expected her to be overwhelmed with grief. But he was quite relieved to find her so practical, so busy with domesticities, and so matter-of-fact. As for himself, his own casualness and lack of feeling until the actual funeral service had made him feel ashamed. Only the religious service itself—both in the parlour and at the graveside—moved him.

Mr. Watson was surprised at Martin's early return to work. "Are you sure you're wise in leaving your mother alone?" he inquired, full of concern.

"Our next door neighbour is staying in the house with her—for a couple of days."

"That's a good thing. But, mind, if you want to take a day or two I can spare you—"

Martin was grateful: he had not expected the newspaper proprietor to be so generous; Mr. Watson had the reputation of being a bit tight-fisted with his staff.

Martin thanked his employer but refused the offer.

"You look a bit tired. You should go to bed early; that's my advice."

So, glad of the chance, Martin left the *Sentinel* office and made for Elm Grove. It was still only mid-afternoon; Miss Garland was out; he had the house to himself. He lay in his room for a while, stretched out in the bed, his head cradled in his arms. He could hear the wind in the trees, whistling. Already the leaves were falling, floating across the sloping lawn and piling up under the hedge. It was very quiet in the house. He began thinking of his father's life, then of his mother's; and then of his own life with them. He had grown away from them. And now that his mother was left a widow he would have to take care of her; and it would mean having to return to Belfast. Well, perhaps the time had come now for him to return home. So better leave the *Sentinel* as soon as possible: better find a job on one of the Belfast papers.

And Elise? He hadn't written to her, indeed he had hardly thought of her. He hoped that she had heard of his father's death: it was quite possible she hadn't.

A knock. He sprang from bed and opened the door. It was Mary. "Excuse me, sir, but would you like some tea?" She was carrying a tray, with the tea things on it.

"Thank you very much, Mary."

She left the tray on the little table by the window. "I'm sorry about your trouble, sir," she said, shyly. And she blushed a little. Then she backed out of the room, quietly closing the door after her, before he could reply.

Nearly a fortnight passed before he met Elise. He saw her quite by chance. He had just come out of the bank and was standing on the shallow steps when he caught sight of her. She was with her husband and they were walking quickly towards him. As they were only ten yards away he could hardly avoid them. He steeled himself for the encounter.

They were talking to each other when Elise looked up and saw him. At once she half turned her head away, and it was George who greeted him. They shook hands; then Martin held out his hand to Elise. She took his hand after the briefest of pauses, and hardly smiled. "Where have you been?" George said. "We haven't seen you for ages, have we, Elise?" Elise shook her head.

"Have you been taking a few days' holidays?"

Martin began to explain that he had been home for some days when George Furness interrupted him. "Just a moment, I want to get some cigarettes in here; then I can hear all your news. I'm dying for a smoke—"

He disappeared into a tobacconist's shop, leaving them alone. Elise immediately returned Martin's gaze, her eyes hard, her mouth tense. "What have you to say?"

Her voice was low, vibrant.

He paused. She looked at him accusingly, waiting for his answer.

"I'm sorry, Elise, but—"

For some obscure reason he was reluctant to tell her of his bereavement. She looked at him, scornfully, anticipating his excuse.

"My father had died."

"Oh."

She turned her head away, the reply was so unexpected; then she put her glove to her mouth and bit it.

"I couldn't get in touch with you. I'm sorry."

"That's all right. I thought—"

"I know what you thought."

She looked towards the shop into which her husband had gone.

"Do you want to see me again?"

"Yes, of course."

"When?"

"I don't know ... Whenever we can ... "

"I can't think ... I can't think now ... I'm sorry about your father—but ... "

She was speaking rapidly, trying hard to control her emotions. And any moment her husband would join them again.

"Tomorrow?" she said, breathless.

"Where?"

"At the café?"

"Yes. When?"

"In the morning. About eleven?"

"Yes, I'll be there."

"About eleven," she repeated.

"Is everything—?" Martin began.

"I'll tell you tomorrow."

George Furness reappeared. He was in the best of spirits because his pupils had done well in the Certificate examinations. There was no hint of tension between him and his wife. He looked relaxed, at ease with his world, in one of his most ebullient moods.

After about a quarter of an hour Elise looked at her watch. "I've shopping to do, George."

"All right, dear. When shall we see you, Martin? Will you visit us sometime this week?"

"Whenever you like."

"Well, say what evening. Thursday? Friday? Or would you rather leave it to the weekend?"

Martin replied that Thursday evening would suit him best; and when they were parting, George gave one of his mock-theatrical bows.

Next morning, just before eleven, Martin left the *Sentinel* office to keep his rendezvous. Elise was waiting for him, sitting at a corner table of the café. He joined her, feeling slightly self-conscious: afraid someone might see them together.

"Good morning." He tried to make his greeting casual, as if he had met her by chance.

"Hello."

He sat down beside her; ordered coffee from the waitress; they lit cigarettes. Elise was dressed in a well-fitting grey coat and a plum-coloured hat; a pair of fine grey gloves lay on the table in front of her. She looked very different from the other women in the café: he could see them eyeing her. Her skin was darker and her movements were quicker and more assured than theirs.

She gave the impression of being more alive. Beside her, the other women were lumpish, only half-conscious.

"Am I late?" he asked her.

"No."

"You haven't been waiting long?"

"I've just arrived."

He was waiting for her to tell him what had happened to her since they had last met. But she made no attempt to do so. At last, bending to sip her coffee, she whispered, "I can't talk here with all these people."

"Where shall we go?"

"How long can you be out of the office?"

"We're not busy."

"An hour?"

"Yes."

"Let's go by the canal."

They arranged to meet at the canal bridge on the outskirts. It was the older and quieter part of the town, with derelict warehouses and boarded-up shops and rows of narrow streets on one side of the canal, and fields on the other. They left the café separately, Elise leaving first. Martin followed after a few minutes.

They walked along the towpath in silence. Then they followed a lane which led to a copse. Halfway up the lane they stopped at an old lime kiln half hidden by trees.

He put his arms round her and kissed her and she took his kisses eagerly, impatiently, arching her body against his.

She roused him by her caresses so that he led her from the kiln into the copse. He threw his coat down on the tufted grass and they lay and made love. Then they stood against a tree and she told him that George had been glad of her return and had promised to be a better husband to her.

"I can't love him any more," she said.

"Why?"

She looked at Martin uncomprehendingly and answered, "Because I love you."

Then they began to walk slowly back towards the town.

On the Thursday he paid his promised visit to the cottage, though he didn't want to.

He felt mean in George's company now, completely ill-at-ease; and he wondered whether George suspected anything. If so, he gave no hint.

They spent most of the evening looking at George's recent paintings and discussing them. Then after supper they played the gramophone—some Lieder by Schubert.

When Elise was doing the washing up in the kitchen Martin told George about his father's death.

"Elise, Martin's father died last week."

Elise pretended not to hear; so her husband walked to the kitchen door and repeated the remark; Elise, drying a plate, came into the sitting-room, her face reflecting concern. "I'm very sorry, Martin," she said.

"And is your mother now left alone?" George asked.

"Yes."

"It is very sad for your mother," Elise said.

"What will she do?" George asked.

"I don't quite know."

"Will you stay with the *Sentinel*?"

Martin paused before answering. Then he said: "I don't think so. I think I'll have to go home—sooner or later. It all depends."

He heard a crash: Elise had dropped the plate she had been drying. At once she fell on her knees to pick the pieces up: she was trembling. Martin and George helped her gather the pieces up. They put them on a coal shovel and threw them into the bin. Elise looked upset; her hair was disarrayed.

"Is it one of our best plates?" George asked.

"No, no," she assured him.

"It gave you a scare," George laughed.

"I hate making a mess."

"Oh, it's all cleared up, isn't it?"

Soon afterwards Martin left. As he said goodnight Elise's face expressed clearly what she was feeling.

At the weekend he went home to see his mother and found her in poor spirits. She seemed to have aged suddenly, to have become almost an old woman. Perhaps it was because she wore a black dress, ill-fitting and too long, which didn't suit her.

Though she had just turned fifty her stooped shoulders and hesitant walk were those of a woman twenty years older.

On Sunday morning, after breakfast, Martin followed his mother into the parlour. It was ten o'clock, and the sun was shining on the opposite side of the street. A few children, dressed in their Sunday clothes, were walking down the street.

"Is that the MacNaughton family?" Martin inquired.

"Yes."

"I'd hardly have known them."

"They're off to their morning Sunday School," his mother remarked.

"Aren't you going to church, Mother?"

She shook her head.

"Why?"

"I don't feel like it."

She was enclosed in herself, and irritable, as if only now she realised her loss.

"Shouldn't you go to the morning service, Mother?"

She made no reply, but looked across the street.

"I'll go with you if you like," he added.

He took her by the arm and led her upstairs.

"It's a lovely morning—you'll enjoy the walk along the road—you weren't out all day yesterday either—come on, get yourself dressed."

Finally she gave in, and they walked down the street together. Martin took her arm and about halfway down the Castlereagh Road suggested they should get a tram: he was afraid she might tire herself too much. Meekly she accepted the suggestion: it was as if she had no will of her own.

The Church service pleased her: and as they left the church, the minister shook hands with them both. Then some people stopped her and she introduced them to her son, proudly. Then, before she returned home she asked Martin to walk by the Albert Bridge: she wanted to see the river and enjoy the breezes coming from the lough. She stood on the bridge for a few moments, clasping the iron balustrade with one hand, her hat with the other.

And on the way back she was quite cheerful.

In the afternoon Martin went with his mother to the graveyard at Dundonald where his father was buried. The day had turned out dull and grey, with rain threatening: and a cold wind swept over the graveyard. His mother was pathetically pottering over the wilting wreaths on the grave which already was beginning to lose its raw newly-turned look.

"You've done enough, Mother."

"Just wait, now. We can't leave it like this!"

She was adamant. Her husband's grave must look well cared for. What would people think of her if she neglected it? For she cared what people thought; she needed their respect.

Martin had laid a Sunday newspaper at her feet so that she could kneel on it; but now it was sodden and he insisted that she would ruin her good coat. She pretended indifference to that; she insisted on leaving the grave fit to be seen by any casual passer-by.

Finally she was satisfied with what she had done; then she looked at her muddy hands. "You'll need to wash them," Martin said. "There's a tap over here."

He brought her to a water tap near a hut used by the grave-diggers and gave her his handkerchief to dry her hands. He dried his own hands too, for he had helped her to rearrange some of the wreaths. And when they took the path towards the main gate the threatening rain was already beginning to fall, enveloping the whole of the exposed graveyard.

Thirty-Seven

THAT AUTUMN MARTIN AND ELISE CONTINUED their clandestine meetings. They usually met on Wednesday evenings in an out-of-the-way pub on the outskirts of the town. On Wednesdays George took an evening class at the technical college, and Elise came in the bus with him. During the two hours he was teaching she was supposed to be at the local cinema. Occasionally, indeed, when the weather was wet, she actually did go and Martin met her there as if by chance. But usually they spent the evening walking along country by-roads and stopping to make love in a secluded spot: a derelict quarry; the porch of a deserted mansion; a pathway, covered with brambles, leading to an ancient Gaelic mound.

He wondered whether George suspected them, but Elise was sure he didn't.

"He's bound to, sooner or later," Martin told her.

"Well, if he does—"

She gave a petulant shrug and said she didn't care.

Sometimes they quarrelled and walked along in silence; and once or twice they decided to break things off but, when the moment of parting came, one or other weakened.

Then at the beginning of December, Martin applied for and was offered a job as a reporter for a Belfast morning paper. He told Elise while they were having a drink. She became very pale and her hand trembled slightly as she lifted her glass.

"You have accepted it?"

"Yes."

They were silent for a short while. Then she said: "You are glad, I suppose?"

"No."

"I know you are."

"I'm not."

He told her he was leaving the *Sentinel* for one reason only: his mother was living alone and she needed him.

"Let's have another drink."

He called the barman and ordered two more gin-and-limes. They drank in silence.

"I'm sorry, Elise."

She made no reply.

They left the pub and walked along without speaking. Martin offered her a cigarette: she refused it. The expression on her face was one of suffering, of hurt pride; Martin was unable to console her.

"I'm sorry, Elise," he repeated.

"Please ... "

She wanted no sympathy from him; she wanted to make him suffer too, the way she was suffering. He tried to put his arm round her as they reached the darkness at the end of the town. She stiffened; he withdrew his arm; she walked along as if his presence no longer meant anything to her. Then, with a glance at her luminous wristwatch, she turned on her heel and they retraced their steps to the ill-lit street leading to the Square where her husband was to meet her.

"Goodbye," she said suddenly.

There was no feeling in her voice and without turning her head she left his side.

He returned to Elm Grove slowly, his hands stuffed in his pockets. So this is how it has ended, he thought gloomily. Well, in what other way could it end? It was sordid and furtive and distasteful. It was everything he detested. He had yielded to his impulses, had given way to Elise throughout. Perhaps he had even encouraged her, though she had needed little encouragement. If he had committed a sin he had been sorely tempted. *Qui s'excuse, s'accuse.* But was the affair so sinful? Shameful; yes, he had felt shame because he had deceived George; and any form of deception was ugly. And now Elise had left him, in resentful fury. The whole miserable business was over and within a couple of months he might be able to forget it.

He walked up the hill towards Elm Grove and through the gate and along the unkempt leaf-strewn drive.

O how warm and soft and beautiful her body ...

It seemed to him that his last four weeks on the *Sentinel* staff would never pass. Winter had set in early, a succession of cold and wet November days.

Mr. Watson was displeased to learn of Martin's resignation. "I'd no notion you intended leaving me," he grumbled. "I thought you were happy with us."

Martin was embarrassed and made no reply.

"I can offer you a rise. If that's what you want, why didn't you ask me?"

It didn't seem to occur to Mr. Watson that Martin was tired of working on the *Sentinel*; was tired of the town; was eager for a change.

Mr. Watson then complained about the difficulty of finding another reporter at this time of the year. "You've left me in a fix—you realise that?"

He appeared to take the resignation almost as a personal insult. He had had no idea that Martin would leave the paper so soon—the *Sentinel* had a reputation for keeping its staff.

"You've definitely made up your mind?"

"I'm afraid so, Mr. Watson."

"Well then, there's no good talking about it any more." And off he shuffled to his desk, muttering.

Martin left Elm Grove with regret: Miss Garland had been kind to him; had given him the run of her house and the privacy he wanted. As he left for the train he shook hands with her and with Mary.

"You'll come and visit us?" Miss Garland said.

"I'd be glad to."

"That's a promise."

"Goodbye," Mary said, shyly.

He had sent his luggage off the day before, and so was free to walk to the station.

The railway station was a whitewashed barn-like structure noted for its draughtiness on even the stillest summer day. This Saturday afternoon a cold westerly wind was blowing and the few travellers paced up and down the platform trying to get heat into their chilled feet. Already the train was five minutes late.

A woman entered the ill-lit platform; she was muffled up and looked inquiringly up and down.

There was something familiar about her; she walked towards him. It was Elise.

She came up to him, along the draughty platform, and faced him.

"I wanted to see you before you left—"

She hesitated. She had been hurrying so much that she was out of breath and could scarcely speak.

"My bus was late. I thought I'd missed you."

"How did you know I was on this train?"

"I rang Miss Garland yesterday."

"She didn't tell me."

"I told her not to. I made some excuse or other. You see, I've no pride left. I had to see you. Will you forgive me?"

"There's nothing to forgive, is there?"

"You're not angry with me?"

"No."

The train could be heard whistling in the distance. It came nearer and hissed into the platform.

"Let me write to you, Martin," she pleaded. "Please let me write to you!"

He jumped into an empty compartment; Elise's pale face looked up at him; he stretched out his hands and took hers. He was filled with compassion for her and bent forward and kissed her.

The train slowly began to move forward and he watched her standing, an isolated figure, on the platform. She waved once, turned, and disappeared into the darkness.

Thirty-Eight

ON MONDAY MARTIN STARTED HIS NEW job. He felt slightly nervous on the first day despite the fact that he already knew most of the reporters and sub-editors by sight and was on speaking terms with those who frequented The Duke. In addition, Edgar Cochrane, who had recommended him to the editor, was chief sub and a person of importance in the building. Edgar had grown corpulent since his marriage (he had married a young widow from Lancashire) and now hated any reference to his slightly Bohemian past. He wore horn-rimmed glasses, bought well-cut dark suits, and had become the successful journalist. On Martin's first morning, Edgar was deputed to show him over the premises. The offices were large and airy, with a main front office as the paper's showpiece. There, in large black-framed photographs, were arrayed former editors: serious-minded middle-aged and elderly Victorian figures hidden behind a tangle of beards and high collars that held their necks imprisoned. Martin was aware of the traditions of the paper he had joined, and was aware, too, that most of his colleagues, when sober, mildly mocked them and, when drunk, bitterly assailed them. He found the reporters and subs on the staff the usual variegated lot: most of the middle-aged ones steady and conscientious, intent on bettering

251

themselves if possible, and interested in their homes and hobbies; some of the younger men as irregular as the hours they normally had to work. They drank a good deal, were fond of gambling, and occasionally enjoyed a wild night out.

In his first few weeks Martin went with one or other of his colleagues into The Duke to spend time during the day. It was a convenient and friendly gathering place with its low wooden ceiling, its two portholes separating the bars, its leaded windows overlooking the narrow tumbledown entry, its atmosphere of a seaman's pub that had mysteriously strayed too far from the docks.

It was to The Duke that Martin brought a letter he had just received from Elise: she had sent it to his office address. But as three other reporters shared an office table with him he was unable to read it in peace. So he slipped out to the pub: at half-past eleven in the morning he found it almost deserted. There he read and re-read it. It began:

Martin darling,

A month has passed since you left me. It has been a terrible month for me and I have tried hard not to write to you. I wanted to put you out of my life. But, in the end, I had to write. I am writing to you on the morning after a night during which I have had little sleep. I found it hard to sleep, just as I find it hard now to think and write. I should have written this to you in French but because we have so seldom spoken French to each other I have written it in English.

Last night George came home drunk again. He began abusing me; and I called him foul names. Then he hit me, and I fell and sprained my wrist. During our quarrel everything came out. I told him I could never love him again, that I loved you, and that we had made love together. I should not have told him anything about us but I did. And now I must decide what I want to do. I love you; I want to live with you; I know I could be happy with you. But you? I don't know what you feel. I know how I feel towards you, and I know my husband is now a stranger to me. Love, says Stendhal, without hope, is bound to die, and perhaps I have no right to hope. I am yours to take if you want to. I write to you what is in my heart even though I may never know what is in yours. I want to see you once more, perhaps for the last time. I will come to Belfast on Friday on the morning train that arrives at 10.15. Will you meet me at the station, please, oh please? You see I have no pride left, only my hunger for you and my loneliness ...

He put the letter in his pocket, finished his whiskey, and walked through Commercial Court into Donegall Street. As he went up the street he bumped against a man in a muffler. "Watch where you're goin', mister!" the man shouted after him. Muttering an apology, Martin hurried along as if dazed by too much sunlight.

He stood waiting for the train; for he had arrived at the Great Northern station nearly a quarter of an hour too early. He had bought a packet of cigarettes at the kiosk, had scanned the titles of the books at the bookstall, had got an *Irish Times* and looked at the first page without taking in a single word of the headlines. And now, the paper screwed up in his hand, he nervously paced in and out of the station. He felt disturbed and worried; he also felt strangely excited. In his pocket he had Elise's letter: he had brooded on it ever since yesterday when he had first opened it; and had experienced shame and remorse every time he had read it. She wanted him to marry her; but how could he? Anyway, did he want to marry her? And what about George?

The train puffed in. The ticket collector opened the gate; doors of compartments were opened; the passengers began rushing out.

The train was full and the platform quickly filled. Martin couldn't see Elise anywhere: perhaps she had missed this train or had changed her mind; or perhaps something had upset her plan. He kept looking along the platform for her.

Suddenly ten yards away he saw Elise's husband staring coldly at him; George was wearing a new cap and a new grey mackintosh.

"Hello."

"Hello."

George stopped and faced Martin. The faces of both were pale and set; and George's jaw was twitching slightly.

"Hello," he repeated. "You didn't expect to see me?"

Martin made no reply. George lit a cigarette and said, "Where can we talk?"

"Wherever you like."

"There's a pub across the way, isn't there?"

"Yes."

Without another word they left the station, crossed Great Victoria Street, and climbed the stairs of Robinson's bar. The barman came towards their table, and George ordered a whiskey for himself.

"What'll you have?" he said wryly. Then, despite the presence of the barman, and before Martin could reply, he added venomously: "You've had my wife—so you'll hardly object to having a drink."

"A whiskey," Martin said.

The barman brought the whiskies.

Then George spoke, his face very pale. "I know all about your affair with my wife, and I want it to stop. That's why I'm here—"

There was a pause. He looked at Martin.

"Well, what have you to say?"

"What can I say?"

"You admit it."

"Yes."

The two men faced each other, equally tense; and Martin thought that George at that moment was going to hit him. Instead he lifted his glass of whiskey, sat poised with it as if he intended throwing the contents in Martin's face, then slowly raised it to his lips and drank it with one gulp.

"You must promise never to see my wife again," he said, his voice hoarse with suppressed anger.

Slowly Martin nodded his willingness; and, finishing his whiskey, said, "I don't want to see your wife."

Both their glasses were now empty, so Martin caught the barman's eye and shouted across the bar: "Same again."

The drinks were brought, and for nearly five minutes the two sat silently drinking. Then George said: "I've known about you and Elise for quite a while."

"Have you?"

"Yes, I have. I didn't interfere because—" Martin waited for

254

him to finish his remark. "—it's not the first time she's laid away. And it won't be the last. I suppose she made the running with you—"

Martin said nothing.

"—I know she did. So I'm not blaming you. Not altogether. I blame her and I blame myself. She'd go to bed with somebody and if it hadn't been you it would've been somebody else. Are you in love with her? Oh, you needn't answer, for I told her you weren't, and I suspect I'm right. But if you are, just say you are. And if you want to marry her I'll not stand in your way."

He paused: Martin said nothing.

"It's bloody funny—" George said, laughing harshly.

"What is?" Martin asked, puzzled.

"Coming down on that train I remembered how we used to talk about women. I think I once called you a Puritan. D'you know why?"

"No."

"Because that's what I am myself. I'm not that much interested in sex. Never was. I'd rather paint a nude than do her."

He raised his hand, called the barman over, and ordered another drink, a double; and as they slowly sipped their whiskey the tension between them began to evaporate.

"You know, I thought something like this would happen. It was bound to."

"Why?"

"I don't satisfy her any more. That's the trouble—we don't come together—and now we don't try. I suppose we'll have to part, sooner or later?"

He became morose: the thought of his failure depressed him; for now his marriage held little promise of fulfilment. As he talked, some of his resentment and anger disappeared. After a while he fell silent: and Martin, though eager to leave the pub, felt unable to make the first move. Finally, after a long interval in which neither spoke, George Furness rose a little unsteadily to his feet.

"Well, that's that," he said grimly. "It's funny, in a way, what happens to us all. We seem to lose in the long run—the whole bloody lot of us."

He struggled into his cap and coat, turned his back, and then made his way slowly down the stairs. Martin stood and watched him cross the street and make towards the pillars of the Great Northern station, his hands stuck in his pockets, his head bent forward, his shoulders hunched.

Once he lifted his head as if to sniff the air; once he seemed to slip on the pavement; then finally he disappeared between the portals of the station.

Thirty-Nine

HE HAD GIVEN GEORGE FURNESS HIS promise: and he intended keeping it. It would not be difficult now that he had a new job. He had plenty to think about without involving himself further in this affair. It was finished and done with: he considered himself both betrayer and betrayed. Elise and George would have to work out their own destinies—together or apart. He had seen the last of both and hoped Elise wouldn't write to him again.

A fortnight afterwards she did write: a pathetic letter describing how her husband had physically forced her to confess about her rendezvous with Martin; and she pleaded with Martin to reply to a *poste restante* address. He tore her letter up and she never wrote again.

But sometimes late at night, while he was reading, his thoughts turned to her. And about a month afterwards he met Sam Houston—now teaching Art in the College of Technology—and was invited to spend an evening with him. He intented to ask Fred and Betty as well.

He accepted and learnt there that George Furness had gone to a job in Canada.

"He's a restless fellow," Sam remarked. "Married a French girl, didn't he?"

"Yes."

"What was she like?"

Martin said that she was very pleasant and that he had often visited their cottage.

"He's a damn good painter," Sam said. "A fine technician, with plenty of ideas, but somehow his work just fails. I don't know exactly why."

As for himself, Sam no longer aspired to be an artist: he was content to teach.

Martin noticed that Betty had grown plump since the days when Martin had first known her and her sister Jean. So he asked about Jean and learnt that she too had married and was now living in Glasgow.

"Her husband owns a garage. I'll be writing to her next week, so I'll tell her I've seen you—she likes to hear all my gossip and, believe me, I haven't so much to tell her these days. I'm not out and about very much, I'm afraid."

She smiled what she imagined to be a secret smile at her husband: Fred had already told Martin about his wife's pregnancy (it was her fourth) and Martin therefore pretended not to understand. Then she added: "I always thought Jean had a soft spot for you."

Martin laughed and questioned the truth of the remark.

"Oh, yes, she had. I know my own sister."

"Women believe they're never wrong in such matters," Fred said.

"We never are," Betty said.

"Never?" Martin queried.

"No, never, never, never."

"Why do you say that?" Martin asked.

"Men are really such fools when it comes to telling how a woman feels."

"I suppose we are," Martin said.

He wondered how much Betty really knew about her own sister. Women could know a lot about one another but they could be ignorant of quite a lot too.

"You must come and see us," Betty said as he was leaving.

"Yes, do," Fred said.

Their invitation seemed to be genuine, and Martin's acceptance equally so, but as he walked along the Stranmillis

Road he wondered whether he would ever visit them. And he thought it unlikely.

Day by day and week by week he reported the significant and insignificant events in his native city. At first he enjoyed doing court work; but after a while it palled. The sight of suffering human beings initially aroused his curiosity—he felt he was vicariously enlarging his experience of life—but finally he began to be scornful of his visits to the Crumlin Road. He was critical of the judgments given by the magistrates and judges; he pitied the juries; his sympathy went to the victims in the dock, the unfortunate, the frightened, the weak, the vicious. They were, all of them, victims of society or of their own passions, and he found it hard to judge or condemn them. He refused to believe himself a sentimentalist: he vehemently claimed to be a realist. Indeed he detested sentimentality and considered the whole process of law-making and interpretation to be a matter for scornful laughter. More and more he became familiar with the faces and voices of the public figures in the city: and after a while he regarded them as ridiculous marionettes. Martin's colleagues, like himself, were completely cynical about the affairs of the city: all the juggling appeared to them merely an intricate and obvious positioning for power. And power meant private profit. And over whiskies and pints the journalists often heartily laughed at the doings and sayings of those on whom they had to report daily.

One evening, late in April, Martin was drinking with half-a-dozen reporters when the talk turned to their own work. "We're intellectual flunkies," said a barrel-like reporter called Gallen.

"What did you say, Joe?" someone asked.

"You heard me, for Christ's sake!"

"Repeat it."

"No!" Gallen bellowed.

"Go on. What's keeping you back?"

"Why the hell should I?"

"You've been repeating yourself for twenty years, Joey boy, up at the big house, haven't you?"

Gallen, goaded, took a deep breath, cleared his lungs, and shouted along the bar—"Flunkies! That's what we are! The whole bloody lot of us!"

"Joe, you said intellectual flunkies—I want to know where the intellectual part comes in. Never noticed it, b'Jasus, myself."

Gallen finished his pint and wiped the froth from his mouth with the back of his hand, staggering and bullocking his way towards the lavatory. On his return, he stood unsteadily by Martin's side, looking helplessly at his smiling colleagues now that he was no longer holding a pint. Martin, standing near the counter, asked, "What are you having, Joe?"

"Do I have to tell you your alphabet?" Joe retorted, his hot breath steaming into Martin's face. Martin ordered a pint.

"You're suffering from premature inebriation, Joe," someone shouted.

Gallen waited till Martin's pint was placed in his hands, nodding his thanks.

"What's that? Repeat yourself."

He gave a belch, and laughter spread down the bar.

"Premature inebriation, Joe."

Gallen smiled a slow rosy smile. "Premature ejaculation you mean."

He broke into a gale of laughter at his joke, juggling his pint as his whole body shook, and nudging Martin with his free hand.

Martin's colleagues had not a great opinion of him as a journalist: they thought he lacked a story-sense, and had no flair for a scoop. Nevertheless they admitted he could write a well-turned article on a subject that interested him—always provided he wasn't writing against the clock. He preferred to write slowly and carefully and often wondered whether he was in the right job. Perhaps he should have been a teacher or a doctor; but he had chosen his work and thought it improbable that he would now change to something else.

His mother had aged a great deal since the death of her husband. She missed him about the house, especially in the evening, and she complained of being lonely, for Martin was often out on an assignment. The evenings he was at home he spent reading and she said he read far too much—it was bad for his eyesight. She liked to talk to him and he would let her chatter away, and in his turn he would ask her questions about her parents, grandparents and even her great grandparents.

"Think back, Mother. Do you really remember your great granny?"

"Oh, yes."

"What exactly do you remember about her?"

And Mrs. Connolly would recall her earliest memories of what she referred to as 'her side' of the family. She also knew a lot about the 'other side'—the Connollys—but she considered her husband's family socially inferior to her own. Her great grandfather had owned a large drapery shop in Armagh City, a fact that she kept referring to. There had once been money in her family, but it had all been squandered by her grandfather who had taken to drink and ruined the family. She had, as a result, a horror of drunkenness and couldn't understand why any man could ever degrade himself by drinking. She couldn't abide even the smell of it. She knew that Martin took a drink and warned him that the habit would get a grip on him, sooner or later.

"I know what I'm talking about, Martin, and nothing you say will make me change my mind."

"But I hardly drink at all, Mother."

"I tell you it'll get a grip on you; you'll get a liking for the stuff; and then you'll find you won't be able to break off the habit—"

He shook his head, annoyed that she had so little trust in him; and he told her sharply he was no longer a child. So they had occasional tiffs—about drink or smoking or late hours or non-attendance at church. His mother believed that his life was not what it should be, and her disapproval irritated him. He tried to see her point of view, but hid from her the activities she disapproved of. So he smoked little while he was at home and occasionally he even attended a church service on a wet Sunday morning. But that was the extent of his compromise to what he considered to be her prejudices or her narrow-mindedness.

He was earning more than his father had ever done; and his mother wondered whether he was thinking of marrying. She broached the subject several times, in a roundabout way, and told him that she would be very glad to see him bringing home a girl: and would indeed welcome her.

"I know you'll want to get married some day, Martin."

"Why are you so sure, Mother?"

"Oh, a mother just knows."

"Well, I'm not thinking of marrying at the moment."

"Haven't you a girl?"

She was unable to conceal her curiosity about his relationships with women. For he never mentioned any girl to her: and this piqued her. She wanted to be in his confidence: and because he told her nothing she suspected the worst—that he might be interested in loose women. When this thought flickered across her mind she suppressed it at once.

"Don't you want to get married?"

"Not at the moment."

He brushed off her inquiries and made clear to her, by his show of irritability, that he had no desire to confide in her.

Sometimes, however, he was able to please her. For instance, he had encouraged her to attend the Philharmonic concerts in the Ulster Hall; and she looked forward to hearing the *Messiah* every December. She always dressed up for this occasion with great care. When she took Martin's arm as they went up the aisle to their seats she was very proud. He also wanted her to go to plays in the Grand Opera House but she always refused his offers. She excused herself, saying that she found plays hard to follow.

Her puritanism was deeply ingrained. That summer she refused Martin's invitation to go with him to France. He suggested that they stay a week in Brittany and a week in Paris; but she said she would much prefer a fortnight in Donaghadee.

"What would I do in France, when I couldn't talk to a single soul there?"

"Then you don't mind going to Donaghadee alone, Mother?"

"Mrs. Magee will go with me."

Mrs. Magee lived four doors away and was also a widow.

So Martin found himself free to go to the continent alone.

Forty

IN HIS LATE TWENTIES HE WAS a well-built, fairly tall young man, rather carelessly dressed. Usually he had a serious expression on his face as he took his short morning walk before boarding a tram to his office. He habitually walked quickly and purposefully, sometimes frowning slightly as he thought how he had wasted the previous evening talking instead of doing something worthwhile. His life was slipping by. Soon he would be middle-aged, set in his mental habits, unable to grasp a new idea or make a fresh attempt to increase his knowledge of the quickly-changing world which it was his concern to comprehend and conquer. He would never be satisfied with himself until he felt as certain as it was humanly possible to be of the 'reality' of life. This word 'reality' was far too difficult: a word that he had struggled with in books of philosophy.

He tried to think of what 'reality' held in store for him at this moment. The morning sun was up, making the tramlines gleam like swords. People were passing. Approaching him was an old woman wearing a black shawl round her head: and carrying a milk jug. He stared at her as she passed, oblivious of his interest. Her face was dried yellow with age, creased into crinkles, her straggling hair a dirty white. He wondered what her thoughts were. Certainly she was absorbed by something. What had been her life? Whatever it had been it was now near its close. He saw her shuffle into a small grocer's shop, muttering to herself. Was her 'reality' his? Had life defeated her?

Du bist wie eine Blume ...

The melody ran through his mind. He tried to think what her life had been but was unable to. Then, on an impulse, he turned to the right at Castlereagh Place and went down Lord Street. He had a sudden longing to see Chatfield Street.

He passed the street known as 'The Gut' which he had once feared to enter. What a slum! He felt indignant that it should exist. Shamefully he glanced into the tiny kitchens, the bare wooden stairways at the front doors.

He reached Chatfield Street. It had not altered since his childhood, except that the doors were more worn, not so well painted, and the brass knockers more tarnished. He saw no-one who knew him. He reached Geary's shop. Above the window was the legend CORNER STORE, and he remembered his mother saying that the Gearys had sold their shop. Incredible that strangers should own this shop, should serve behind the counter, should handle the scales he had watched a thousand times. But Geary's was no more: this simulacrum struck him as a ridiculous substitute! He hurried past the pub with its peeling brown gable against which the drunks used to stand brawling and singing 'Nelly Dean' into the dark night.

This July morning the street and corner and shop and pubs that belonged to his boyhood seemed so changed that he wanted to erase them at once from his mind. He stood for five minutes at the tram stop at Templemore Avenue looking extremely thoughtful, conscious that his boyhood was far behind him, that what his imagination still cherished was more splendid than the tawdriness he had just seen.

He arrived in the office and learnt that he had a 'marking' for the afternoon—a Corporation meeting at the City Hall; in the evening the Opera House. He turned over the paper to the advertisements and noted that the play was an amateur production of *Candida*. Well, he would enjoy Shaw after the certain boredom of the Corporation. He looked out of the dust-stained window into the sunlit street and began to wish that he'd taken his holiday in July rather than in August; this year he couldn't decide where to go. Indeed, he'd no overwhelming desire to go anywhere. And yet he must go somewhere. He needed a change ... He listlessly watched the passers-by on the pavement opposite; all seemed so absorbed in their own lives, he thought, and looked so careworn and worried. As if their existences mattered! They were born, existed, and died.

Most of them were quite unconscious of the multitude of social and historical facts and values that had conditioned them; were content to try to solve their immediate petty problems; were only dimly aware that their society was fundamentally wrong and ill adapted to their needs and must be changed and they themselves with it ...

Suddenly he jumped up from his chair, overturning it with a crash. He had just seen Claire! She had passed by on the pavement opposite! His heart was thumping against his chest, like a soft hammer, making him breathless.

He dashed out of the office and ran down the stairs, his hair flying, his legs hardly seeming to touch the ground. He found himself in the street. Where was she? Where had she gone? Had he missed her?

He ran across the road, after taking one wild glance at the traffic, and raced along the pavement in the direction she had gone. He ran about two hundred yards, dodging in and out like a footballer, aware that people were looking at him as he passed. But he didn't care in the least what they thought: he was obsessed by a single thought—Claire Taylor was back home, and he had actually seen her, for one fleeting, almost miraculous moment; and he must see her again; must see her and talk to her and hear her voice. His whole being urged him towards her.

Suddenly he took a stitch in his side. He slowed down to a walking pace. He'd missed her. She'd disappeared down some side street or entered a shop or had crossed the road or ... He looked round despondently, his hair falling over his forehead. His moment of exaltation was over; he was experiencing now a moment of despair. He stopped at the Junction, looking up Castle Street, at the shoppers entering Anderson & McAuleys and he stood for at least ten minutes.

Slowly he walked back to his office, in utter dejection.

And slowly the remainder of the morning passed, her image before his eyes. He ate a tasteless lunch in a café in Wellington Place, a book propped up, unread, against a salt-cellar. He attended the meeting in the City Hall and heard words spoken and replied to: they might just as well have been spoken in a language he was incapable of understanding. And coming out of the City Hall he ran into a procession of men and women carrying makeshift banners and shouting slogans: "We won't pay! Not a penny more!" The procession was parading round the city in protest at an increase in rents. He watched the working-class marchers. Instead of passing him, their leaders turned towards the front of the City Hall.

"Good for them!"

The sight of three or four hundred men and women fighting for something that mattered moved him strongly. Many of them were unemployed and drably dressed; most of the women and girls looked ugly and coarse, and their voices, raised in unison, sounded raucous.

"Good for them," he repeated, as the tail of the procession passed him.

The Opera House was less than half-full; and the audience seemed more interested in the players than in the play; and the players too seemed more interested in themselves than in the play. But Martin was incapable of passing judgement on anything: being totally devoid of interest in play, players, or audience. At the interval he left and returned to his office to write up his copy. He did so quickly and as briefly as possible. He looked at his watch. Five past ten. Should he telephone her? Should he write to her? Already he had looked up the telephone directory to check if the Taylors were still at the same address. Or had they fallen further still?

He put his hand on the telephone, but it rested there.

Wasn't Claire Taylor now called Mrs. Mansell? She was the wife of an English doctor. A married woman. Perhaps a mother. He had no right to intrude on her life again. He was behaving foolishly and irrationally, but he wanted to see her again, wanted to hear her voice. And why not?

But his hand remained on the telephone, his courage failing.

A night and a day passed; and her image was constantly before him as he went about his work. When he walked along the street he imagined that she would appear before him, and that she would be alone, and that what he longed for would come about. It was intolerable to think that Claire and he were living in the same city, and that he had seen her but hadn't spoken to her. He must meet her.

So, a couple of evenings later, he walked along the Malone Road and reached the avenue where the Taylors now lived.

He passed up and down in front of the Taylors' house at least six times without seeing a sign of Claire; and in a mood of depression he walked back towards the centre of the city.

Passing Sandy Row he noticed a group of small boys carrying planks and boxes and then he remembered the date— the eleventh of July: the night that bonfires were always lit. As a boy he had enjoyed gathering wood for the 'eleventh night' and had enjoyed watching the blaze flaring up as high as the roofs of the houses. Most of all he had enjoyed the singing and dancing round the fire into the early hours of the twelfth of July morning when with smoke-sore eyes and grimy face he had fallen exhausted into bed: to be awakened after what seemed only a few minutes' sleep by the sound of the bands and the marching of the Orangemen along the Albertbridge Road.

Now the annual demonstration in the city held no excitement for him: he had long ago rejected all it stood for. It seemed to him that his native city had betrayed its true tradition, the tradition of 1798, when Protestants and Catholics had proclaimed their faith in a 'brotherhood of affection' among all Irish men.

Exhausted by his long walk across the city he stretched himself out on the sofa and closed his eyes in weariness. He felt miserable and made little effort to hide his misery.

His mother, the *Telegraph* on her lap, regarded him.

"You were workin' late, Martin," she said, taking off her glasses, her tone a little sharp.

"Yes, I was," he snapped.

He took off his shoes, sighed, and put a cushion beneath his head.

"What's the matter, son?"

"I'm tired. That's all."

"Are you hungry?"

He told her he wanted no supper. He would go to bed almost at once; he had to be at work early in the morning. She brought him a glass of milk and told him to drink it. To please her he did so. Then he rose to go to bed.

"Are you unhappy, Martin?" she asked.

"Unhappy?" he repeated, his voice bitter.

"Yes."

"Why should I be?"

"I don't know, Martin. But you are. You never smile these days—or laugh—or anything. I've watched you. There's something troublin' you. Why don't you tell me what it is? Mebbe I can help you."

He shook his head, denying his misery; but his mother was so persistent that he became irritable and told her to leave him alone.

"I'm too tired to talk."

"All right," she replied, hurt. "I'll lock up."

He left her and walked up the dark narrow stairs to his room, feeling drained of any desire for life.

He was in torment. He felt he could endure it no longer. He decided to risk telephoning Claire.

He did so two mornings later, when the office was quiet. He was trembling as he spoke.

"May I speak to Mrs. Mansell?"

"Speaking."

It was her voice.

His mouth was dry: he was unable to utter a word in reply, and he heard Claire's voice again.

"Hello. Who's speaking, please?"

"Martin ... "

"Who?"

She appeared not to have heard properly.

"Martin ... Connolly ... "

"Oh."

A pause.

"How are you, Martin?" she asked, her voice warm and friendly.

"Very well."

"It's very nice to hear you. How did you know I was home?"

"I saw you the other day."

"Where?"

"In town."

"Really. Why didn't you speak to me?"

"I couldn't. I tried to, but ... "

"Oh, I'm sorry. We must meet—" She hesitated. "That is if you'd like to—"

"Yes," he said. "Yes, that's why I'm ... I'd love to. We must ... Where?"

In his excitement he was unable to suggest a meeting place.

"I've to call in at the Linen Hall library this morning—"

"At what time?"

"About half eleven."

"Good. I'll see you there ... "

He looked at his watch. In less than an hour he would see her. Slightly trembling with excitement he lit a cigarette and began walking about the paper-strewn office, his imagination on fire.

Forty-One

HE CLIMBED THE STAIRS OF THE Linen Hall library and looked round the desk where the books were received and returned. He could see no-one remotely resembling Claire either at the desk or at the shelves. He looked at the old-fashioned clock and checked it with his watch. He was early: only twenty-five past. So lifting a book at random he sat down at a desk by a window and waited.

Punctually, at half eleven, she appeared. She stood at the top of the stairs looking round, her back to him. Then she turned and faced him. He rose and walked quickly towards her and she came forward with outstretched hand.

He experienced a feeling of intense joy: all his senses preternaturally alive. He gazed at her: and she was smiling: and still they had nothing to say to each other. Then she spoke.

"Have you been waiting for me long?"

The commonplace question made him smile and he gave her a smiling answer.

"For years, I think."

"Well, we can't stand here much longer," she replied, laughing. "Where shall we go?"

"To Campbell's."

"Oh, so you still go there?"

"Yes, occasionally."

Campbell's—one of the cafés they used to frequent—was only a few steps from the Linen Hall library. They took a table on the ground floor; Martin went to the counter and got the coffees; Claire opened a packet of cigarettes.

"Do you smoke now?" he asked, a little surprised.

"Yes, I'm afraid I do."

"When did you start?"

"Oh, a couple of years ago."

He lit her cigarette. As he did so he noticed her wedding ring: she followed his glance and blushed.

"I suppose you disapprove."

He thought at first that her remark referred to her marriage, but then decided that she intended only to refer to her smoking.

"Yes, I do! Though why I should I don't know. It's quite irrational—if a man smokes, why not a woman?"

"I disapprove of myself," she said.

He looked at her: and she added quickly, "Oh, I've changed."

He looked into her face. She had been a girl when he had last seen her—a virgin—and now she was a mature woman of twenty-seven. She certainly had changed: indeed her face had lost some of its freshness and its youthfulness. She looked paler and thinner.

"I don't find much change in you, Martin."

That she had just called him Martin, as she used to do, gave him pleasure.

"Don't you?"

She shook her head.

"No, except—"

"Except what?"

"You look—well ... you look more confident of yourself."

"Oh, I've more self-conceit," he said, lightly. He felt extraordinarily happy in the presence of this woman who now was beyond his reach. She had always given him happiness; with a look, with a word, with a touch of her hands. And now, he still wanted her, to love and to cherish.

His longing for her was still intense, a feeling he couldn't control. It was beyond his will to do so. And yet he knew she had never really been a beautiful woman: and now, after her

271

marriage, she might be thought almost plain. She'd certainly lost some of her complexion; her hair was mousey; her face expressed suffering. He continued to look at her, in wonderment, hardly seeing what she wore or hearing what she said. To be in her presence was bliss.

And he became aware of Claire's own pleasure in his company. She must love him: her candid blue eyes told him so. And he'd never known her guilty of deception.

They gossiped; they drank two more cups of coffee; an hour passed. Claire asked him questions about people they'd known; she asked him about his work; and she talked about her own family. Her mother had died three years ago; her father had retired from business, was now in poor health and lived with Claire's sister, Ruth, who hadn't married. Her father lived a very quiet life now, occasionally playing bridge with his neighbours and seeing a few of his former business friends. His linen business had slumped badly just before his retirement and the family wasn't well-off. As for Claire's brother, he had given up his political ambitions, was married and doing well at the Bar.

Eagerly he listened to her bits of domestic news. Of her own life she hardly spoke. Where was her husband, Dr. Mansell? Was he in Belfast with her? She hadn't mentioned his name yet. Had she borne him children? Was she a mother?

She looked at her wristlet watch: it showed half-past twelve.

"I must go, I'm afraid."

She rose. The thought that perhaps she was leaving him for good terrified him. He must see her again; he must tell her so; he must find out if they could meet somewhere, somehow.

"Please, I must see you again, Claire," he pleaded. "May I?"

They looked at each other. He was appealing to her mercy. He was completely in her power. He desired, above all, to share her life.

"Why not? We've always been friends, haven't we?"

"Yes. But your husband?"

She remained silent for a moment. Then said, "I've left my husband."

As she spoke, a flicker of pain passed over her face, and her eyes were brimming with tears.

"I didn't know, Claire. I'm sorry—"

But in his heart he was rejoicing.

Before they parted they agreed to meet on the following Saturday; he suggested they could have a light lunch at Campbell's and afterwards set off for somewhere along the coast. Then, formally, like acquaintances, they shook hands and she disappeared into the Saturday shopping crowd.

He returned to Campbell's and climbed the stairs. Round a table at the window sat a group of people he knew slightly—a freelance journalist, two or three schoolteachers, an actor, and a couple of young businessmen. This part of Campbell's—the top floor—was the centre of the meagre intellectual life of the city. One of the schoolteachers signalled him to join the group: and he did so. The talk was about a new magazine that might be started.

"It should criticise everything," someone said.

"Exactly."

"Didn't Plato say something about that?"

"Don't ask me—I wouldn't know—but I'm sure he did, if you say so—"

"You mean something about the unexamined life being no life at all."

"I suppose Plato meant that ... yes ... "

"But, tell me, what should this magazine be called?"

"Why not *Criticism*? Just that. Isn't that what we're after?"

"No, that wouldn't do."

"You're a journalist, Connolly. Any ideas?"

Martin shook his head and tried to feign interest in the discussion. But he'd heard only a jumble of disconnected phrases. He suggested that the choice of title was important, and everybody agreed; and then the group began to drift away and he found himself alone. Normally he would have been interested in the founding of a new magazine: but this morning had been far from normal. He was quite unable to think normally, and even to behave normally was an effort. Gossip about local journalism or politics or theatre or music hadn't the slightest interest for him. He was entirely absorbed in thinking about his reunion with Claire. Everything else seemed trivial and irrelevant. He decided that Claire had changed, subtly changed, so that she might well have been a different woman. When he had known her first she had been immature, unsure of herself, conventional. And now—now she struck him as

273

being a woman of experience, of self-knowledge, and self-confidence. The failure of her marriage must have hurt her deeply. And yet she hadn't soured: she hadn't the look of an aggrieved woman, a woman whose view of life was jaundiced. She looked, on the contrary, a woman who had learnt to face herself and her problems with courage and equanimity. He loved her: he would always love her. Of that he was sure. And he was intensely curious to know what her life had been since they had parted over ten years ago. He wanted to know everything that had happened to her: he felt that her life, her experience, her pain, was part of his own life, his own experience, his own pain.

Forty-Two

SATURDAY AFTERNOON ON THE LAST WEEKEND of July they lay side by side below the Bloody Bridge. They had taken the train to Newcastle and walked along the winding coast road. It was a warm day. Below them the Irish Sea reflected an unaccustomed blue; above them, far off and high, the Mournes were purple with heather, and lower and nearer yellow with whin. The road itself, by the bridge, flushed scarlet with fuchsia.

They walked in silence, the sea chopping against the huge slabs of jagged granite strewn at the foot of the cliffs.

Martin was holding Claire's hand as she talked; caressing it gently as she told him her story. She told it simply, with little emotion, almost as if what had happened was something that had happened to somebody else a long time ago. She lay, eyes closed, as if she were talking in her sleep ...

She had married Bill Mansell because he had fallen in love with her, and because her family had approved of him, and because she had been flattered by his attentions.

She had always had a girlish admiration for doctors; and Bill had wanted to marry her: and she had wanted to be married. Bill had told her that if she refused him he would join the Army Medical Corps; but if she would accept him he would settle down and work for his FRCS and specialise in surgery. He believed he could become a great surgeon if Claire would only help him and encourage him. He pleaded that he needed her help, her encouragement: without it he would have no chance of fulfilling his ambition. She believed him; and she believed in him; and so they married.

At first they had been happy—perhaps for a year. They hadn't much money because Bill had an ill-paid post with a hospital at Hammersmith. They rented a tiny flat near the river and though she had to endure her own company all day, and was lonely at times, she didn't much mind. She lived for Bill's return home in the evening: she was content to mould her life to his. But everything had turned out wrong: Bill failed his fellowship once; then twice; and then he lost heart. He became extremely irritable; they had a few quarrels; finally he gave up studying for his fellowship and blamed her for his failure. To show his feelings he had an affair with a nurse and told Claire he wanted a divorce. So she left him and came home.

Claire paused: then said, her eyes still closed, "Perhaps I was to blame too—I don't know ... They say there's always two sides to any story, particularly to a marriage. There must be, mustn't there? I must have let him down. Anyhow, I ... "

She was unable to continue. Martin looked at her, his heart full of compassion. The tears were streaming down her cheeks. He gave her his handkerchief; and after a while her sobbing ceased. At last she murmured, "I'm sorry ... I'm very sorry ... "

She gave him back his handkerchief and he stuffed it into his pocket.

"That's all," she said, calm now.

They sat in silence. The sun still shone out of a blue sky; on the horizon, a large cargo ship, half-hidden in a dark grey haze, was steaming across the Irish Sea.

"You should have married me, Claire."

For some seconds—it seemed to Martin an interminable length of time—Claire made no reply. Her face gave no indication of what her thoughts were. He had just spoken his own thoughts: and he had spoken them firmly. He wanted her: he was determined to have her. He loved her. What had happened to her since she had left him was of no significance whatsoever—except that he'd a feeling of black venomous hate towards this ridiculous man—a doctor too!—who'd been so insensitive, so foolish, so egocentric as to undervalue her!

He waited for her answer. What he'd just said demanded an answer. He was making her an offer of marriage. She must know that. At last she answered him, very calmly: "Yes, I should have married you."

"You really loved me, Claire," he went on, putting his arm round her and kissing her hair.

"Yes."

"We were fools!" he said fiercely. "Marry me!"

She shook her head.

"Why not? I want you! I've always wanted you! You've always wanted me!"

He took both her hands in his. He kissed her hair, her cheeks, her eyes; then he kissed her on the mouth, passionately.

"I'll never let you go!"

She told him that her divorce wouldn't take place until the spring—there could be no question of their marrying, so it was best for them not to think of it.

"I'm frightened of marriage, Martin."

"Of course you are, but—"

She laid her hand on his.

"Please let's forget about it."

"All right, darling—so long as you know what's in my mind."

During August they couldn't meet: Claire was holidaying in Portstewart with her father and sister; Martin had to go to Donaghadee where his mother had rented a fisherman's cottage for the month. He'd arranged to stay for a fortnight; then his mother invited a neighbour to take his place.

Glad to be home by himself, he spent the evenings reading: and he wrote long letters to Claire. He felt lonely, in need of her company. He felt, too, that his life at last had a meaning. Then, too, his editor had asked him for a series of articles on the history of Belfast. He had also been elected secretary of his 'chapel' of the NUJ. In his letters he told Claire all this. He wrote to her:

277

I miss you very much. Every day I think of you, sometimes for hours. But, curiously, not in a way that makes me unhappy. I always think we are in this world to be happy—we must be, else why are we here?

I count the days till you return and in the meantime I spend most of my free evenings in the Reference Library in Royal Avenue, looking up old books and pamphlets about our native city. *Odi et amo*: that's the only way I can describe my feelings about this place. The Industrial Revolution has blighted us in some way—but of course it also brought us into being! What a midwife! I feel that this 'black' city has now forfeited its birthright: it belongs nowhere: is indeed a lost city. One day it'll have to find itself again. I'm reading our only mystic—Æ—and I like him more and more. He was—perhaps you know this—a first-class journalist and a first-class organiser for the Irish Co-operative cause as well as being a poet. Altogether a wonderful man! But I wished I enjoyed his poetry more: I don't think it's very good. Still, Æ was the greatest man to come out of the North in this century, and we must read his books together sometime ...

During the autumn Martin's articles were published. They caused quite a stir. Some readers wrote congratulating the paper on publishing them; others objected to them, saying that the writer was emphasising the seamy side of the city's history. For a while the correspondence column was full of the controversy.

One morning the editor brought Martin into his office.

"I want to make a booklet of your articles. What do you think of the idea?"

Excited, Martin accepted the proposal, and as he was leaving the office the editor added: "We'll give you a bonus of course."

A fortnight later the bonus—a cheque for twenty-five pounds—arrived on Martin's desk. And that evening he showed it to his mother.

"What are you going to do with it?" Mrs. Connolly inquired.

"Spend it, of course."

Mrs. Connolly shook her head gravely.

"You should put it in the Post Office. It'll come in handy some day."

But he refused to do what she desired and she was piqued and said: "Money that's easy got is easy spent."

"We should have a real blow-out, Mother."

But she would have nothing to do with such an outrageous idea. So he gave her ten pounds for herself: the rest he proposed spending on a trip to Dublin, though his mother protested that such extravagance was sinful.

"You won't be able to spend all that money?" she said, incredulous.

"Maybe not, Mother, but I'll have a good try."

The idea of such wastefulness so offended her sense of propriety that he put off his Dublin trip to placate her. In any case he had changed his mind: he intended to holiday in Austria or Italy next summer.

By the autumn Martin was going out with Claire two or three times a week: they went to concerts and plays and political meetings; they explored unfamiliar parts of the city—the Falls Road area where the Catholics lived, and the streets off the Shankill Road, mostly inhabited by Protestants.

"You see why I'm a socialist," Martin said.

Claire nodded her head, gravely, in agreement. To her these walks were something of a revelation. At first she had been nervous exploring the tangle of mean streets with their swarms of ragged children, their groups of unemployed men at pub corners. As a girl she had scarcely been aware of such wretchedness.

"Are these kitchen houses or parlour houses?" she asked, as they went along a street off Carrick-hill.

"They're kitchen houses. Aren't they dreadful?"

"But you told me you were brought up in a house just like these?"

"No, I wasn't, idiot," he teased her, unsure whether she was being really serious. "I told you I was brought up in a parlour house. D'you imagine I come from a slum like this?"

"But you told me there wasn't a bathroom in your house."

"Neither there was. Do you imagine every house that isn't a slum has a bathroom?"

"Yes, I thought that—"

"You are a fool—as well as a bourgeois!"

She squeezed his arm affectionately. That they were also able to joke about class differences gave him a great deal of satisfaction; certainly he was the more class-conscious. He found it hard not to be envious of Claire's social graces.

"Well, I can't help being middle-class."

"No, you can't," he said, ruefully admitting the fact.

"Your trouble is that you're an inverted snob," she went on.

"At least that's better than being a real snob, like you."

"I'm not a snob."

He took her arm affectionately and kissed her.

He now contributed articles to a local socialist paper which had been appearing irregularly for over a year; he was also helping to produce *The Playboy of the Western World*, to be performed just before Christmas. The play was to help finance the magazine. One evening he asked Claire if she would take part in the production.

"But I've never acted before, Martin."

"Most of the cast hasn't, so you'd be in good company."

"Well, I'd be afraid to."

"Of course you wouldn't."

At first she didn't believe he was serious, but he insisted that the dramatic society was indeed short of players, and that they would welcome her help.

"Oh, I'd like to help," she conceded.

So Martin brought her to a rehearsal in the party's rooms in York Street; and after a while she was persuaded on to the stage. She discovered that the rehearsal was taken so light-heartedly that her nervousness soon vanished, and she accepted a minor part—Sara Tansey.

At the final rehearsal Claire wanted to know how the play was shaping.

"It isn't bad, I think," Martin said, without much conviction.

"Honestly?"

"Well ... What do you think?"

They both burst out laughing and Martin said, "Well, the mixture of Irish accents is really quite funny, but what does that matter?"

"Are we making fools of ourselves?" Claire asked, her confidence a little shaken.

"I suppose so. But to be a socialist here means you're regarded as a fool. Anyway the whole idea is to make a few pounds for the paper."

Yet Martin, despite his enthusiasm for the socialist cause, didn't actually belong to the party; he had a streak of non-conformity that made him reluctant to join. And one Saturday in January, soon after the play had been performed, Claire asked him: "Shouldn't you join?"

"I suppose I should, but if I did I'd feel I'd lost something."

"What do you mean?"

"I wouldn't feel so free. Maybe it's just that I'm not a party man. I like to feel free to change my mind about anything."

Still, he considered it a weakness not to belong. As for Claire, she was now convinced that a belief in socialism was merely common sense.

"It just seems right, doesn't it?" she said one Sunday afternoon when they were on a walk. When she confessed her conviction Martin was agreeably surprised: and male-like, he considered himself responsible for her conversion, though he had consciously tried to refrain from proselytising.

"What convinced you? You weren't a socialist years ago?"

"Indeed I wasn't. My father's a true-blue tory."

"Your whole family is."

"Yes, I know. Well, it was Bill changed me. He was always reading Shaw—he really admired Bernard Shaw."

"Really," Martin replied, his voice scornful.

But he was genuinely surprised; he had always assumed that Claire's husband was as little interested in politics as the average doctor was.

"Oh, you'd have liked him."

Martin turned on her, incensed.

"I'd like to tell him what I think of him!"

"Why?"

"The way he treated you was ... "

Martin shook his head. Words failed to express his contempt for Dr. Mansell.

"Oh, I think you'd like him," Claire insisted.

"He messed up your life, didn't he? And you actually think it possible that I'd like your ... husband?"

He paused before pronouncing 'husband' but the word had

forced itself out. He hated to think of the man as Claire's husband; he hated to think of the man at all. He considered that Mansell had now no claim on Claire; any claim that he once had was now forfeit. Claire had every right to be free; she was no longer in bondage; the legal tie was a mere formality. Morally, she was free.

So Martin rounded on her, venomous at the thought of her husband.

"Don't you hate him?"

"No."

Claire's reply was exasperatingly calm.

"You don't?"

"No, Martin."

"Well, you should! He deceived you! He deceived himself! The man's a fool!"

"I married him," Claire said gently.

"You did! And that's why I—"

He didn't continue. He had hurt her by his outburst; wounded her pride; been insensitive to her innermost feelings. But it was for her sake, and because he loved her. If he was insensitive and unthinking it was only because he—

"Let's forget about him," Claire said, taking his arm.

They had reached the old Stranmillis Road when a shower of rain which had been threatening all day began to fall. They took shelter under the trees at Cranmore.

"He means nothing to you?" Martin asked as they stood together, facing each other.

"I'll forget about him some day," she said solemnly.

"Promise?"

"Yes, I promise."

Forty-Three

THE WINTER WAS NOT YET OVER. It was early March, and recently there had been a heavy fall of snow, and afterwards a week of slush. It seemed that the winter would never end. Impatiently Martin waited for the coming of Spring: for by March or April Claire would likely have her divorce. She would be free; and then they would get married. Curious, but they had never really discussed marriage; Claire had always avoided the subject; and once when Martin broached it she asked him not to talk about it just then; so he refrained from talking about it at all. She knew, of course, that Martin wanted to marry her; but because, legally, she was still another man's wife, she felt tied to her husband. Her marriage vows had meant a great deal to her; so until her divorce was through she wanted to be faithful. She confessed to Martin that for her own peace of mind she needed to be chaste. It was her code—perhaps ridiculous and archaic, but it was how she must behave. She was the creature of her upbringing and its traditions, at least in this.

They were often seen together and so were inevitably the topic of a good deal of gossip: and Martin's colleagues sometimes dropped hints about the advantages of having an affair with a married woman. He took their banter good-humouredly and said little by way of reply. Let them think what they wanted to think!

A fortnight later, during the last days of March, the spring came. A week of bright sunny days followed the snow and slush. On the first Saturday in April he took Claire to the Giant's Ring and they walked along the grassy mound circling the megalith.

They had the large saucer-shaped meadow to themselves, and having circled it several times they took the path to the megalith and leant against the great tilted stones. Martin looked at Claire thoughtfully. That morning she had heard from the solicitor that her divorce was through.

Taking both her hands he kissed them, murmuring: "Well, it's all over, darling."

"Yes."

"Aren't you glad?"

"Yes, of course I am."

"Happy?"

She didn't look happy. The news had excited him much more than it had excited her. She returned his gaze and replied, "Deep down, yes, I'm happy. But now—just now—I feel stunned."

He kissed her on the mouth; and opening her coat he caressed her body. For a while Claire lay in his arms, quiescent, her eyes closed. Then she said at last, her voice so low that he hardly heard her, "I want you, Martin."

They went across the meadow to the circling mound and there, under the trees, made love for the first time.

His life continued to be bounded by his home and the newspaper office—except that now he saw Claire nearly every day. He had told his mother about Claire's return to Belfast, and had hinted that he was seeing her. His mother disapproved and was frank in her disapproval. She detested the idea of her son having anything to do with a woman who had left her husband.

One evening, a month after the divorce, Martin mentioned that Claire had got her freedom.

"Has she indeed?" his mother said coldly.

"Yes, mother."

It was teatime, and a silence fell between them. Martin had

just come in, and in less than an hour's time he had to set out to report a meeting of railwaymen on strike. After the meeting he had arranged to meet Claire.

"So your lady friend's now divorced," his mother said, pouring herself out another cup of tea.

He nodded; and his mother added, "I wouldn't like to be in her shoes! She'll never be happy herself, an' she'll never make anybody else happy."

Martin made no comment: he had mentioned the divorce because he was anxious to have his mother's reactions.

"It's a terrible thing for a woman to do—to desert her husband," his mother went on.

"It is," Martin said, "But it's not always wrong."

There was a constrained silence which he broke.

"I'm seeing Claire tonight, and I want you to do something for me."

His mother held her peace: she looked up at her son, waiting to hear what he had to say.

"Will you?" Martin said.

"What d'you want me to do?"

"I want you and Claire to meet."

Martin saw his mother's face go pale; she put down her cup, she was trembling slightly.

"No, son, I can't do that."

"Why not?"

"I have no desire to meet your lady friend."

"But I want you to."

He faced his mother: determined now to have this out.

"Why not?" he added quietly.

His mother shook her head.

"Well ... " he began.

His mother suddenly spoke.

"Why can't you stop seeing this—this woman?"

"Why should I? What has she done wrong?"

"She couldn't be a good woman."

He flushed, furious that his mother should dare to make such a judgment.

"Who says so?"

"I do. Your mother."

"You've no right to say that! So please don't say it again."

"If I think it I'll say it."

"Not to me!"

"Yes, to you, son. I'm in my own house an' I can say what I like."

Their voices were rising. Martin realised that he was on the verge of losing his temper. Breathing heavily, like a runner, he paused. His whole body was tense. He had decided that it was now or never.

His mother's Pharisaism had stung him into cold suppressed anger.

"Then I must tell you something ... "

His mother sat looking out of the window, her lips tight, her head slightly tilted, her whole posture expressive of her obduracy.

In this matter it was crystal-clear that she had made up her mind irrevocably; it was crystal clear that nothing he might say would make her give way in the slightest. For her no compromise could possibly be admissible. Martin had challenged what she cherished in her innermost being: her belief in what was right. Divorce was wrong, no matter how common a practice it might become: it was wrong in God's sight and in the sight of the church. Devoutly she wished her own church was as uncompromising in this matter as the Roman Catholic church was. But her son had no respect for the teachings of any church; he had cast them aside as if they were of no importance. She found it hard to understand how anyone could be so presumptuous as to risk the danger of eternal damnation. So she had prayed for him, night after night, on her bended knees, by her bedside, that he might be led to see the error of his ways. It was not that there was evil in his heart, it was only that he—and now this was what all his presumptuousness was leading to!

She waited for him to speak, and when he spoke it seemed as if his words were coming from a great distance.

"I want to marry Claire."

He looked at her. Not a muscle in her face moved and he marvelled at her self-control.

"Did you hear what I said?"

She rose from her chair and stood before him, firm in her faith. Nothing he might say could possibly move her.

"Mother, did you hear me?"

"Yes, I heard you."

Her voice was dry, as if drained of emotion.

"Well?"

She must answer him. He got up and stood before her.

Then, with great deliberation, she spoke: "I'll have nothing to do with her."

She moved away from the table and as she did so he caught hold of her arm.

"Listen to me—!"

With a motion expressive of scorn and anger she twisted herself free of his grasp and marched out of the room, her head high.

She went upstairs to her bedroom. Martin then left the house, slamming the front door after him.

He walked along the street with lowered head, his eyes blazing with anger. Well, the situation had now come to a climax. He had known that his mother would think and act as she had thought and acted: she could behave no differently, her life being what it had been. Yet he blamed her: blamed her for her stupidity and her obstinacy. Her intolerance had infuriated him so much that his whole body was still quivering. Life with her had become unbearable! He would endure it no longer! He had the right to be his own master; he had his own life to live; and he must choose his own future in so far as deliberate choice lay within his power.

That evening he was unable to give the whole of his attention to the mass meeting of railwaymen on strike. Seated at a table immediately in front of the Ulster Hall platform, Martin and half-a-dozen other reporters impassively listened to the speeches, the resolutions and the arguments between the officials and the rank and file in the body of the hall.

Towards the end of the meeting, however, the atmosphere became more tense: it was announced that an attempt was being made to break the strike by means of blacklegs, including dozens of university students. Shouts of 'Shame' echoed round the hall and strikers rose to their feet waving their arms and demanding more rigorous counter-measures in face of the unscrupulousness of their opponents.

Afterwards Martin met Claire and told her about the plight of the railwaymen. It seemed likely now that the strike would fail.

"The same thing happened in the General Strike in Britain in 1926," he said, "the students took the side of the employers."

"Why did they do it?" Claire asked, puzzled.

"Because they knew no better," Martin muttered, adding bitterly, "and they are the ones that should know better."

As they walked along Bedford Street discussing the strike he refrained from mentioning his own quarrel, though all the time it lay at the back of his mind.

"You think the strikers will have to give in?" Claire asked.

"Probably."

"It's a shame, isn't it?"

He nodded.

"Oh, there'll be some sort of a compromise," he predicted. "But it'll really be a defeat."

"I think it's a shame!" Claire's tone was vehement. She told Martin that earlier in the evening she had listened to some friends of her father's denouncing the strike and she had hardly been able to keep silent.

"But you didn't say anything?"

"No."

"You should have spoken out."

"I know I should have, but I didn't."

Her concern for her father had made her keep silent. She was attached to him and hated the very idea of hurting him. Her divorce had come as a great shock to him and now she wished to upset him as little as possible.

All this she freely admitted. Perhaps she was wrong to be silent; perhaps she should blurt out at home what her true feelings were.

"I suppose I'm just a coward," she said.

"No, Claire, it's not that."

"It is, it is," she said passionately.

His only reply was a shake of the head; for if she was a coward he was lost.

More and more he was aware that he was leading a life which was difficult to live. He was failing to adjust his actions to his vision. The strike had failed and he felt implicated in its failure; his mother hardly spoke to him these days, so great was her resentment of the life he was leading; and even in Claire's company he was occasionally moody and irritable.

Also he was getting little satisfaction from his work. The leading articles of his paper disgusted him: they had helped to form public opinion against the railwaymen; more and more he disliked working for such a paper. He thought of resigning and going to London in search of a more congenial job. Yet he was reluctant to leave his own country: to get to England was to go into exile and he preferred to stay where he belonged.

He felt he would soon have to decide what to do. He wanted to get married; and he knew Claire would be willing to marry him. But she didn't want to live in London: she associated it with her husband too much.

"I know how you feel," he said, squeezing her hand tenderly.

"If you must go, you must," she said, a distressed look on her face.

Martin had now begun calling for Claire at her home. He had seen her father, now an invalid, sitting wrapped up in rugs in an armchair. Mr. Taylor was obviously a dying man—his face ashen grey, his hair white, his light blue eyes lustreless.

He couldn't recall who Martin was, though he had pretended to when Claire reminded him about Martin's visits, as a schoolboy, to their old house.

"Ah, yes, yes of course," he said, shaking his head slightly and trying in vain to recall which schoolboy this particular young man could possibly be.

Martin had remembered Mr. Taylor as a well-dressed man, fond of golf, and with an air of self-confident breeziness. He had then regarded Mr. Taylor with awe: and now he regarded this man, dying of cancer, with pity.

As for Claire's brother and sister, they received Martin very coldly and very politely; their disapproval, though masked by their manners, was perfectly obvious to him. They spoke only a few conventional words before making an excuse to leave the room. Martin, inwardly furious, said nothing to Claire: he suspected that she was aware of their attitude to him just as he suspected that she was aware of his own mother's attitude to her.

During the months of May and June they were constantly

together. To see her for even a quarter of an hour made all the difference to his sense of living. A day without her seemed to him a day wasted, a day without point or purpose: he needed her presence to give reality to his own existence. He neglected his newspaper work so much that Claire was worried on his behalf.

"They'll give you the sack," she warned, "if you don't watch out."

"I don't care."

"But you should care."

"No, I shouldn't. What's a job like mine worth?"

In a mood of lightheartedness he gave her a wry account of some of the reporting he had done during the week: the courts, the Corporation meetings, a Rotary conference. And he compared reporting to scavenging, mimicking the speakers he had listened to, until Claire burst out laughing at his antics. Still, he confessed to her that reporting suited his temperament—he liked the irregular hours and the unpredictability of the work; and anyway it was the only job he was fitted for. He insisted, however, that to take journalism over-seriously was ludicrous—especially reporting for the newspaper he had the misfortune to serve.

His real life was lived, for the most part, outside his job. Reporting was a way of earning a livelihood—that was all. His real life was lived in Claire's company. With her, he seemed doubly alive; with her, all his senses were heightened. She made him more aware of clouds, sea, sky.

Together they discussed books and plays and concerts; and made love in the woods outside the city.

Nevertheless he was conscious that their relationship was incomplete. And he longed for marriage.

Forty-Four

THE SUMMER CAME. MARTIN APPLIED FOR several reporting jobs in England, but without success. Jobs in journalism were hard to come by and he became discouraged and almost reconciled to living at home. Still, he was anxious that his way of life should change, the sooner the better.

In the second week of July the annual procession of Orangemen marched through the city, and Martin was involved in a street incident.

In the early evening of the twelfth of July he was wandering about Royal Avenue. Claire was away on holiday with her family; without her he felt lost, dispirited. In the morning he had reported the procession as it left the city—banners waving, bands playing, tens of thousands of men marching in their regalia—and now he was weary of the sight and sound of the parade. Yet it had a fascination for him. The gay silken banners, orange and blue and red, held proudly aloft to display portraits of Queen Victoria and William III; the flute, reed and brass bands in their bright uniforms; the rank after rank of solemn-faced Protestants, all believing that they were defending their civil and religious liberties—it certainly was an impressive sight. He had grown up with it; it had become part of his life; the twelfth of July was the single day of pageantry that enlivened the city. A day of ritual; of rudimentary poetry. Yet always it profoundly depressed him. For he saw this procession as a complex symbol of the deeply-rooted division of his native city—indeed of his native country. It divided ordinary people on religious grounds: it created suspicion and distrust between Protestant and Catholic families, generation after generation.

Earlier in the day Martin had reported the proceedings—the pious resolutions passed to defend the Protestant faith—and had dutifully handed in his copy. Then, after a drink at The Duke, he was standing in Donegall Street almost opposite the cathedral when he heard shots coming from York Street. Immediately he ran in that direction.

The procession was still passing by.

"What's happened?" he asked.

"Somebody's shot," an old woman answered.

"When?"

"Just a couple o' minutes ago."

He pressed through the crowd, to find that the procession had come to a halt. A buzz of chatter rose from the spectators. It was rumoured that an Orangeman had been shot and was now lying wounded at the top of Lancaster Street.

"There'll be trouble about this," someone said.

More shots rang out. The crowd began to disperse. The procession now divided, one part continuing to march along York Street, the other part halted by the police at the entrance to the street. Then quickly the long street cleared. Along with half-a-dozen people Martin took refuge in the hallway of a drapery shop. Suddenly the plate glass shattered and bits of the window powdered the pavement and splintered over women's coats on display inside.

"God almighty," said an old man, his pipe clenched between brown stumps of teeth.

Martin peered along the street which was now quite deserted, except for two figures on the opposite pavement, one walking about three yards behind the other. Both were middle-aged men, poorly dressed, in dark blue dungarees.

"What are those idiots doin'?" he asked a black-shawled woman beside him. She was about thirty-five, with a lined coarsened face that made her look prematurely old. Clutching her shawl and wrapping it tightly round her as if for protection, she gazed up into Martin's face. "I dunno, mister," she said, her voice hoarse with fright. "They'll get shot!"

The two men walked directly along the opposite pavement, lifting their legs awkwardly, as if they were unaccustomed to walking along a street.

"They're sailors from one of the boats," the old man with the pipe said.

"They must be fools!" Martin said, looking towards the two men. He could now see their brown expressionless faces: the man in front was carrying a small brown parcel; the other, his head lowered, was staring at his companion's heels. Both seemed quite unaware of what was happening; could have been deaf and blind.

The black-shawled woman gave a nervous titter as the two men approached.

"They're Lascars," the old man said.

"Bloody fools," Martin answered.

A shot rang out. The Lascar in front halted and his companion nearly tripped over him. Martin saw their lips moving; they looked round as if in bewilderment. After a short pause they walked on slowly, down the street.

"Hey!" Martin shouted, but they took no notice of him. Cursing them he ran across the street, his heart pounding with fear.

He grabbed one of the Lascars by the arm and hustled him into a doorway, signalling to the other to follow them.

"This is a riot!" he shouted.

"Mister?" one said, looking frightened.

"D'you want to get killed?"

They both looked at him, bewildered.

"Killed!" he shouted at them, as to incredibly stupid children.

An hour later Martin was saying goodbye to the two Lascars. He had tried to explain the background to the riot but had only succeeded in further mystifying the already thoroughly mystified sailors. Their replies to Martin's explanations were repeated nods of miscomprehension. They had told him that they had just come off their ship and were trying to do their shopping. No, they had never been in Belfast before—it was a very strange city—and they shook their heads sadly.

During the last hour the two Lascars had seen armoured cars; had seen the arrival of ambulances to collect the casualties; had seen gunmen in action; and now they wanted to get back to the safety of their ship as quickly as possible. They were sure that the people of this city were mad: just as mad as this young man who had talked to them for the last hour, telling them the most incredible things.

At last the traffic had begun to move—people were now walking along the pavement, trams were lurching along as usual, everything was ordinary again. The strange-looking young man bade them goodbye and they nodded their heads and made for their ship.

Martin, having left the two Lascars, walked towards the side street—Lancaster Street—which had been the centre of the riot. It was a Catholic street, inhabited by unskilled labourers—many of them unemployed—and their families. He learnt this from one of the bystanders, who blamed the Catholics for starting the riot and vehemently asserted that the peaceful procession had been attacked by gunmen.

"I'd chase the whole bloody lot o' them out t'hell o' this," the man said, walking away.

Martin returned to The Duke and found the bar full of excited men arguing about the riot. He joined a couple of journalists, one of them a Catholic called Harry Kinelly. Kinelly sat drinking whiskey, his face pale and worried-looking. He was a man of about thirty, was popular with his colleagues and noted for his liberal views. Martin knew him slightly and liked him.

"Have you just come from York Street?" Kinelly asked as Martin sat down.

Martin nodded.

"What did you see?" Kinelly said.

"I saw two Lascars," Martin replied.

"Don't try to be funny!" Kinelly retorted.

"No, I actually saw two Lascars. They were the only sensible people I saw."

"What do you mean?" Kinelly snapped.

Martin related his experience; and Kinelly listened, but

without much interest. He was obviously thinking of something else, or perhaps had already drunk too much.

"Did you yourself see anything?" Martin asked.

Kinelly paused, finished his drink, and looked straight into Martin's eyes.

"I saw a young man shot dead. That's all."

"Who shot him?" someone at the counter called out.

"I don't know who shot him," Kinelly replied, "He's dead. And there'll be others shot dead tonight and tomorrow night and maybe the next night."

Harry Kinelly's prophecy turned out to be true. The rioting in the city continued till there were thirteen dead, scores wounded, and hundreds of homes wrecked or burned. All the old antagonisms and hatreds and fears between Protestants and Catholics came to the surface. The local newspapers in their reporting and editorials were so partisan that most of the journalists were disgusted. Martin, furious with the policy of his own paper, retaliated by writing an article for a socialist weekly published in Glasgow. When this article was published Harry Kinelly was enthusiastic about it.

"You've been impartial. You're the only journalist that's tried to be fair to the Catholic side—and to your own side as well."

Martin's mother read the article and thought him foolish to have written it. She was frightened that something might happen as a result of it.

"What could possibly happen, Mother?"

She shook her head, amazed at his lack of common sense.

"You're asking for trouble," was her reply.

"I don't think so."

"I'm warning you. You'd no call to write like that about the place you live in."

She was afraid of his being attacked in the street and beaten up; and he was unable to allay her fears.

"There's no need to be frightened," he assured her. But his carefree assurance only annoyed her the more.

"I'm your mother, and though you'll pay no heed to me, you'll rue the day you didn't."

She burned the article as soon as Martin went out, hoping that not many people had read it. After all it had appeared in a paper she had never seen before or even heard of.

Mrs. Connolly was now turned fifty and looked an old woman: her figure was plump, her hair grey-white, her clothes drab. More and more she was turning to religion for consolation: she often went to weekday prayer meetings.

One evening when Martin returned early from work he found his mother in the parlour entertaining a Mr. and Miss Scott. The Scotts were brother and sister; and both of them belonged to Mrs. Connolly's church. Daniel Scott—a dark-faced man who sat bolt upright—owned a small grocery shop: he was a widower with no family. His sister Ida was unmarried. With Martin both the visitors were self-contained and stiff, as if on their guard. The talk mostly centred on church affairs, in particular about their minister who had just undergone an operation in the Royal Victoria Hospital. Martin hardly spoke; he looked at the Scotts with curiosity. They were prim and ill at ease in his company; so his mother did most of the talking. Just before ten o'clock Mr. Scott remarked that it was late and time they were away. Then, having thanked Mrs. Connolly for her hospitality and shaken hands with Martin, they departed. Mrs. Connolly saw them to the door.

"Who are they?" Martin asked.

"Friends of mine," his mother replied.

He looked at her. She was wearing a blue dress he had never seen before; she was flushed with the heat of the parlour and the excitement of entertaining her visitors. As she tidied up she told him that the Scotts had invited her to supper on Sunday, after church.

"I'd like you to come, Martin."

"But on a Sunday evening I always go out."

"I know."

She knew where he went on Sundays—she knew he was with Claire Taylor.

"I wouldn't enjoy going. You know that. And the Scotts wouldn't enjoy having me. They're just trying to be polite."

"Martin ... "

He looked up from his book. His mother had taken off her shoes: he noticed she was wearing a new pair.

"Yes?"

His mother sat down beside him.

"I've something to tell you."

He waited. His mother took a deep breath.

"Mr. Scott wants to marry me."

Martin tried to take in the news without changing the expression on his face.

"Does he?"

"Yes."

He waited. He looked at his mother's face. Her eyes seemed larger; a stray strand of grey hair had fallen across her forehead. He suddenly felt warm and sympathetic towards her.

"And you want to marry him?"

"Yes."

He paused.

"Then you must do so, Mother."

He rose. And suddenly she put her arms round him and she was in tears. He stood before her, mutely sharing her joy.

Forty-Five

A FORTNIGHT BEFORE CHRISTMAS MARTIN'S mother married Mr. Scott. They were married in a country church in County Down, with only a couple of dozen of their friends present. It was a misty mild day, and the lights of the church were lit though it was still the early afternoon.

For Martin the whole of the proceedings was unreal and dreamlike, and he was conscious of himself playing a part in a slightly ridiculous ceremony. He found it inconceivable that his mother was now a Mrs. Scott, the wife of this dark-faced anonymous grocer whose interests were confined to running his shop and attending religious gatherings.

As soon as the wedding was over and his mother and stepfather had departed to Rothesay on their honeymoon, Martin felt a sense of liberation. He walked along Castle Place in the direction of the City Hall, breathing in deeply the sharp wintry air—the mild afternoon had finally turned cold. He was glad that the wedding was over. Perhaps his mother would be happy with this man so unlike her first husband, his own father; at least she wouldn't suffer from loneliness—and it was loneliness that she had most feared.

He walked home. The house was cold without her presence. He lit the gas stove in the parlour and warmed himself before it. It was his mother's parlour: the curtains, the furniture, the wallpaper, everything reflected her taste: except the shelf full of books that belonged to him. The house, too, was hers; he would certainly clear out within the next week or so and find somewhere else to live. He was free now to mould his own life.

The empty house oppressed him. He looked at his watch. Only nine o'clock. He felt the need to be moving, to be outside, among people.

Few people were out; a crescent moon was shining over the city. He reached the end of the tramlines and climbed the winding country road up the hill. The city lay beneath, glittering with lights, a long phosphorescent yellow snake winding between the dark hills.

He felt lonely. Already he missed his mother: he was surprised to discover that he was already suffering from a feeling of deprivation. Outwardly his mother had meant little to him. He had grown away from her; she had often irritated him. Certainly he had been thoughtless and neglectful, had taken her presence for granted, had failed to give her the filial affection she needed. He felt guilty for his failure as a son, and the consciousness of his failure depressed him all the way home.

By the spring of the New Year his life had changed. He had left his mother's house on the Castlereagh Road and taken two small rooms in a shabby Victorian terrace off the Dublin Road; bringing with him a tea-chest full of books and an escritoire. His mother had wanted him to have the money realised by the sale of the furniture, but he had refused her offer. With fifty pounds of his own in the bank he thought himself quite well off.

His mother seemed happy in her marriage: she was now serving in the grocery shop alongside her husband. Martin paid a dutiful call and chatted for an hour or so. The Scotts were friendly; and his mother didn't inquire about his private life. He didn't tell her that he was planning to marry Claire at Easter.

His life, without the foundation of marriage, had no meaning. To go on much longer living as he was would be intolerable. But Claire's family were less than lukewarm about the idea of her re-marrying: she had quarrelled with her sister and brother about it.

"And your father?" Martin inquired.

"I don't know about Father," Claire said, "I really don't know—but he doesn't seem to mind."

Claire's father was too ill to care. Once, after an evening at the Opera House, Claire suggested that Martin should come home to speak to her father.

"Do you think he'll want to see me?"

"Yes. He asked me where I was going tonight; I told him to hear *Rigoletto*."

"You told him you were with me?"

"Yes."

Mr. Taylor was seated in a chintz-covered armchair: cushions supported his arms, back, and head; his legs were hidden beneath a tartan rug. He greeted Martin with an almost imperceptible nod.

For a few minutes he inquired about the performance of *Rigoletto*. Then he fell silent, staring into the fire. Claire left the room in search of her younger sister.

"Mr. Connolly—"

Martin bent forward, hardly able to hear Mr. Taylor's voice.

"I want to ask you a question."

Mr. Taylor paused and looked at Martin.

"I understand you're a journalist—" Martin nodded "—and that you want to marry Claire?"

Again Martin nodded.

"My question is: can you support my daughter?"

Martin was so surprised at the old-fashioned conventional ring of the question that he was unable to reply. At last he said, limply: "I hope so."

A pause.

"Then I see no reason why—"

But Claire had entered the room and Mr. Taylor said no more.

On the following afternoon—a Sunday—Martin and Claire walked along the Lagan towpath and Shaw's Bridge. It was their favourite walk. The narrow river reflected the trees choked with ivy on the opposite bank: above them, on the right, stood a line of tall beech trees stretching towards the grey sky. The towpath was deserted.

Martin had told Claire about her father's remark.

"Well, can I support you?"

Claire laughed and took his arm, squeezing it affectionately. Martin kissed her and said, "Did I tell your father a lie?"

"Did you intend to?"

"No."

"Then you didn't."

But they agreed that Mr. Taylor could have been misled by Martin's answer.

They walked, sometimes in silence, as far as the village of Lambeg. Once they halted beside a deserted cottage and Claire asked: "Are you sure, Martin?"

"Sure?"

He looked puzzled.

"Do you really want to marry me?"

"Yes, I do. Very much."

He took her hands and kissed them. Then he kissed her on the mouth, passionately.

It was less than a fortnight to Easter. Already there had been a few spring days and the cold damp winter would soon be forgotten. But the aftermath of the summer riot had remained, poisoning the life of the city for months. The newspapers had reported in full the details of the interminable court cases that followed. In addition the industrial life of the city continued to suffer from paralysis. Shipbuilding and linen manufacture had almost ceased. Daily, thousands of men and women thronged into and out of the unemployment exchanges. Only the pawnshops flourished.

More and more Martin was caught up in political activity. He found it impossible not to become involved, not to protest against the social degradation that diseased everything. He attended socialist meetings in various dimly-lit halls, spoke once, haltingly, at the Custom House steps, and wrote a bitter pamphlet on the conditions and wages of young workers.

Yet, although he was politically active, he made few friends in the movement. It was, he decided, his own fault: he had not yet conquered an innate feeling of shyness, of unease in the company of acquaintances. He was reluctant to serve on committees and to accept office.

"I'm not really interested in politics," he told Claire one evening, "not deep down, I mean."

They had just left a lecture given by a London speaker—an intense professor of mathematics—to an audience of about twenty workers.

"Why do you say that?" Claire asked.

"It's all a waste of life somehow—this constant wrangling about means and ends—"

"But it's necessary."

"I know it is."

Claire, now a firm socialist, was a bit troubled at Martin's moodiness: he was occasionally like this—depressed by the apparent lack of progress the movement was making.

"I don't understand you," she told him.

"I think the whole universe is unjust—"

"Yes, but—"

"It's a depressing thought, isn't it?"

Then, after a pause, Claire said: "We can't help the universe, but at least we can do something to help ourselves. Can't we?"

She looked up at Martin, her voice a little plaintive. He smiled and took her gloved hand.

"Yes."

She then released her hand, took off her glove, and they continued walking, hand in hand, in the direction of her home.

A couple of days later Martin had an afternoon off and Claire and he took the train to Helen's Bay and walked along the coast towards Bangor. They had called to see a furnished bungalow at Carnalee, which Martin thought might suit them for the summer. They had inspected it and told the owner that he would have their decision the following day. As they walked along they discussed the bungalow. Both were keen to live for at least six months by the sea.

"Well, shall we take it?" Martin said.

"Are you sure you won't mind travelling up and down to Belfast?"

"No—not during the summer."

"All right then. I think we should take it."

They walked through Stricklands Glen and soon arrived in Bangor. He brought her to the pebble-dashed little street where he had spent part of his childhood and showed her the house where he had lived. They went to a café near the pier and had tea.

It was growing dark as they returned to Helen's Bay. The tide was high, the lough choppy; a small collier was on its way out to sea. They watched it as they stumbled across the soft damp sand. Then the moon came up, full, throwing a long knife of moonlight across the dark water.

Both were thinking of their marriage now only a few weeks away. They felt a little apart, afraid of the future: each was aware of a sense of foreboding, of withdrawal, like the ebb and flow of the tide.

"You haven't spoken to me for a long time," Claire said.

"I'm sorry."

"What were you thinking about?"

Martin shook his head and smiled.

"Go on—please tell me."

"Of the future—that's all."

They reached the end of the beach. On the opposite shore of the lough they could see the twinkling lights of Carrickfergus and the intermittent flashing of the lighthouse at Black Head.

"Are you afraid?" Claire asked. She looked at Martin's face.

"No," he answered, "I'm not afraid."

They walked along a wooded path towards the castellated station at Helen's Bay and stood waiting for the train.

It was cold on the platform; the train was late; at last the black gleaming engine hissed into the station, giving them a glimpse of the red glowing firebox.

They entered an empty compartment. For a while Claire gazed out of the window into the darkness; her face pale and disconsolate. She looked forlorn: so Martin took her hand and caressed it gently, tenderly.

"I need you," he said, kissing her on the forehead.

She squeezed his hand in return, comforted now a little.

"You believe me?" he said, awaiting her assurance.

She nodded.

And then through the darkness, they saw the lighted city.